Jennifer Brown is th[...]
several middle-grade and young adult no[...]
including her acclaimed debut, *Hate List*.
Additionally, Jennifer is the author of four Love
Inspired novels, including the *Publishers Weekly*
bestseller *Kidnapped in Kansas*. Jennifer is also
the nationally bestselling author of women's fiction
novels under the pseudonym Jennifer Scott.
She lives in Kansas City, Missouri. Visit her at
jenniferbrownauthor.com.

Books by Jennifer Brown

Love Inspired Inspirational Mountain Rescue

Rescue on the Ridge
Peril at the Peak
Hunted at the Hideaway

Love Inspired Inspirational The Protectors

Kidnapped in Kansas

For Scott, first love, last love, forever love

Acknowledgments

When I decided to write a novel featuring a sexy, sensitive, bighearted cowboy, I knew that I was going to need a whole lot of trail leaders to get me through this ride.

First, I want to thank an actual trail leader, and my leader through all things publishing, Cori Deyoe at 3 Seas Literary Agency, for making sure I understood how horses work and for encouraging me to go ahead and hop on up. I promise you, one day we will ride together for real.

I would like to thank the entire team at Harlequin for giving me a chance to tell the small-town stories that live deep in my heart. Thank you, Johanna Raisanen, for riding by my side, gently letting me know when I've diverted from the path and helping me get to the really good scenery.

A huge, galloping thank-you to Kirsten French, program director at Northland Therapeutic Riding Center, for sitting down with me to explain how equine therapy works and for giving me a behind-the-scenes tour of the center. Your help and knowledge were invaluable to me and to this story.

Thank you to my family for always riding with me, regardless what animal we're on or where the trail leads. I love you.

Finally, thank you, reader, for visiting Haw Springs and taking the ride with Morgan and Decker. Without you, Haw Springs couldn't even exist.

CHAPTER ONE

MORGAN GRIPPED THE handhold above the open passenger-side window for dear life as her sister, Marlee, careened out of Haw Springs. Highway lines and telephone poles and trees whipped past, blowing the scent of pine and blacktop and sunshine through Morgan's hair. She was glad to be back to the comfort of home and family but had envisioned perhaps a little slower pace.

"What's the rush, exactly?" Morgan's voice felt pulled from her by the wind, as if it, too, was in a hurry to get where they were going.

Marlee glanced at her. "No rush. Why?"

"Because you're driving like a maniac."

"No, I'm not." Marlee laughed. "I'm just driving."

"This is *just driving*? At least slow down when you get to the country roads with all those switchbacks. I'll end up flying out the window, and then what kind of impression will I make when we get there?"

"The city has made you slow, little sister. Although, from the sound of things, your imagination has greatly improved." Morgan could have sworn that her sister pushed the gas pedal even closer to the floor. That would be just like Marlee—as devilish as the day was long and always happy to put an exclamation point at the end of a sentence.

"Isn't that the opposite of how it's supposed to be? Aren't country folk supposed to be slow-paced and city folk supposed to always be in a hurry?" Morgan asked.

"That's just a stereotype on TV. People are people. And you used to think this was normal, so, when it comes to you, the city made you slow."

Morgan didn't feel slow. Most of the time she felt rushed and revolving, like a cog in a very complicated machine. Being a single, working mom of a five-year-old son on the autism spectrum was not exactly what Morgan would consider leisurely. That was exactly why she needed this summer back home to begin with. To recalibrate. To slow down.

When Marlee suggested that Morgan put Archer in an equine therapy program and take a leave of absence from work to catch her breath a little, Morgan could think of nothing that sounded better. But apparently, to Marlee, slowing down was figurative. If Morgan intended to spend a lot of time with her sister while she was here, catching her breath was going to have to happen on the fly.

"Besides, if I remember correctly, you got way more speeding tickets than I ever did, back in the day," Marlee said. "I'm just trying to catch up to you."

"I did not!" Morgan protested, but they both knew that she most definitely did.

Morgan's son, Archer, let out a delighted squeal from his car seat in the back seat. Marlee checked the rearview mirror. "Your son likes the way I drive," she said, then raised her voice. "Don't you, Archer?" He squealed again. "See? You. Got. Slow."

"That's a terrified squeal."

Archer let out a peal of laughter. Traitor.

"Nice try, sis," Marlee said. "He loves it."

Not a fair test. Archer loved everything Marlee did. And Morgan couldn't blame him. She'd looked up to her older sister her entire life. Marlee lived her life the way she was driving this car right now—exhilaratingly and determined. She always seemed to know exactly where she was going and exactly what she was doing at all times. Being in a room with her was like being in a cold room with a roaring fire; you just wanted to sit next to it, let it soak into you. And with Morgan deciding that, two years after her husband, Cody, split, it was time to move on from her disastrous marriage and get her life back on track, she needed a fire to sit next to. She needed Marlee's determination to soak into her.

"Are you ready for your interview?" Marlee asked, tapping the brakes just slightly to turn onto a gravel road. She and Morgan rolled up their windows to keep out the dust, and now the car seemed strangely silent. Archer made a noise of protest in the back seat. "What am I thinking, Miss Big-City Ad Exec? This is just a summer job—of course you're ready."

"One, I'm not an ad exec. That makes my job sound so much more important than it is. I'm a marketer, and just above entry level at that. I'm lucky that my boss is understanding and gave me a leave of absence."

"You're selling yourself short, as always," Marlee said. "I know better. You're amazing at what you do, and you can try to deny it all day long. It doesn't change the fact."

"Two," Morgan said, moving on, "it's not just a summer job. It's a chance to get Archer a new kind of therapy, and you know I can't afford it on my own. So, yeah, I'm ready, but I'm also a little nervous."

"Still no child support from Cody?"

"Still no anything from Cody."

Marlee made a *tsk* sound and shook her head.

She glanced in the rearview mirror again. "He really has no idea what he's missing out on. Archer is the best. Aren't you, Archie?" Archer babbled back at her and she raised her eyebrows. "Exactly. I couldn't have said it better myself. Whoever called him nonverbal didn't know what they were talking about."

Morgan let out a laugh, grateful for how immediately and fully Marlee loved Archer. He wasn't like other kids, but Marlee didn't care.

"So you've seen the ranch," Morgan said. "What do you think?"

Marlee shrugged. "It's ranchy. But, you know, not in a salad kind of way."

"Very helpful, thank you."

"You know what I mean, though. You've seen one ranch, you've seen them all. Some big buildings, a bunch of grass and dirt, pretty trees blowing in the breeze, a whole lot of whinnying going on in the background. Ranchy."

Morgan stared out the window and rubbed her bottom lip—a habit she had whenever she was deep in thought. Archer had never seen a real-life horse, and Morgan had no idea how he would react when he saw one. She wasn't even 100 percent sure how he would feel about grass and dirt, trees and wind. At times, it seemed like the only thing Morgan could predict when it came to Archer was that she couldn't predict anything when it came to Archer.

As if she could sense Morgan's trepidation, Marlee reached over and patted her sister's knee. "It's gonna be great, Morgan. He's gonna do great. It's a ranch, not a prison. If he hates it, you can just spend the rest of your summer at the community pool, working on your tan. There are worse things. Or you could come work for me. I can always use help in the flower shop."

Morgan sighed, her hand falling away from her lip and dropping in her lap. "I know you're right. I'm overthinking it."

"You're just trying to be prepared. But the owner seemed to know an awful lot about autism. He's got all the certificates—I saw them on his wall. Archer will be safe there. And I would bet the guy knows everything there is to know about horses, too. And probably enough first aid to get by. Like how to set a broken leg, what to do if a horse careens off a cliff with a kid on it, that kind of thing." She glanced at Morgan, took in her alarmed face and laughed. "Relax! I'm kidding."

"Ha ha ha," Morgan deadpanned , but she, too, couldn't keep a giggle at bay. "I'm being serious, though. I'm handing my kid over to him, saying, 'Here you go, stranger. Take the most precious thing in my world, put him on a thousand-pound animal who could very well be sick and tired of carting kids around all day, or…or could decide that it doesn't like the way Archer smells, or feels some weird vibe off of him and just decides to gallop off into the sunset. Hope it doesn't decide to career off a cliff. Have fun, good luck, bye-bye!'" She waved.

"Bye-bye," Archer echoed from the back seat and waved out the window.

"Are you finished freaking out?" Marlee asked.

"Yes," Morgan said. "No. I don't know. I think I'm just a little worried about trusting this man. I've never met him. What if he's not a good guy?"

"Not all guys are Cody, Morgan."

"I know that. I do. But…just tell me what this guy is like again?"

"Well…" Marlee thought about it. "Confident. Kind. Really good with kids. Especially kids on the spectrum. He's got a partner—like a ranch-hand kind of guy—with ASD who lives on the property and works for him, and they're total besties. I think Archer will probably love him. Won't you, Arch?"

"Yes," Archer said from the back seat—his new favorite word. He answered every question in the affirmative.

"That's right, buddy. Oh, and he seemed pretty

excited when I told him about your experience working with sales. I told him you could sell ads to a dead person."

"Oh, great, so his expectations are high."

"Also," Marlee said, turning another corner, from gravel to dirt road. Clouds of dust billowed all around them; Morgan wondered if her sister could even see through the windshield. "Alllsooo..."

"Oh, no. I know that grin, and I know that *alllsooo*. Nope. No. First the guy stacking cantaloupes at the market, and then your assistant at the flower shop, and now Mr. Alllsooo the Rancher. You're not going to do this to me all summer, are you?"

Marlee's grin grew wider. "Do what?"

Morgan pointed at her. "That. You're not going to try to set me up with every single guy we see, are you?"

"Who said anything about setting you up? Jumping to conclusions much? Maybe you're actually a little teensy bit interested in a handsome, single rancher. Besides, you said you're ready to move on."

"I am. In my own way. In my own time. I don't need your help. And I don't need to go falling in love with anyone in Haw Springs."

"Well, good thing this isn't Haw Springs. It's *technically* Buck County."

"*Technically*, I'm only here temporarily. Kansas City is three hours away."

"But he's really good-looking," Marlee said. "Dark hair that curls up from under his cowboy hat."

"Nope."

"Broody brown eyes."

"No."

"Dimples for days."

"No."

"Muscles that positively torture his poor T-shirt."

"Marlee!"

"What? He's supercute is all I'm saying."

"If you like him so much, why don't you go for it?"

Marlee waved Morgan's suggestion away. "He's not my type."

"Who says he's *my* type? Maybe I don't like cowboys."

"Yes, you do. I believe your last weekend before college was spent frolicking around the fall festival with a cowboy."

Morgan felt herself blush. "We didn't frolic. I don't even know how to frolic. Cowboys most certainly don't frolic. It's against Cowboy Code."

"You frolicked. I literally watched you frolic. I'm just saying, maybe this is your chance to move on. Maybe this cowboy likes to frolic, too. Maybe he goes against Cowboy Code, even though that's not a thing and you just made it up."

"Okay, okay, enough. What's this guy's name again?"

"I can't remember, but the name of the ranch is Pathways. Like, maybe he will be your *pathway* to love."

Morgan groaned and rolled her eyes as Marlee laughed uproariously, eliciting another round of laughter from Archer. "You're not funny."

"I'm a little funny. Oh, come on, sis. Lighten up. You're about to meet the man of your dreams."

"I think I'm just aiming for meeting the man with a summer job."

"Well, that, too. And look. We're here."

Marlee slowed as she pulled through the Mc-Bride Pathways gate.

DECKER LED TANGO into the barn, where his ranch hand, Ben Werth, had already groomed and stabled Comet, Ziggy and Sugar. Ben was busily brushing Scout, his favorite mare, and talking to her in a soft, cooing voice, while Decker's old hound dog, June, snoozed on a blanket that Ben kept for her in a corner. June's head popped up at the sound of Tango's approach. Her tail thumped the stall wall, but she stayed put on the blanket.

Tango let out a soft snort, catching Ben's attention. He turned and dipped his head slightly, an acknowledgment to Decker, before going back to the brush.

"What do you think, Ben? Are we ready for the start of summer session on Monday?"

Ben dipped his head again. "Yes."

"Scout looked a little skittish today. Probably need to keep her back for the more experienced kids, don't you think?"

Ben stroked Scout's neck. "She likes kids. She'll be careful with them. I'll make sure."

Decker nodded. He'd been counting on Ben since they were sixteen years old. If Ben said he would make sure his horse was calm with the kids, there was no question that he would do it.

Decker clipped a cross-tie to Tango's halter. "You think you can untack Tango for me? I've got a meeting."

"Is it with David?"

Decker paused. "Is he here?"

"I saw him."

Decker sighed. He loved his brother, David, but lately things had been tense between them. David, co-owner of the ranch that had been left to them when their father died, had been pressing Decker to sell and move Pathways to someplace smaller.

Both boys had been raised alongside animals, but David's passion for them had led him to veterinarian school. He was a good vet. A great one, actually. And the boom in his business reflected that. Now he not only had loans to pay off but also was in dire need of a bigger space for his practice. But expansion required money, and, in David's estimation, Decker was sitting on a big pot of untapped funds, half of which belonged to him.

When their father died, David had wanted to sell the ranch and split the profit. But he'd understood that Decker didn't want to let it go and had agreed to let his little brother get his dream business up and running. They shelved the idea of selling until they'd given Pathways a fair shot. After Pathways became solvent, they agreed, Decker would simply buy David out.

But neither of them had really defined "fair shot," and now David's need for those funds had become urgent. But income from McBride Pathways Therapeutic Riding Ranch was sparse, to say the least, and Decker couldn't afford to buy his brother out.

The ranch was run on volunteers, grants and the backbreaking work of Ben, who was modestly paid, but accepted it because he loved the work and was allowed to live in the tiny ranch-hand house near the pasture for free.

"Thanks for the heads-up. You going home when you're done with Tango?"

"After I make sure all of the welcome kits are correctly packed."

Decker smiled. Ben had gone over the kids' kits a million times already. They were as right as rain. "Okay, just don't stay too late. Check in with me before you go?"

"I will."

Decker made sure Tango's cross-ties were secure, gave him a quick pat on the neck and left the barn. June resumed her nap.

David was waiting for Decker behind the check-in desk in his blue scrubs, casually flipping through the Summer Pathways pamphlet. He glanced up when Decker stepped in, the glossy booklet still spread out in front of him.

"Professional," he said, tapping his finger on the page. "Looks great. How much did it cost you?"

"I called in a favor. Got a discount."

"Good. Discounts are good." David turned another page, read for a bit, then closed the booklet. He came out from behind the desk and crossed to the observation area that was furnished to look like a snug living room. He sank into a chair and rested his forearms on his thighs, his fingers tented together.

"Is the summer program full?"

"Not quite. But we're getting there. How's your schedule looking these days?"

"Overfull." Decker saw weariness set in on his brother. David was usually great at hiding his fatigue, but his clinic had gotten so popular, it seemed to Decker that lately his brother was working around the clock. "And I'm about to lose Leo."

"Your vet assistant? Why?"

"He's about done with school. I would love to offer him a full-time spot. That's why I'm here. Have you had time to think more on what we've talked about?"

"I've thought about it."

"And?"

"And I can't afford it yet. I need more time."

"How much time?"

"I don't know. I'm building a following, but this is only my fifth full season. I'm sorry. I know that's not the answer you want to hear."

David leaned back in his chair and rubbed his forehead. "I know we've been over this before, but are you sure you're not just hanging on to the land for sentimental reasons?"

Decker had no response for this. They both knew it was true. The McBride land was important to Decker. In some ways, it was everything.

"Right," David said, dropping his hand in his lap. "And are any of your students getting a 100 percent discount?"

"A couple. We're working on grants. Scholarships. That kind of thing."

David hung his head and gave it a shake. He let out a chuckle. "You are softhearted, aren't you, brother?"

"Should I be hard-hearted? Would that be better?"

"Of course not." David stood. "But it's not hard-hearted to take care of yourself. You have to eat. You have to live. And so do I."

Decker crossed his arms. "And I suppose you don't take care of a single sick animal for free? What about the Langhorst farm? Aren't you there every single day looking after those animals? You charging old Vera Langhorst for every visit, are you?"

"That's different. I can give away an hour without giving away everything." David gestured with his arms to indicate the entire ranch.

"I'm not giving away everything. And I'm not having this conversation again. These families need resources, not more bills to pay. If they can pay the full fee, I take it. If they can't, I take what they can give me. Come around sometime while we're working with the kids, and you'll see. Some of them couldn't even tolerate being outside when they started here. Some of them were terrified, and I could barely get them to pet the pony, much less get on a horse and ride. It's about strides, David. It's about quality of life. It's not about dollars and cents." He lowered his voice. "You remember what Ben went through."

David sighed, a concession. "I understand, Decker. I really do. I know the importance of what you do." He approached the counter, facing Decker. "Look. I know it means a lot to you. I know your heart is in the right place. I've been patient, and I would continue to be patient if I could."

"I know."

"I've got a lot of loans. I've got my own business to run, and I can't move forward. I want to grow, just as much as you do."

"I know that, too."

"Okay, well…can we not just see if we get some offers?"

Decker groaned.

"I can get a Realtor on board. You won't have to do anything. Why don't we just see what we can get for the place? You can take your half of what we make and find a smaller ranch. Restart your business on a less grand scale."

"Five horses and a pony is hardly grand."

"You can still help plenty of people without all that extra space."

Decker knew that David was right. The McBride ranch was huge. He didn't use half of it for the Pathways program. But the program wasn't the only thing keeping him here. It was land that had been in the McBride family for generations. He'd promised his father.

"Can we just explore our options, Decker? Please?"

The brothers stared into each other's eyes. Decker knew that David was being sincere. He would never want to take away anyone's dream unless he really felt that he was in a tight situation. But Decker wasn't ready to call it quits on the ranch. Not yet.

"Give it to the end of the summer. I'll turn it around. I'll get enough to buy you out. If, at the end of the summer, things don't start to look better for Pathways, I'll be the one to reach out to a Realtor myself."

David thought for a moment, and then gave a slight nod and offered his hand. "Okay. Deal."

Decker shook his brother's hand, relieved to get another ten weeks' reprieve. "Thank you. I won't let you down."

David checked his watch, then pushed away from the desk. "I need to get back." He stopped with his hand on the doorknob. "What exactly do you think is going to change in two and a half months?"

"Remember how we talked about bringing in someone who can do some fundraising? I have an interview in about five minutes. She's supposedly really good. And I'm not paying her. Her son is going to be in the program, and in return, she's going to do some fundraising. She's going to get us in the black."

"This woman is from Buck County? How did you find her?"

"No, she's visiting from Kansas City. Her sister came in one day out of the blue, practically demanded an interview. It's promising, David. If she's even half as good as her sister claims, this ranch will be rolling in donors in no time."

"What's her name?"

"I can't remember. Something that starts with an *M*. Marty, maybe? Marlee. No, wait—that's her sister's name. Hang on, I know she told me. It's M—"

There was the sound of footsteps ascending onto the wood porch and scuffing toward the door, the low murmur of two female voices punctuating each step. Both David and Decker turned to look. David's hand fell away from the doorknob. He took a step back just as the door opened.

Three shapes were silhouetted in the doorway. One, a short, slender woman in a sundress and cowboy boots, holding the hand of a small boy. Decker recognized her as Marlee, the sister who'd come in earlier. The other woman was taller, with long, impossibly shiny brown hair;

she was dressed in a pair of sleek black slacks and a snug button-down shirt with the sleeves rolled up. All big-city business.

"Hello," Marlee said, stepping inside. The taller woman followed her in and shut the door behind her, blocking the sunlight and bringing them into full view. Decker blinked twice, almost unable to believe what he was seeing. The confident grin that almost looked like a dare, the squared shoulders ready to take on the world, the wide blue eyes with the longest eyelashes he'd ever seen. It was like being transported backward in time. He barely registered Marlee was still speaking. "Hopefully you remember me? Marlee West? And this is my sister—"

"Tweety," Decker said.

CHAPTER TWO

IT WAS THE end of summer when she met him the first time. Morgan had been feeling the pressure of leaving the only home—the only town—she'd ever known. She was headed to St. Louis for college, which, okay, wasn't a million miles away or anything, but it was far enough that visits would be *an event*. Her mother had spent weeks upon weeks softly sniffling while buying totes and bottles of Tylenol and Band-Aids and a cute pink shower caddy, dutifully checking items off a list while Morgan tried to pretend that nothing was happening.

Morgan was also checking off a list. Things she wanted to do one last time before leaving home. People she wanted to see. Experiences she wanted to have. It was almost impossible to believe that she'd lived in one tiny spot for eighteen years, and yet there was so much she hadn't done.

When Marlee and a few friends announced they were going to the Buck County fair, Morgan begged to tag along, with no plans other than to soak up the scent of funnel cakes and the feel of soft grass worn to bare dirt under her feet one last time.

He was with a group of friends, and they were playing a game on the midway, trying to knock down fur-fringed puppets with baseballs, throwing hard, the *thwump* of the ball against the rubber backdrop followed by their groans and cheers reverberating through the fair. She slowed as she passed them, noting the cute little curls that wisped up from under his baseball cap, the taut shoulders straining the back of his T-shirt, rippling with each throw, and when he turned to playfully taunt his friend, she spotted dimples and nearly melted into the grass right then and there.

One of his buddies noticed her lingering and elbowed him. "You've got an admirer." The cute boy turned and nodded toward her, that smile a beam of light in the twilight.

Morgan wasn't traditionally forward with boys, but there was something about her imminent move north that urged her on. That unfamiliar sense of time slipping by that made her reckless.

"You should win me that Tweety Bird," she said.

He leaned forward. "Pardon?"

She pointed at a metal rack filled with prizes. "That Tweety Bird. I want him."

He raised his eyebrows and chuckled. "You want him."

"It's basically the only thing I want in life right now." She heard Marlee make a fake retching noise behind her, but she didn't care. He was talking to her, and that was all that mattered at the moment.

He rubbed his chin and nodded. "I see. You a big fan of Tweety?"

Morgan felt a tug on her sleeve. "Come on. Let's go." But Morgan didn't budge. "We're leaving."

She waved her sister off, unable to break eye contact with the boy. "You go. I'll catch up."

"Suit yourself, lover girl." With a collective huff, Marlee and her friends slipped away into the carnival crowd.

"You didn't answer my question," the boy said once they were gone. "You a big fan?"

Morgan bit her bottom lip shyly and said, "Oh, yes. I'm the biggest fan."

He rubbed his chin again. "Hmm. Okay. And if I win you that Tweety…"

"If you win me that Tweety, I'll let you take me over there to that truck and buy me a snow cone, Baseball."

He laughed out loud. "Well, that's the best

deal I can think of." He handed a five-dollar bill to the man running the game and gestured for the baseballs. He turned to his friends, who were buzzing and snickering and bumping shoulders. "Watch out, y'all. I'm gonna win this here prize for…" He turned back to Morgan. "You got a name, or…?"

She shrugged. "Maybe. You'll have to win to find out, I guess."

The fellas around him oohed and cackled. "Okay, well, then, if you won't tell me, then I get to come up with a nickname for you."

Ten minutes later, she and the boy she'd simply called Baseball were sitting at a picnic table with snow cones. Morgan had a giant Tweety Bird and a new nickname.

A nickname she hadn't thought of in ages.

Until she was standing in a dim, dusty log building on a ranch in Buck County, facing a man with little curls wisping up from under his cowboy hat, and a set of very familiar dimples.

"Tweety." Decker breathed memories and history and life into Morgan with that one word, the years and the fair evaporating from her daydream. The midway tumbled away with its squeals and its roar of metal on metal. Time had slipped by again.

Marlee's gaze bounced between the two of

them, just like it had back on the midway. "Wait. Do you two know each other?"

Morgan ignored her sister. She was too busy trying to come back to the present. "Hey, Baseball," she said, her voice coming out as a bitter croak. "Long time no hear."

It took a moment for Marlee to absorb what was going on, and then her eyes grew wide. "This is Baseball?" Marlee asked. "*Baseball* Baseball? The fair frolicker? No way!"

The man standing next to Decker let out a snort. "Fair frolicker?" Recognition set in on his face. "Oh! I totally forgot about that."

It was this that finally snapped Morgan fully into the present. So many images from that perfect weekend, and the hurt weeks afterward, were swirling through her mind, threatening to take her breath away. She cleared her throat, stood tall and lifted her chin, trying to adopt her usual composure. She prided herself on her professionalism. She'd adopted a hard exterior when Cody left, and she sure wasn't going to soften it for the man who was her first real heartbreak.

The man in the scrubs stepped forward, offered his hand. "David McBride. Decker's brother. I don't think we've ever formally met."

Decker. That's right. She'd called him Baseball, but his name was Decker. The name reverberated through her. *Decker McBride.* She hadn't allowed herself to think or speak it for a long time.

"I didn't know Decker had a brother," she said, reaching for his hand. As she said it, she became fully aware there were a lot of things she didn't know about Decker McBride, even though he'd played such a big role during her whirlwind final weekend at home and her first weeks at college. For instance, that he had a brother. And that he apparently owned an equine therapy ranch in Buck County.

Another thing she didn't know about Decker McBride? Maybe the most important thing? She didn't know why he broke up with her out of the blue all those years ago. One moment, he was the boy she was quickly falling in love with, talking about a future with; the next moment, he was bowing out. With no real explanation. *It's just not working out.*

"Nice to meet you, David. I'm Morgan West. I'm here for an interview."

"Technically, we've met before," David said. "I was there. At that fair. I was one of the guys he ditched after winning you that bird."

Morgan felt a blush coming on. "Oh. Well, nice to meet you again. I was sort of oblivious to everything but that Tweety Bird in the moment."

"It was a long time ago," Decker said, sounding a little dazed.

Archer let out one of his groans that Morgan knew meant he was getting impatient. He tugged on Marlee's hand; Marlee tapped Morgan's shoulder. "I'm going to take this as my cue to make myself scarce. Arch and I will wait for you outside?"

Morgan nodded absently. She knew she was going to get the third degree once she got in the car again. This was going to be a Whole Thing.

"Is it okay if we go into the barn to look at the horses?" Marlee asked. "I think Archer would like that. Has he ever seen one in person, Morgan?"

"Huh? Oh, uh, no, I don't think so."

"Sure thing," David said. "I'll walk you there." He nodded to Morgan. "Nice to meet you, Morgan…again. Or should I call you Tweety?"

"No, please don't. Morgan is fine. And likewise," Morgan said, her stomach twisting into knots as she became fully aware she was about to be alone in the room with Decker McBride for the first time in over a decade.

The three of them disappeared, letting in a swath of sunlight that bathed Decker's face, reminding Morgan of sitting on a picnic blanket in a clearing surrounded by trees, just the two of them, nibbling on peanut butter and jelly sandwiches and cheese cubes. He had kissed her that day—her very first kiss—a sweet memory that she'd taken to college with her and brought forward every time she was homesick. She'd day-dreamed about coming home and seeing him again. Going on more picnics. Getting more kisses.

But that had never happened.

"So that's your son?" Decker asked.

She nodded, offering a steely smile. "Archer."

"Nonverbal?"

"For the most part, but he'll babble and echo, or try out a new word. Right now he's rocking the word *yes* like nobody's business."

"He looks like you."

"If you saw his dad, you wouldn't think that."

"Will I? See his dad? I mean..." He tipped his face to the counter, and Morgan could have sworn he was blushing. *Don't do that*, she wanted to say. *Don't you dare, after all these years, do that.* She'd spent so long pining over him, wishing he would reach out to her. Then, when he didn't, and the realization set in that he'd moved on, wishing she could see him so she could give him a piece of her mind. Letting him know he broke her heart. "I'm just asking because we do require an ID if anyone other than you comes to pick him up. It's a safety thing."

"You won't need to worry about that," Morgan said. "Cody won't be coming. He's not in the picture at all. But I'll let my parents and sister know."

"Okay. Good." Morgan tried not to read into that *Good*, while again Decker stared down at the papers on the desk. He finally looked up and toggled a finger between the two of them. "Is this going to be weird?"

Morgan swallowed, squared her shoulders, put on her boardroom persona. "Absolutely not. Archer needs this. I need this for him."

"But our history—"

"Is in the past. Long past. We were teenagers with a little crush."

But it was so much more than a little crush, she thought, even as she said it. *So much more.*

JUST A LITTLE CRUSH, Decker thought, feeling heaviness in his chest. It wasn't. But he could hardly make that argument now. After all, he was the one who'd ended it. And he knew he'd ended it poorly. He was young. He was scared. He was falling for her too hard, too fast. He was still aching every day for his mother, who had walked away from the ranch and never come back. Just vanished, without so much as a goodbye for her husband and two sons. He was bitter and confused and was certain that he would be his father—alone, heartbroken and scrambling to juggle it all—if he let himself be vulnerable to any woman. Morgan was beautiful and bold, and things between them were so easy. Too easy. Which would make losing her down the road too hard. It was anything but *a little crush*.

But none of those things were an excuse. He'd bailed on her—that was the long and the short of it. Morgan was standing in his lobby, and the feeling was surreal. For a moment, he thought he might be dreaming. He had, after all, dreamed about Morgan a million times since he broke it off with her. Every dream was like a stake to the heart.

"I'm a professional, Mr. McBride," Morgan said, approaching the desk as she pulled a file folder out of her bag. "What happened between us in the past…is in the past."

"Please. Call me Decker."

He could smell her before she even reached him. She smelled the same—like honeysuckle and coconuts and fresh laundry. He felt woozy. She laid a paper on the desk in front of him. A résumé. He glanced at it but couldn't absorb any of the words. All he could take in was that honeysuckle. That fresh laundry. Those blue, blue eyes.

When he'd asked if this was going to be weird, maybe he'd been asking the wrong person. Maybe *he* couldn't make this anything but weird. Maybe he couldn't let go of her.

But he thought he *had* let go of her, years ago.

"I have extensive experience in client interface. I know how to make a client feel like they're the most important person in the world and that our business would crumble without them. I know how to talk someone into wanting to give their money by convincing them that it's the best thing for them. I'm the youngest senior team lead in our firm's history, and I will tell you that I worked hard to work my way up. I can sell, Mr. Mc...er, Decker. If you're looking for donors and sponsors, I can promise you I'll find them."

He nodded. "Do you know anything about horses?"

She shook her head. "But I can learn. And I've been researching. For Archer's sake." Her voice softened. "It's important work you do here, Decker. I'm really excited about it. As a mom."

The sound of boots scuffing along the wooden porch drew their attention. The door opened, and Ben walked in with June at his heels. He blinked, took in Morgan, tipped his head forward and touched the brim of his hat. Decker tried, and failed, to suppress a grin. Ben wasn't always good at knowing proper social etiquette, especially in new situations, but he was great at mirroring. When he'd started at Pathways, he only knew about cowboys from books and movies. And one of the things that he'd learned was to tip his hat in greeting. *Just like John Wayne*, he'd said the first time Decker observed him doing it.

"Ma'am," Ben said, and Morgan nodded in his direction.

"All finished, Ben?" Decker asked.

Ben came forward, skirting around Morgan. "I didn't get to finish brushing Tango. Mr. David told me I could go. But I didn't get to finish brushing."

"We'll brush him a little extra tomorrow," Decker said. "We'll get on it first thing in the morning. We won't do anything else until he's ready."

This seemed to satisfy Ben. He took off his hat and held it in front of him. "But I think you should know that there are people in the barn." He glanced at Morgan uncomfortably. "A lady and a boy. Should I stay to make sure they don't hurt or steal the horses?"

"They're fine. They belong to Morgan here." Decker gestured at Morgan, who gave Ben a shy wave. "They won't hurt or steal the horses."

Ben didn't wave back. He took two steps closer to the desk. "But you don't normally let students in the barn. It's not safe, remember?"

"Normally, that's true. But they're just looking around. They'll be safe. I think we can trust them."

"His name is Archer," Morgan offered. "The little boy. He's going to be a student in the summer program. I hope…?" She glanced at Decker, shooting some sort of energy through him. Yes, this was going to be weird. It was going to be more than weird; it was going to be hard.

He'd let her go. But he'd never truly let her go.

Ben clutched his hat. "Ma'am, if he goes into the barn, all the other people will want to go into the barn. It's called the slippery-slope argument, coined by turn-of-the-century philosopher Alfred Sidgwick, only he called it 'the objection to the thin edge of a wedge.' But it's the same thing."

"Oh. Wow." Morgan looked delighted. "I didn't know all that. You learn something new every day."

Ben gave the nod again, looking very pleased with himself. "Yes, ma'am, I do."

"Oh. I didn't mean you specifically. I meant me. Or everybody, really."

Ben looked thoughtful but didn't answer. Decker knew that look to mean he was trying to figure out something he'd never considered before. Morgan was going to be a challenge for Ben. And Decker liked that. Ben was certainly more than capable of meeting challenges. Ben had gotten Decker through more challenges than he even realized. Including the challenge of losing Morgan all those years ago.

"They'll be just fine in the barn," Decker said. "You can go on home. Is David still here?"

Ben tapped his hat back onto his head. "No, he drove away. He said there was too much history floating around in here. I don't really know what he meant by that. History is a concept, or perhaps a noun attached to an item, like a musket bullet or a piece of ancient pottery."

Or a stuffed Tweety Bird, Decker thought. *Or a pair of wide blue eyes that invite you to just fall inside and tumble and tumble and tumble forever.*

Or a fear of hurt and rejection that leads to a breakup.

Hard for history to float if it never really got off the ground.

Ben continued. "Or sometimes someone will say that something is 'history in the making,' which makes 'history' a noun in the sentence, but really, it's still just a concept. Regardless, none of those things float."

"David just meant that Morgan and I met years ago at the Buck County fair, that's all. He was speaking figuratively."

Ben gave his head a scratch, mulling it over.

"So I'll see you tomorrow morning. We have to finish this interview," Decker said.

"Okay." Ben headed toward the door, June tagging along. "I'll start by brushing Tango," he said without turning around. "Since it didn't get finished today."

"You bet," Decker said. "Thank you, Ben."

Ben left the office, and once again the air felt still and heavy with anticipation. Decker took a deep breath and pretended he was reading Morgan's résumé, while his mind reached for ways to make this less awkward. After a moment, the floor creaked with her shifting weight.

"He's really smart," she said. "And charming. I think Archer would take to him."

"Ben? Oh, yeah, he's great," Decker said. "We've been friends since high school. He was the equipment manager for our baseball team, but right away I knew that he was capable of so much more than that. People assume that just because someone is autistic, they're limited. But Ben isn't limited. He's the smartest person I've ever known. He's really the reason I started Pathways in the first place, so it was a no-brainer that he was exactly who I needed to help me on the ranch."

"And me? Am I who you need? To help on the ranch, I mean."

"Right, we should talk about that." He placed the résumé on the counter. "Your sister told me that you'll only be here for the summer—is that correct?"

"Yes," she said. "I'll go back to Kansas City

in August. Archer's pre-K starts toward the end of the month. I can be here for the full summer session."

"Okay. And for pay? Marlee mentioned a trade."

"I don't need a paycheck, if Archer can participate for free. I promise you I'll bring in sponsors."

Decker rubbed his chin, his thoughts careening all over the place. He wanted to send her on her way, keep the ties that he'd cut years ago severed. He wanted an excuse to tell her this wouldn't work, without admitting that the real problem was it would be too hard, too emotional to let her hang around.

But if she made good on the promises she was giving him, she would be the savior he needed to keep McBride Pathways up and running, maybe help Decker bring in enough money to buy out his brother.

And then there was Archer. He didn't know the little boy, but if there was a chance that the horses could be a positive step forward for Archer, he had to give it a try. Decker's own best friend was proof of how capable someone could be, if only someone else believed in them and put the time and effort into helping them. It had taken Decker a lot of years to realize that Ben had come into his life for a reason, and that working with autistic kids was his calling. And then a lot of studying, test-taking, licenses and sinking every cent he had into making it happen. He had to give Archer this chance.

Besides, he couldn't help it.

As difficult as this was going to be, a part of him just plain wanted Morgan there.

"Okay," he said, meeting her eyes. "You can start Monday morning."

CHAPTER THREE

HAW SPRINGS HAD changed very little since Morgan left. In some ways, it was a town frozen in time, and Morgan liked it that way. There was comfort in coming home to the same place that you remembered. She longed for familiarity.

There had been a few notable updates on Main Street, though, including the introduction of a kitschy, cloud-themed coffee shop called The Dreamy Bean, run by a soft-spoken, tie-dyed and macramé-clad young woman named Ellory DeCloud. Ellory herself had a dreamy quality about her that made her shop make sense. The Dreamy Bean had pushed out a dank and dusty antique shop full of smelly furniture and grimy glassware and replaced it with an airy, spacious hangout filled with pastels and patchouli and pastry. It was a good move forward for Haw Springs. Especially welcome if you were a transplant from Kansas City who loved a good coffee shop to park yourself for a good, long think.

Morgan had quickly made The Dreamy Bean

her go-to stop in the mornings while her parents plied Archer with frozen waffles slathered in peanut butter and apple juice on ice, precisely the way he wanted it.

"Hey, look who it is," Ellory called when Morgan entered the shop the Sunday before the Pathways session was to start. "Tea or coffee this morning?"

"Tea, please." Morgan held up her laptop bag by the strap. "And maybe a scone? Got some reading to do. I need sustenance to keep me awake."

"Gotcha."

Morgan sank into a white, puffy chair at the back of the store—her most favorite spot to sit and ponder with a warm cup of tea resting between both hands in her lap. The chair was situated with a perfect view of the square in the morning sun and was directly under the speaker, which was frequently playing mellow 1960s folk music.

She opened her laptop and tried to focus, but found her mind wandering back to Decker again and again.

It hadn't only been that one night at the fair. When the midway had shut down around them and security had waved everyone out, Decker had walked her to the parking lot, where Marlee and friends were waiting in the car impatiently.

He'd carried the giant Tweety on his shoulders, and they'd talked and teased and bantered like they'd been friends their whole lives.

"No way you just said *Twister* is the best movie of all time, Tweety. *Twister*?"

"I did. Because it is. Have you seen it?"

"Everyone's seen it."

"But have you?" A pause. "That's what I thought, Baseball! You haven't even seen it. It's got everything. Romance, action, flying cows. What more could you possibly want?" Morgan made a *tsk-tsk* noise. "Baseball, Baseball. You disappoint me. Next you're going to tell me that you never saw *Holes* or *Hocus Pocus*, either. *The* movies of our generation."

A laugh and a shrug. "I was busy!"

"What! You're kidding me. Busy doing what?"

"Anything but watching those movies." More laughter as Morgan socked him in the shoulder.

They'd reached the car and stopped, turned to each other. His fingers brushed against hers, giving her butterflies.

"I have so much to teach you, Baseball."

He raised his eyebrows. "Is that so?"

Time stilled between them. Morgan ignored Marlee and friends, who were giggling and making smooching noises inside the car. When Marlee finally honked, Morgan broke away with a start. And suddenly she was shy and nervous.

"Gotta go. Bye."

"Wait." He snatched her wrist and tugged her back. In her mind, he swept her into his arms and gave her a long, romantic kiss, and music swelled around them, and an unexplainable wind blew through her hair, and her heart sounded like tumbling waves, sweeping them away. In reality, he swept the stuffed animal off his shoulders and pushed it into her arms. "You can't leave without your prize."

"But that was going to be my excuse to see you again tomorrow," she said, hugging the bird against her stomach. "I was going to have to hunt you down on the midway and demand another one. You ruined the plan."

"Ah, I see. But what if I'm not here tomorrow? Then what?"

Marlee honked again and Morgan jolted. "You will be."

She trotted to the car, hearing his laughter, and then, "See ya around, Tweety," at her back.

They met again on the midway the next night. And then again on the third night. After running out of dollar bills and riding all the rides at least twice, they'd moved up to the DJ tent and danced for hours. And then they had the picnic the next day.

And the kiss. It was almost what she'd imagined it to be. Only better. If she closed her eyes and thought about it, she could still remember every single detail. His thumbs brushing her jawline. Her heart beating out of her chest. The scent of summer enveloping them, along with the calls from the birds in the trees.

She didn't want to leave for college, but she had to. It seemed tragically unfair that, though they'd gone to the same high school, the years between them, and the different crowds they circulated in, meant they didn't know each other at all.

We could have had more time together, she'd complained.

We have our whole lives ahead of us, Tweety.

When just a few weeks later, sitting in her dorm, feeling homesick, she received the text— it's just not working out between us—she'd felt so silly for thinking he'd meant they had whole lives ahead of them *together*.

"Your London Fog and scone, my lady."

Morgan startled, her eyes flying open. Ellory placed her order on the little table next to her.

"I'm sorry. I didn't know you were asleep. I wouldn't have bothered you."

Morgan waved her off. "I wasn't asleep, just daydreaming. I'm kind of having a hard time concentrating. My mind just wants to wander and wander these days." She picked up her tea. "This is exactly what I need, thank you. I was

reading last night—well, researching, I guess—
and it got late."

Ellory sat on a nearby ottoman and crossed
her impossibly long legs. Today she was wearing a pair of chunky, sky blue heels over white
tights, with a frilly, blue-and-white-checkered
dress. She reminded Morgan of a lavender-
haired Alice, in a caffeine-fueled Wonderland. "I
thought you said you came back to Haw Springs
to relax, not to work."

Morgan took a sip of her tea and nodded. "I
know. But I got a job."

"A job! Congratulations! But don't you already
have one? Back in St. Louis?"

"Kansas City, yes. And I shouldn't really call
this a job. It's just a summer thing. More of a
trade. My son, Archer, will get to do a summer
program for free in exchange."

"Ooh, that's fun. What's the program?"

"McBride Pathways. It's equine therapy for
autistic kids."

A slow grin spread over Ellory's face. "Oh, yes,
I know it. The McBride brothers." She hugged
herself around the middle, scrunched her face
up and smiled.

Morgan laughed. "What does that mean?"

"Just that they're the most eligible bachelors
in Buck County, and I don't even think they
know it. A veterinarian and a cowboy. How

much better could it get? David has an office
down the street, and when he comes in, he puts
the *Dreamy* in Dreamy Bean. He's all, 'What
do you recommend today?'" Ellory mimicked
a smoldering voice and wiggled her eyebrows.
"I always want to say, *I recommend a date with
me.*" She tossed her hair over one shoulder se-
ductively.

Morgan tried her own mimicry. "What's hot
today, Miss DeCloud?"

Ellory twined a lock of hair around one finger.
"Why, you are, Mr. McBride. Everyone knows
that."

They both laughed. Then Morgan set her tea
back on the table and picked up the scone. "And
Decker? What's he like?" She bit into the scone,
trying to look nonchalant, but her heart was
working double-time just mentioning his name.
She wasn't exactly sure why hearing the words
most eligible bachelor dredged up a pang of jealousy in her. Why did she want to know about
him? They would never have anything beyond a
memory of the fair, so what did it matter?

"Just as dreamy," Ellory said. "But a lot qui-
eter. Keeps to himself. He never comes in here
alone. Always with David. And he always looks
like he'd rather not be here." She leaned forward on the ottoman. "But let me tell you, if he
wanted a companion who wasn't his brother, he

would have no trouble finding one. Wherever he goes in those cowboy boots and jeans, all eyes follow, if you know what I mean." Her eyes widened. "Oh. You *do* know what I mean! Are you and Decker…?"

"No! No. Absolutely not. No way. Uh-uh." Morgan felt all the blood rush to her face. She knew that she was protesting too much, but she couldn't make herself stop. "I mean…but I guess I can see the attraction. If, you know, that's your thing."

"Handsome, broody cowboy with a killer smile? Yeah, that could be my thing, for sure."

There was that weird, misplaced jealousy again. *He's not yours, Morgan. He never was. Change the subject, change the subject.* "Anyway. I realized that I know absolutely nothing about horses. My job isn't really going to have much to do with them, and to tell you the truth, I'm kind of afraid of them, but I figured I probably should at least know the difference between a…" She glanced at her computer screen. "A pasture and a paddock."

"Honey, you know what you need to know. That's what really matters. Decker knows the horses, trust me. You'll be fine."

"I hope you're right."

"With that kind of scenery, how can anything go wrong? And I don't mean the ranch." She gave Morgan a wink, just as the door opened, and in stepped David McBride. "Perfect timing," Ellory whispered. "Do you feel that? It just got super dreamy in here." She giggled, stood and hurried to the counter. "Good morning!"

Morgan held back a laugh. Ellory was a hopeless flirt. But she wasn't wrong.

She went back to her reading. This job was going to be impossible if she didn't let the past go. She had work to do. She had Archer to focus on.

"Horses, horses, horses," she murmured to herself, then began reading. "'Cannons. A horse's lower legs from the knee to the ankle. Similar to a human shinbone.' Well, then why not just call it a shin?"

Should she have told Decker about her weird hesitation around horses? She wasn't sure if it would have made a difference or not. After all, like Ellory said, she wasn't going to be riding; she was going to be making phone calls and putting together spreadsheets and designing banners to hang on fences.

"I hear you're going to be working for my brother." David approached her, a steaming to-go cup in his hand. It was the weekend, so he'd ditched the scrubs for jeans and a T-shirt.

"I am," she said, offering a meek smile.

He held up his cup in a toast. "Congratulations. Welcome to McBride Ranch."

"Thank you." She lifted her mug and took a sip. David made her nervous, and she couldn't quite pinpoint why.

"You've got a big job ahead of you. Pathways needs all the sponsors it can get. We've never really had someone dedicate their time solely to that, so I have no idea how it's going to go for you. Haw Springs is pretty tiny. Buck County isn't much bigger itself."

"I'll give it everything I have. There are surrounding towns. Even Kansas City is a surrounding town, if you don't mind driving for a few hours."

He took a sip and gazed out the window at the square, which was slowly picking up in traffic. "That land belonged to my parents," he said. "And it belonged to my dad's parents before him, and even their parents before them. Generations of McBrides have spilled blood, sweat and tears into the very grass that you'll walk on there."

Morgan closed her laptop. Suddenly, this seemed like the education she really needed.

"It was Dad's baby. He raised and sold cattle there. Grew some corn. But never had a business big enough to really make it, you know? We worked a lot of roadside stands. Decker and I have walked every square inch of that land a million times over. So has Ben. We've hunted it, and cared for it, ridden on it, lived off of it. It's been an important part of our lives. But, make no mistake, we had hard times there. Hard times that I'm more than happy to leave behind." He tore his gaze away from the window, almost as if he was tearing himself away from a memory, and took another contemplative sip of his coffee. "That ranch has always been more important to Decker than it was to me. Not that there's anything wrong with making a living using the land that our ancestors gave us. I can appreciate the history behind it, and the beauty of it, and why it's so important to our family. But it's not an easy life to maintain, and I want something different. You know what I mean?"

Morgan knew exactly what he meant. She had, after all, left Haw Springs to chase something different herself. "I do."

He turned so he was facing her. "I'm glad you do. When Dad died, I wanted to sell right away, maybe put a couple cell phone towers on it. I could have used the money to get my practice off the ground, pay off debt. I could have started in a bigger office right off the bat, maybe even attracted some partners. If I'd started bigger, maybe I wouldn't be in the position I'm in now, needing to upgrade before I really have the funds for it. But Decker refused to sell. And I let him refuse, because I love him. He's my brother, and he loves that land. And then he decided to turn it into this therapy ranch. Very admirable. Very Decker. And he's gotten that business off the ground, and it's getting more popular all the time."

Morgan gave a thin smile. "Word of mouth."

David nodded. "Yeah. Everyone loves the quiet cowboy with the soft heart. He wants every autistic kid to get a chance on those horses, whether they can afford it or not. Pathways is the kind of business that's going to rely on fundraising and donors to keep afloat. But Decker's so busy, he doesn't have time to do that. And, if I'm being honest, he's not good at that. Schmoozing. Moving and shaking. The only moving and shaking he does is on a horse. He needs someone who can spend all their time talking people into investing."

Morgan dabbed at some scone crumbs with her forefinger and brought them to her mouth. "My specialty."

"Good. Because I've got cats and dogs coming out of my ears."

Morgan's tea had grown cold, but she took another sip anyway. She didn't know what else to do with herself. Her fingers lingered over her scone, but she found that she no longer had an appetite.

"I'm telling you all of this because I want you to know that you've got a big job ahead of you.

You're going to have to pack a lot of work into just a few weeks. Decker will never tell you this, but you're sort of his last hope."

"I am?"

He nodded again, looking a little forlorn. "I hate it, but reality is reality. If you can't get the ranch solvent, we will be forced to sell. Decker will lose the McBride land."

TUCKED AWAY IN the farthest southwest corner of the McBride ranch, surrounded by trees, was a small glade in which Decker had discovered countless treasures from McBrides past, from colorful marbles to spent bullets to fishing lures. On the other side of the southernmost line of trees was the untouched tip of the Langhorst farm, which was now just fields, and home to a handful of animals that rarely strayed this far north. If you wanted to be alone on the McBride land, this was the place to go. It was the hidden patch of ranch that Decker visited most often, from the time he could mount a horse and take off on his own.

It was the perfect spot for taking naps, his back pressed against the warm grass, his hat tented over his face to shade the sun. Or for lying out at night and peering at the stars, imagining a day when he would be the one in charge. Or for letting out a few tears when he was most missing his mother.

Or for spreading out a blanket for a picnic and a first kiss with the most captivating girl he'd ever met.

Or for thinking about his mistakes when he was missing that girl and knew he couldn't allow himself to reach out to her.

It had been quite some time since Decker had visited the glade. He was busy studying for and then testing for his Certified Therapeutic Riding Instructor credential. And, when he passed, he was busy planning and building Pathways. He had precious little time for stargazing and daydreaming. And no time for picnics. And what was the point of missing his mother, anyway?

Tango let out a snort as Decker dismounted him and gave him a pat on the neck. Decker suspected it was also a favorite spot for his horse. Lots of grazing to be done.

"Go for it, buddy," he said, disconnecting the reins from Tango's hackamore and looping them over the saddle horn. "Just stay close." It was already hot, and summer had barely even gotten started. He sank down in the shade, leaning his back against one of the trees. He pressed the heels of his boots into the earth, plucked a piece of grass out of the ground and fidgeted with it while staring at a ladybug that was traversing her way into the sun.

Decker had spent the bulk of his night brushing up on his knowledge and training. Truth was, riding was so natural to him, and getting special-needs kids onto horses made so much sense to him, he could do it all as automatically as breathing. He knew that once the kids arrived and he and Ben and their volunteers began to teach them how to saddle and mount a horse, he wouldn't even need to think. But there was always that doubt in the back of his mind. Maybe he just hadn't yet met the kid who would push him to the point of surrender. Maybe this would be the group that would throw him off balance.

The rattle of wood clattering against wood across the clearing captured his attention. A rope ladder blew in the breeze and *thunked* repeatedly against the trunk of a tree. One side of the rope had snapped and the ladder hung askew. He pulled himself off the ground, gave Tango a quick glance to make sure he was still happily grazing and went to it.

What is it with boys and trees? You two will knock your heads open yet. And when you do, don't come running to me. You go to your father. It was his big idea to let you build that thing—he can take you to the hospital when you're bleeding. Decker chuckled at the memory of his mother, standing at the bottom of the rope ladder, staring up at David and him as they teetered around on branches building their tree house. She had one hand against her forehead to shade her eyes from the sun. *We're fine, Ma. Don't worry*, David had kept saying, but even then, Decker could tell that his brother wasn't as comfortable up in those branches as Decker was, and could hear in the waver in David's voice that he was maybe trying to convince himself as much as he was trying to convince her.

Decker caught the blowing, broken ladder and peered up at the tree house above. It was weatherworn but still looked pretty sturdy. He couldn't know for sure, though, without going up. The snap in the rope was near the top. He would need to cut down the whole thing and re-rope it if he wanted to fix it.

He did want to fix it.

He wanted a lot of things.

But, mostly, at this very moment, he wanted to climb this tree.

"Who needs a rope, anyway?" he said aloud. He angled himself under the lowest branch, just as he had done on countless trees as a kid, and jumped. He felt the bark of the branch against his palms, and it was like being transported back in time. *Why do adults stop climbing trees?* he thought. He pulled himself up until his hips were level with the branch and straddled it. From there, he was golden. He balanced one foot on the branch and then the other, then slowly stood, a higher branch already in his sights. The soles of his boots were stiff and slick against the wood, and he found it much more difficult to steady himself than he remembered. He lifted his leg to move to the next branch. *Steady, steady...*

"Tango is not secured."

Decker spun at the sound of the voice and, in doing so, lost his footing. His arms whirled in the air, but it was pointless. He fell from the tree and landed on his back on the ground. Ben towered over him, sitting on Scout. He held on to Tango's reconnected reins; Tango drifted along beside him, happily munching grass.

"That's why adults stop climbing trees," Decker groaned, pausing for his brain to catch up with his body. He didn't think anything was broken, but he was going to hurt everywhere tomorrow.

"Are you okay?" Ben asked, his eyes wide as he stared down at Decker. "I have not climbed a tree in a very long time, but I seem to remember that a primary rule of climbing one is that you should hold on at all times while doing so. To avoid falling."

"Thank you. I'm fine," Decker said, finally rolling over to his hands and knees. He got to his feet. "I'm good."

"Tango is not secured," Ben repeated.

"Sorry, yes, I know."

"You always say it's best to hold their reins or a lead rope when they're grazing and keep them close to you."

"That's true. I do."

"But you're not holding Tango's reins. And he wasn't even close to you. He was over there."

Decker reached out and took the reins from Ben's hand. "You're right. I should have been holding them. I was sitting right next to him, but this drew my attention, and I guess I just got caught up in something."

Ben's brow furrowed. "You mean that metaphorically, of course. You don't seem to be caught in anything. Your hands and feet aren't bound. If they were, your fall from the tree might have been much more serious. However, if you were bound, you probably would have never gotten up there in the first place."

"I mean it like I got distracted and forgot about what I was doing."

"So you were daydreaming."

"More like remembering."

"What were you remembering?"

Images of Decker's mom flashed through his mind. Picking blueberries for a summer pie, humming while her hands worked. Boots crunching through snow as she hurriedly brought an

empty box and blankets to a birthing mama cat
in the barn. Sitting in dim light at the kitchen
table, softly sobbing into a dish towel after she'd
thought everyone had gone to sleep.

For the longest time, he missed her more than
he could say. More than he would dare to say.

But now she was just a memory. One that
roiled his stomach and made him feel pity. He
took a deep breath and changed the subject.

"I guess the wind must have snapped this,
huh?" he said, tugging on a ladder rung.

Ben studied the ladder. "Over time, the ele-
ments can make things brittle."

"But it can be fixed," Decker said. "Next time
I'm out here."

Back to the furrowed brow, and Decker knew
he'd said something confusing again. "You cannot fix a snapped rope. You could tie a new knot,
but that's adapting the rope, not fixing it. If you
glued it, it would not be strong enough to hold
the weight of a climber. And that's still only
adapting it. To fix it, you would have to reweave
it, and I do not think it is worth the time and effort it would take to do that, because rope is in-
expensive. Especially since you have much more
rope in the barn."

Decker grinned. "I suppose you're right. I
should just replace it, shouldn't I?"

Ben nodded at his fidgeting fingers. "A new

rope would be the least time-consuming and safest option in this particular scenario."

Decker let go of the ladder; it softly slapped against the tree trunk. He gave Scout's nose a quick stroke and took Tango's reins from Ben. "I wish I thought like you, Ben. You're so good at breaking things down."

"Another metaphor."

"Yes, another metaphor."

"I have not broken anything."

"I know." Decker hoisted himself onto Tango. The horse chuffed, unhappy that his grazing time was about to be over. "I'm guessing you came looking for me because students have started to arrive."

"Yes. The volunteers, too."

"Then I should get moving, huh? Are you nervous about the new session, Ben?"

"Sometimes it is difficult to tell the difference between excitement and nerves," Ben replied. "Cindy says that. She also says that you can experience both at the same time. I am experiencing both."

Cindy was the Applied Behavior Analysis therapist who worked with most of the students who came to Pathways. She lived in Riverside, a bigger town an hour and a half away, and would arrive a little later, after the students had been introduced to the ranch and to the horses. Decker's big score during the last session was adding her to the team, convincing her to donate her time twice a week. Sareena, the speech therapist, would also arrive later. Sareena came with her niece, and was happy to donate her services to all of the children, reminding Decker that by and large Haw Springs people were good people.

He nudged Tango's sides with his legs. "Let's go." The horse obediently began moving forward. Ben and Scout rode next to them. They plunged into the trees, heading home.

"Are you experiencing both?" Ben asked. "Excitement and nerves?"

"Nah, I'm mostly just feeling bruises from that fall," Decker said, but he was lying, and he knew it. He was more than just nervous—he was petrified. New students, new parents, new therapist on board.

And Morgan. The very thought of her sitting in his office made his stomach clench with nerves.

And maybe a little excitement. Just the tiniest twinge.

DECKER AND BEN popped out of the woods on their horses. Morgan had already arrived and stood on the outside of the round pen, watching Annie Allbrook, one of Decker's best volunteers. Annie was a high-functioning autistic person, and had a great day job working in the office at the elementary school in town. But during school breaks, she was first to head back to the ranch to work with her beloved horse, Sugar. When Annie first arrived at Pathways, she took to Sugar immediately, murmuring to the mare as if she'd finally met someone who understood her completely and she had loads of secrets to share. If Decker didn't know better, he would have thought Sugar felt the same way about Annie. *Finally. My someone.*

And, Decker had long suspected, Annie was also there to work alongside her beloved crush, Ben.

"Annie has arrived," Ben said, pushing Scout a little faster.

Annie gave Decker an awkward wave as soon as she saw them pop out of the trees. Seeing the wave, Morgan straightened and shaded her eyes to watch them ride in. Decker could feel himself push Tango a little faster, as if he were a teenager showing off for a pretty girl.

Okay, so maybe he wasn't experiencing both excitement and nerves. Maybe it was just plain nerves rolling around in his gut.

When he got close to the training area, he swung himself off Tango, gave him another pat and waited for Ben to dismount Scout.

"Mr. Decker!" Annie had dismounted her

horse and was chugging toward the fence, her boots kicking up a cloud of dust. She stepped up on the bottom rung and reached over for a fist bump.

"Annie Bananie! Good to see you! How you doing?" He thumped his fist against hers.

"Sugar remembers me," she crowed. "I gave her a carrot and she kissed me."

Decker laughed. "She's a good girl," he said. "And she has a good rider. Of course she remembers you. You're her favorite."

Annie beamed, pointing her face to the ground the way she always did when she was embarrassed by too much attention. "I'm going to bring her another carrot tomorrow, too."

"That sounds like a great idea."

Ben sauntered to the fence, having tied up Scout and Tango in preparation for class. He tipped his hat to Annie. "Miss."

Annie dropped back to the ground and wiped her hands on her jeans. "Hi."

Decker had suspected for some time that Ben was a little taken by the tiny, energetic brunette, because wherever she was, Ben was nearby. But Decker very much doubted that Ben would ever admit it, even though Annie wore her feelings for Ben all over her face.

"The welcome kits are in the office," Ben said. "I would like it if you helped me bring them outside. All of the students will have arrived soon, and Decker doesn't like to keep them waiting."

"Yes, I would like to help you with that."

Annie left Sugar to wander around the pen and joined Ben. They walked away without another word to Decker, as if he no longer existed.

"They seem like a pretty good team." Morgan had sidled up next to him. Tension rose in him as the breeze brought the scent of her to him, her hair shiny and billowing, little currents catching the elegant ruffled sleeve of her shirt, the legs of her crisp slacks.

"They've been working together for a while now," Decker said. "They seem to just get each other…" He trailed off, realizing that the last time he'd used the term *just get each other*, it was on a picnic blanket in the glade with the only woman he ever took back there. *This is going to be impossible*, he thought.

Archer squealed at their feet. Morgan whipped around, a mother who knew the sound of her child in distress without even seeing him.

He was a few feet away, lying on his back in the grass, June standing over him, licking his face.

"June! Off!" Decker scolded, but Morgan put her hand on his arm.

"No, no, this is good. Look at the smile."

She was right. Archer smiled, even as he pawed

away June's attention. The squeal was delight, not distress. Decker even heard a few giggles under the squeals. After a few more seconds, Archer rolled away and got to his knees. He held out his hands to June, who happily began licking them, too. The giggles turned into belly laughs.

Morgan chuckled. "Okay, Archer, that tells me we should probably go wash your hands." She turned to Decker. "He's obsessed with pancakes and peanut butter, and I guess we were in such a hurry this morning, we forgot to wash up before we left the house. Bathroom?"

Her cheeks were the same pale pink as her shirt, and the breathless way she talked about her son, the sparkle in her eyes when she said his name, made Decker almost unable to move or speak at all. He had to force himself to snap out of it. "Uh, yeah, there's one in the main building. I'll show you."

With great force, he made his boots move forward, hoping that he would, at some point, be able to leave the past behind. But he had no idea how he would do that with the past and the present so entwined...and so...beautiful.

CHAPTER FOUR

AFTER MORGAN WASHED and dried Archer's hands, she splashed some cold water on her own face. Maybe it was the sun that got her so flushed, but she suspected it was seeing Decker ride in on his horse and his sweet interaction with Annie that did it.

Get a grip, Morgan.

She dried her face and looked at herself in the mirror, trying to focus on the positive. June wasn't just licking Archer's face and hands. She was connecting with him. And he was connecting right back. Morgan shifted her eyes in the mirror to her son, who was happily spinning in circles. It wasn't easy to break through Archer's exterior, but June had seemed to do it with ease. If the dog could do it, who knew what a horse could do? This was an amazing development. A big deal!

"Hey. How about that puppy dog out there?" He kept spinning. "Arch? Arch. Archer." She touched his shoulder lightly and he stopped. Still, he had a huge grin on his face. He may be tucked way in deep, but wherever he was, he was frequently happy in there, and that was something she hung on to desperately as she navigated parenting a child on the spectrum. She crouched to his level. "Did you like that doggy?"

"Yes!" he exclaimed, rocking that favorite new word again.

"I think she liked you, too," Morgan said. "She was giving you kisses, wasn't she?"

"Yes!"

"Are you ready to meet the horses?"

"Yes!"

"Me, too. I think you're going to love them. Do you think you're going to love them?"

"Yes!"

She nodded, brushed his hair out of his eyes, stood, took his hand and headed back into the sunlight, determined to let her grudge against Decker go. This was all about Archer, and the horses he was about to fall in love with.

He hates the horses, Morgan texted.

No! Marlee responded. I thought he would love them.

You and me both. I'm pretty sure he thinks this is the worst idea I've ever had.

What happened?

Morgan paused. The observation room was dominated by two big windows facing the outdoor arena, and another two on a different wall facing the attached indoor arena. Windows for staff to keep an eye on things, in case someone had an emergency, and for parents to watch their children grow.

Or, in the case of Morgan, watch her child fling himself on the ground and wail inconsolably.

Morgan sighed and texted: Meltdown City, that's what happened.

I thought you said he had bonded with one. June?

June is a dog.

Oh.

Yeah.

Hard to ride a dog. But not impossible.

You're not very good at consolation. He's literally rolling around in the dirt.

He will wash.

Yes, but he can roll around in the dirt at home.

Give the kid a chance. He'll warm up.

I hope you're right. Morgan knew that Archer needed time to warm up to a lot of things. He wasn't great with change. And riding on top of a giant animal was definitely a change in his daily routine. It would have been more shocking if he'd jumped right up on one and taken off. But she also knew that sometimes he just never did warm up. Sometimes he made up his mind and that was that.

Morgan's phone buzzed again. Better subject— how's the job going? You and Baseball engaged yet? I'm not trying to tell you how to run your wedding, but as your maid of honor, I just want you to know that my best color is blue. Makes my eyes really pop.

Ha ha ha you are not funny. I've barely spoken to him. No sparks. Sorry. And I like yellow. Sorry again.

Who needs to talk when you have history and chemistry and…why does falling in love sound like going to school? Weird. Anyway, I'm sure you're dazzling him with your mad sales skillz.

Morgan was feeling a little like her job hadn't started yet, so she hadn't dazzled anyone with anything. Morgan didn't know where so much as a stapler might be hiding. So far, she'd only stood in front of the window, gazing out at her kid like all the other parents, and had only given nervous, sidelong glances toward the desk.

Do you think I should go out there and deal with Archer?

You mean helicopter him? No.

I mean make everyone's life less miserable by putting an end to the meltdown.

I think you should let the professionals work their magic. I'm sure this isn't the first meltdown they've seen.

Are you saying I'm not professional?

Are you trying to sell Archer ad space?

Fine. Point taken. I'll let someone else rescue him.

As if on cue, Decker appeared out of nowhere and crouched next to Archer, resting his fore-arms on his knees. Morgan watched as Archer writhed away from him, but then slowly calmed. She could tell that her son was listening to what-ever it was Decker had to say.

After a few minutes, Decker lowered himself so that he was sitting on the ground next to Ar-cher. June got up and bounced a few laps around

Decker, then plopped onto the dirt and rolled to her back. Archer laughed as Decker scratched the dog's belly, and then he reached out to pet her, too, at first clutching a handful of the dog's fur, then changing to a hard pat and finally flattening his hand to a soft stroke as Decker continued to work with him.

Morgan gazed at them, filled with so many mixed emotions. She was relieved that Archer was no longer crying. She was happy that he was making a connection with June. She wanted to be nothing but thrilled and hopeful for him, but she was guarded. These were the kind of moments she'd dreamed for Archer to have with Cody. But Cody had disappointed her. Now here was Decker, living up to the moment in a way that Cody never could, yet he, too, had disappointed her.

How was she going to expect Archer to trust Decker, when she herself didn't?

If I let Archer roll around in dirt at home, I wouldn't have to spend my entire day with a visual reminder of being rejected.

You may be holding on to an unreasonable amount of angst over Decker McBride.

I'm definitely holding on to something. I think it's called bitterness.

Healthy.

For real, I think this was a mistake, Morgan typed, but her finger hovered over the send button without pushing it. She watched as Decker stood, brushed off his jeans and held out a hand to Archer. To her surprise, her son took his hand and followed him to the fence. Decker lifted the little boy up to stand on a fence rail so he could get full view of the training ring, where Annie was busy riding Sugar in circles, showing off for the more timid kids. Decker pointed and talked, his arm around Archer, holding him in place. Archer watched, following Decker's finger.

He isn't going to get on a horse today, but maybe just not hating them is a good goalpost. Morgan was great at moving goalposts so her son could get the occasional score. It was all just so exhausting. But she was accustomed to exhaustion, so it was time to forge ahead.

She deleted what she'd typed. Gotta go. Trying to pretend that I'm cleaning up and doing actual work instead of just helicopter parenting.

Multitasking! Very nice! He'll love that about you!

Again, not funny.

She maneuvered herself behind the desk and began looking around, which felt a little like snooping, except all she was looking for was a pen and maybe a ledger or notebook of some kind. A contact list would be nice. Computer passwords. A phone. How was it possible he didn't have a phone? No, there was a phone number. She specifically remembered seeing it on the website. The phone was just hidden somewhere beneath the paperwork or maybe in a drawer or something. Had to be.

She quickly pulled up the Pathways website and dialed the number. She waited silently for a beat, then heard a muffled ring that matched the ringing in her phone. She began shifting papers, opening drawers, looking under things, but she couldn't find the source of the ring.

Until the call picked up at the same time that the door opened, and Decker stepped inside. "Hello?"

She quickly hung up and pocketed her phone.

"Hello?" He examined his phone screen, then glanced up at her with confusion knitting his brows. "Was that you?"

"Where's Archer? Wasn't he with you?"

He glanced through the window. "He was, but the phone rang, so now he's with one of the volunteers. Is something wrong?"

"Well, for starters," she said, feeling silly, "your

office doesn't have a phone. How do you run a business with no phone?"

He wiggled his cell phone in the air. "Right here."

"It's not in your office."

"Neither am I 90 percent of the time. If it was in here, I would never answer it. What's the point of a business phone if nobody is answering?"

She paused. This made sense. "Right."

He walked to the desk and laid the phone in front of her. "Trust me, you can have it. I'll happily leave it inside while you're here."

He leaned against the counter, and Morgan tried not to inhale too deeply. She remembered his scent—an intoxicating blend of leather and wood and something green and natural. She remembered the way he moved—purposeful and at the same time loose-jointed, almost as if he needed to put no effort into his movements because his body always just seemed to know what to do. She remembered the way he held the baseballs, casual and light, but then threw them with tight precision and intensity that flickered alive in an exhilarating instant. She ignored the pull to stand closer to him.

"You getting settled in?" he asked. "What do you need from me?"

She shook her head, partially trying to shake away the memory of Decker throwing those baseballs. For her. For that Tweety Bird. What had happened? What had she said or done to make him dump her?

No. Those were questions she'd stopped asking herself years ago.

"You okay?"

"It's just hard to concentrate when I can hear Archer having a meltdown and I'm not right there. I'm used to being the only one." She cleared her throat, trying to recover. "He hasn't had a big blowout episode like that in ages. You worked wonders with him just now, though. Thank you."

Decker glanced out the window. "Horses can be intimidating. Nobody's going to make him get on one if he doesn't want to. The meltdown is part of the process for some kids. We'll get him past it. Just might take a few days. He's a great kid, Morgan. He's going to be just fine."

What Morgan wouldn't have given to hear Cody say those words. Instead, it was always, *What's wrong with him? Can't you shut him up? Why is he like that? Just once I'd like to have a normal kid.*

Normal kid. That was the one that burned her up more than anything else. *What's normal?* she used to shoot back. *Not you. Not this.* Cody was never able to see just how remarkable Archer really was, yet Decker already had all kinds of faith in him.

"So…" Decker said, glancing at the paperwork on the desk. "First step?"

"Clean this up," Morgan said.

Decker nodded. "I haven't been as organized lately as I once was. A lot going on, what with working to get Cindy and Sareena on board, getting a new session up and ready, taking care of the animals and so forth. If you have some ideas on organization, I'd love to hear them. What else do you need?"

"Well," Morgan said, "do you have a list of contacts? People who currently donate to McBride Pathways, so I don't waste my time hitting up current donors?" A cloudy look passed over Decker's face. "You don't have a list?" Morgan asked, aghast. He pressed his lips together apologetically. "Oh. You don't have donors. Really? Not a single one?"

Decker spread his hands wide, as if making a concession. "Time" was all he said. "I'm a one-man show here. We had donors at first, but I didn't have time to keep asking. Plus I hate asking. Feels like begging."

Morgan took a deep breath and let it out in a gust. "Okay. Well, I don't mind asking. So, step one, clean this up. Quickly. Step two, get out there and get you some donors. Step three, get some big money rolling in. I only have a few weeks, but I promise you, by the time I leave, Mc-

Bride Pathways will be more than afloat. It'll be a cruise ship chugging off to exotic destinations."

Decker's grin deepened, and Morgan felt the pull of it in her chest. It was that same pull she felt standing at the carnival game all those years ago. "I like the way you think, Tweety."

"Morgan," she said, the admonishment popping out before she could even think about it. "Please."

"Of course. Morgan." She saw something sour pass over his face, something that tightened his brow and stiffened his jaw.

"What?"

"Nothing. You're right. I shouldn't… I just… I thought you said things wouldn't be weird between us."

"They're not."

"That felt weird. Tweety is just a nickname. Doesn't mean anything."

That one stung. Morgan felt it deep.

"But it's not just a nickname," she said, pressing her palms flat against the counter, trying, and failing, to dampen what really wanted to come out. "At least not to me. It does mean something." *It once meant everything.*

He straightened, pulled away from the counter, physically distancing himself from her. "My apologies. You won't hear it again."

"Decker, I intend to keep things professional. I'm just asking that you do the same."

"Message received. I guess I was just hoping we could be professional *and* be friends. But you're right. You're here for business, not friendship. Is there anything else we need to air out? If so, I'd like to know now. I don't want to be walking around my own ranch on eggshells."

There was an indignant snap to his voice that Morgan didn't like. This was not going at all like she'd planned. How dare he act put out? How dare he make it so *she* was the one on the defensive?

She was the one left filled with questions that she'd assumed would never get answered. Questions that she'd pushed down and tried to tell herself didn't matter.

Well, they did matter.

And she deserved answers.

"Eggshells? Really? Just because I don't want you to call me a pet name at work? Okay. We're doing this," she said. "Why?"

"Why what?"

"You know what, *Baseball*. One minute we were telling each other that we were falling in love with each other, planning to see each other as soon as I could get back down to Haw Springs, talking about a future together. And the next minute, you were telling me that it isn't working out. No explanation, just *isn't working out*, and then you were gone. Like you never existed. Like *we* never existed."

"I didn't want to lead you on," he said.

"Too late. You already had. I was in love with you. We were in love with each other. It *was* working out. We were figuring out how to make it work out."

"You were hours away."

"It was college. I was planning to come back. Was it that you just couldn't possibly wait for me? Another woman, maybe?"

"No, of course not."

"The very least you could do is give me a real explanation. Why, Decker? Why wasn't it working out all of a sudden? What happened?"

The air was thick between them, and Morgan could tell that there were things he wanted to say, but for some reason wouldn't. In some ways, she felt as if she knew Decker McBride better than she'd ever known anyone, and in other ways, he was a complete stranger. She started to wonder if maybe she'd just had it wrong all along, if she'd been the only one to feel the pull between them.

But, no, that couldn't be. Because she could still feel it now. It wasn't one way. The way he looked at her, the way he said her name. The way he called her *Tweety*.

"It was a long time ago," he said. "And I had my reasons."

Morgan's mouth dropped open, incredulous. "That's it? That's your explanation? That it was a long time ago and you had reasons?"

"I wouldn't have been able to give you what you wanted," he said.

"You didn't even know what I wanted. Not totally."

"I'm sorry, Morgan," Decker said. "Truly. And I'm thankful for your help here. But if you don't want to be here, I understand."

Morgan looked deeply into his eyes. He was passionate. Something she'd once loved about him. But she could see clearly now that she wasn't his passion. Not anymore.

If she ever was.

No matter what she said, it wouldn't make a difference now, all these years later. The end result would be the same. He didn't love her, and pushing to know why could cost her the chance of being at Pathways. It could cost Archer the chance of growing. And Archer was what was most important in her life.

After a long, silent moment that felt like an eternity, she turned her eyes back to the desk. "Like you said, it was a long time ago. I was young and seeing a future where there wasn't one. And you're right—it wouldn't have worked. We obviously went on to live two completely different lives. I won't bring it up again. Just, um…the nickname."

Decker cleared his throat and turned away from the counter. "Of course. Yeah. Makes sense. Guess I should get back out there. See if Annie and Ben need anything."

"Right," Morgan said. "Don't worry about me in here. I've got everything under control. McBride Pathways is about to be a household name."

He removed his cowboy hat and scratched his head, looking shy and beautiful, those curls tumbling loose against his neck. "Well, I don't know about that. But I'd love to give it a shot. Thank you, Morgan. And, again, I'm sorry. I wish I could explain it to you."

He put the hat back on his head and walked out, his boots clunking against the wood floor like exclamation points slicing through her heart. Exclamation points that she didn't want there at all but felt powerless to keep away.

"You could," she said after the door had shut. "You just won't."

IT WASN'T LIKE Decker to feel so off balance and distracted during class. He couldn't get thoughts of Morgan out of his head. *Is she watching right now? What is she thinking? Will she forever hate me for what I did? What if she decides Path-*

ways isn't for Archer and doesn't come back? It seemed that he barely got class started before parents were streaming to the arena fence to pick up their kids, the day over.

He didn't blame Morgan for being hurt. He'd never told her about his childhood and how he didn't trust love. He didn't divulge his fear that she would leave him down the road with an irreparable hole in his heart, just as his mother had done to his father. He didn't know how to explain that he'd chosen the hurt of losing her when they were just getting started over the hurt of losing her later, when she was the very air that he breathed. How could he make her understand that? He'd barely been able to understand it himself.

"I think I'll take off," Cindy said, sidling up to him after the last of the kids had gone. Only Archer remained, and he was happily lying on his side on the ground next to June under her favorite oak tree, picking at leaves of grass. Pathways was all about horses, but Decker would never be convinced that June didn't also have a hand in helping many of the kids who came through.

Cindy followed Decker's gaze. "I'll work with him some more tomorrow. He'll get there. I'm pretty confident about it."

"He will," Decker agreed. "He's not my first kid to shy away from the horses."

"And he won't be the last. That's what makes this good work, though, you know? You get to really make a difference in someone's life." She pointed toward the barn, where the teen volunteers stood in a loose group, some chatting, but most quietly lingering, staring at their phones for the first time all day. "Speaking of making a difference. I'll let you get to the eager crowd."

Decker chuckled. "I don't know about eager," he said. "More like tired and hungry crowd. I'm guessing they'd like to go home for dinner."

"That makes two of us." Cindy walked to the oak tree and squatted next to Archer. "Archer, I'll bet you're ready to go home, too, huh? Would you like to come with me to find your mama?"

Archer, hearing the word *mama*, scrambled to his feet and followed Cindy to the office. Decker loped toward the group of teens. Ben stepped out of the barn to meet him, always the leader looking for something to lead.

"The horses are all taken care of, but I told everyone that they needed to stay until you give the A-OK." He gave a timid thumbs-up.

"You're the leader here. Did you give *your* A-OK?"

"I did. Cheyenne forgot to fill Sugar's water bucket, but I caught her mistake. Sugar has plenty of water now."

"Good catch," Decker said. "Anything else?"

Ben shook his head. "They're experienced and willing workers. Salt of the earth. Which is an idiom, meaning that someone is honest and reliable and a good, loyal worker, even if they don't necessarily look like they will be those things."

Decker smiled and gave Ben's shoulder a pat, then addressed the group. "Everyone, thank you for being here today. Did anyone have any problems or issues that we need to discuss?"

The kids milled toward him, looking up from their phones, but nobody engaged. Decker was used to that by now. If there was a problem or issue, he would have to rely on Ben to find out and bring it to him, or he would find out himself when the issue boiled over.

"No? Okay, then I'll see you all here tomorrow. Come in early enough to grab a pancake or two in the main building. Ben and I will bust out the griddle." He saw the look of alarm and confusion on Ben's face. "We're not actually busting anything. I just mean that you and I are going to cook pancakes for everyone in the morning. Do you know how to cook pancakes? Because I don't."

Ben's hands were twining nervously; he placed them on his hips to stop the motion, giving himself a look of authority. "I can study how to make pancakes tonight," he said. "But I can't guarantee that I will have it all memorized before tomorrow morning. Not if I intend to engage in the recommended eight to ten hours of sleep. I may have to use a printed recipe or perhaps my phone. And, of course, with it being my first time making them, I cannot guarantee results."

Annie giggled and covered her mouth. Ben shifted his weight uneasily and crossed his arms tightly across his chest.

"I was just kidding," Decker said. "I know how to make them. I just need a little help, if that's okay."

"Who will tack up the horses?"

"Choose an assistant to come in early with you and help you out. I'll also help. Together, we'll get them squared away."

"Squared…?"

"It's another idiom. It means we will have them all ready to go in plenty of time. Besides, some of the returning campers can start learning how to tack up their horses tomorrow. You want to teach them?"

Ben straightened with pride. "Yes, I do."

"Excellent. See? We have tomorrow all planned already. Come hungry, everybody. See you tomorrow. And thank you for a great opening day."

Decker left the teens to run toward the parking lot, where their parents waited in their cars, and headed toward the office to shut down everything else. This was his dream, as long as he could remember. A warm summer evening wrapping up a successful session, horses in the barn, dog at his heels...

Wife and son waiting for him to call it a night.

He paused and shook his head. So maybe he didn't have the entire dream. But he had most of it, and that mattered.

And he had Ben, which also mattered. And in many ways, Pathways was as much Ben's dream as it was Decker's.

In high school, Decker had spent a lot of time defending Ben against the cruelty that awaited anyone who wasn't exactly like everyone else. He met every mouthy classmate with fists clenched and jaw jutted. In turn, Ben had defended Decker against himself, refusing to allow Decker even the slightest moments of self-doubt. He believed in Decker's abilities more than Decker did.

Decker was immersed in thought as he pulled open the office door.

Archer knelt in front of the coffee table, playing with a set of plastic animal figurines. He made soft animal noises while he played, floating deep in his imagination. Morgan looked up from the desk and gave a tentative smile.

Decker had a sense that he should say something, but words evaded him. The scene, right on the heels of his thoughts of his dream of having a family, seemed perfect and cruel. Morgan was the wife he'd imagined. She was also the reason he shut down that dream and accepted he would never have what he truly wanted. He must have paused a beat too long, because Morgan's smile faded into a look of concern.

"Everything okay?" she asked.

Feet forward, he told himself. *Snap out of it. Get it together, McBride.* He cleared his throat, determined to ignore the earlier dustup between them and get back to whatever was going to be their version of normal. "Absolutely. Did you have a great first day, Archer?"

Archer completely ignored him.

"Did he ever get on a horse?" Morgan asked.

"Not yet. Cindy will keep working with him," Decker said. "Some kids need a little extra warm-up time, but— Whoa!"

Morgan jumped back from the desk, panicked, her arms flying in the air. "What?"

Decker pointed. "The desk. There's…" He grinned. "There's a desk there."

Morgan slapped her hand on her chest and let out a breath. "You scared the daylights out of me. I thought something was wrong. Or there was a mouse or something."

"You're afraid of mice? I had no idea. They're tiny little creatures."

"They're…they're hairy. And have pointy little toes and tails and beady little eyes."

Decker laughed. "Thank you for describing what a mouse looks like. I thought they had horns and long noses that drag the ground. Giant, gnarly beasts, those mice."

Morgan crossed her arms. "They can scurry up your pant leg and they can bite and they can transmit diseases like…like the Black Plague." She said the last meekly, trailing off as Decker gave a skeptical look.

"I think you might be thinking of rats. And Ben will tell you that it was actually fleas on hamsters that carried the plague."

"What does Ben know?" she asked.

They locked eyes for a beat, and then both answered at the same time. "Everything."

"Anyway," she said, "I tried to organize things as best I could. I'm going to bring in a few supplies tomorrow. Something I can take notes in, and something to organize business contacts. And a coffeepot. Maybe some bottles of water for the parents who stick around? Make it a little more welcoming in here. Not that it isn't already beautiful. It's just…rustic." She ran her hand along the edge of the desk. "And dusty. I'll bring some cleaning supplies, too."

"Morgan, I don't expect you to clean my office."

"*Our* office," she corrected him. "At least for

a few weeks. And it's my pleasure. Consider it a tip for the extra childcare from June."

"Aw, June's just an old, lazy hound. She's happy to have someone scratch her belly for a while."

"She occupied Archer for a good, long time. Trust me, that can be work, belly scratches or not."

Decker thought it over and chuckled at the thought of June working as a nanny. "Seems like a good deal for me. June does all the work, and I get the spruced-up office."

But no matter how hard they tried, the air between them still felt stiff. Decker tried to think of the right words to say. He felt such familiarity with Morgan, but at the same time, like they were complete strangers. Like everything he tried to say would fall flat under the weight of missing years. Like no matter what he said, she would forever only remember the heartbreak.

"Anyway," Decker said.

"Archer, it's time to go. Aunt Marlee is waiting," Morgan said at the same time, grabbing her purse from under the desk. "Tomorrow I'll hit the ground running. I'll probably go into town, start talking to local vendors about sponsorship opportunities. Name on a banner and all that."

"Sounds good."

"People just love to see their names on banners." She bustled out from behind the desk, her high heels in one hand. Something about watching her shuffle in bare feet endeared her to Decker; he couldn't help smiling. Morgan was unapologetically who she was. She always had been.

She crouched next to Archer and helped him scoop the tiny animals into a bag, letting him keep one in each hand for the drive home. Archer headed for the door; Morgan paused just long enough to stuff her feet into her shoes, and then she followed him.

"See you tomorrow," Decker said.

"Mmm-hmm," she responded. At the door, her hand on the doorknob, she paused and turned as if she was trying to decide if she should speak or not. "Forget about earlier, okay? I just… I guess wondering what happened between us got the better of me. I think I needed to air it out."

"I'm the one who should apologize. I didn't want to hurt you. I hate that I did. I don't know how to make it up to you."

She waved him away. "You don't need to. Everything's great. I promise. See you tomorrow?"

He dipped his head in affirmation; she slipped through the door into the evening air, pulling Archer along behind her.

Alone in the main office, Decker realized how tired he was. The first day of a new session always wore him out, without the conflicting feel-

ings of a long-lost love waltzing back into it with
no warning. He sank onto the little couch and
propped his feet up on the coffee table where
Archer had just been playing.

He felt bowled over by his past. Not just his
past with Morgan, but his entire past.

Decker was ten the last time he saw or heard
from his mother. Images of her face swirled in
his memory, young and sturdy and beautiful. He
remembered the sobbing episodes, the yelling
fits, the fights between her and his father. He re-
called the silver buckles on her suitcase, the red
of her shoes that perfectly matched her finger-
nails. The bounce of her curls as she walked out
the door, away from his dad. Away from David.
Away from him. Forever.

Maureen, I've got my hands full here, his dad
had cried.

I've got my hands full.

Decker shook his head to chase away the memories and sat up. Morgan tried to press in on him,
too, and he shook his head a second time. He
needed the past to just stay in the past and stop
haunting him.

"Yep, I've definitely got my hands full. Way
too full."

He got up, turned off the lights and stalked
out of the office, headed for home.

CHAPTER FIVE

"I'M OFF TO see Dr. LaSalle," Morgan said, handbag looped over one shoulder. She wore a pale yellow sundress with a cropped white cardigan, and a pair of cork wedge sandals, just tall enough to let everyone know she was headed for work and not the beach.

Marlee, who was busy putting together a puzzle with Archer, glanced up at Morgan and gave a low whistle. "You trying to make Dr. LaSalle fall in love with you or what?"

"Ha ha." Morgan brushed her skirt with her hands, loving the tiny white flowers with little dots of blue for centers. The dress was literally every color that Morgan looked best in. She felt great in it. "This is professional work attire. I'm not trying to make anyone fall in love with me."

Okay, maybe it wasn't quite the work attire that she would wear to her actual job. Those outfits were more black and gray slacks and buttondowns and boring, chunky, sensible shoes. But she was in Haw Springs in the summer—things were more laid-back here. Relaxed. Sunny and whimsical. She couldn't go stomping through Main Street offices in dark, dreary suits and expect the same results that she'd get in one of the giant corporate offices in the city.

Plus, if someone fell in love with her, it might not be all bad.

Just not Decker. Maybe.

She was so confused by Decker right now. He was the same guy she remembered him to be, and she definitely loved that about him. Joking with him had felt good—maybe too good. And also bad—definitely too bad. He'd had so many opportunities, including just yesterday when they had to have the whole Tweety conversation, to just be up-front with her. Yet she still had nothing.

Jerk.

So, yes, she wanted him to fall in love with her. So that she could not want him in return, and he could see how that felt. And not tell him why she was pulling away. And, yes, she knew that was an immature reaction on her part, and she didn't care.

The dress, sweater, sandals ensemble was more See What You Could Have Had If You Hadn't Dumped Me attire. *Unjustly Jilted: a new clothing line by Morgan West.*

"Good, I'm glad you aren't trying to snag him, because Dr. LaSalle is mine, all mine," Marlee said.

Morgan's eyes grew wide. "You're dating him and you didn't tell me? That could have been awkward to find out during a business meeting."

"Relax. No, we're not dating. He doesn't even know I exist. I have an appreciation, is all. His clinic is right around the corner from the flower shop, and I may or may not find myself needing some fresh air at the end of the workday so I can watch his comings and goings with interest."

"*An appreciation* and *interest*. I think you mean a crush."

"He's an excellent doctor, from what I hear. I think I just might be coming down with something serious." Marlee gave a few weak coughs. "I need medical attention."

"He's a pediatrician. You're tiny, but you're not five. And you're perfectly healthy. He's not going to give you medical attention."

"He took an oath. If I show up in his office in dire need of medical care, he has to provide it, no matter how old I am."

"I don't think dying of a crush exactly qualifies as dire need," Morgan said.

"I may need mouth-to-mouth resuscitation." Marlee flopped over onto her back dramatically, one arm flung out, her eyes closed. Archer took this as a sign to tackle her; he pounced, toppled over her middle. "Oof!" Marlee's eyes flew open, and she didn't miss a beat; she crooked her fingers into claws and began tickling Archer until he squealed and rolled away. "Tackle me, will you? Then face the consequences!"

"Besides, what do you want with some old doctor, anyway?" Morgan asked, trying to be heard over their commotion. "There are plenty of cute, young guys in Haw Springs."

Marlee sat up. "What do you mean *old* doctor?"

"You told me he's *the original small-town doctor*, and he carries one of those old-fashioned doctor's bags and everything. I'm envisioning a stooped old man with round spectacles, and shaky hands that he uses to pat your knee to comfort you while he calls you *child* and *dear* and, like, gives you a good bloodletting with leeches."

Marlee's cheeks puffed, and then she burst out laughing. "Okay. Yeah. That's what Matthew LaSalle is like. Exactly. I wish I could be a fly on the wall when you meet him."

Morgan checked her watch and jumped. "Meet him! I'm supposed to be there already. Gotta go. Thanks for taking Archer to Pathways. Love you, buddy." She gave Archer a peck on the top of his head. "And I love you, sis!"

"I can't wait to hear all about old, stooped Dr.

LaSalle," Marlee called as the door shut behind Morgan.

It was a perfect early-summer day in Missouri. The sun was as pale as Morgan's dress, and lapped her face with warm waves. She sat in her car and closed her eyes against it, just taking a moment to breathe in the sweet scent of dew-laden, freshly cut grass. Later in the summer, it would become unbearably hot. Bugs would cloud the air, the ebb and flow of cicada calls would wrap around the city like a stifling blanket, and the grass would be dry and crunchy and no longer needing to be cut.

Those dog days of summer would forever remind her of Decker. Festival season. She planned to be long gone from Haw Springs before so much as the first trailer pulling a carnival ride arrived.

But today…perfection. She started her car and drove into town.

She barely saw the plain, wooden LaSalle Pediatric Clinic sign hanging unassumingly from the eaves of an ordinary house. She pulled into the driveway, which led to a small parking lot around back. Also around back, the entrance to a yarn store. A sign taped to the door said Forgot my breakfast! Back in 5 mins!

Only in Haw Springs, Morgan thought as she got out of her car and tromped across the gravel lot, trying not to let the pebbles topple her over in her wedge shoes.

Wouldn't that be lovely? Me, sprawling on the ground with a broken ankle, my sunny yellow dress all covered with dirt and gravel dust.

She pushed open the door, feeling a little as though she were barging into someone's home. In fact, she was 90 percent certain that the upstairs was actually Dr. LaSalle's home. *Not a bad commute*, she thought. She found herself in a small waiting area filled with toys and books, and a TV that showed a cartoon movie with the sound muted.

She checked in with the receptionist, whose nameplate read *Mary LaSalle*, and remembered Marlee telling her that Dr. LaSalle's retired school secretary mother was his receptionist. Together, they were a two-man show. Quaint.

All checked in, Morgan barely had a chance to sit down before the door to the exam rooms opened.

"Morgan West?"

Dr. LaSalle stood in the doorway, long white coat hanging on his slender frame. Marlee wasn't wrong—he was the kind of handsome it was hard to look away from.

"Yes, that's me. Thank you for seeing me." She stood and stuck out a hand.

"Thank you." He gave her hand a quick shake,

and then ushered her through the door. "I appreciate you being willing to come in before we start seeing patients."

"Oh, no, I'm the appreciative one. I'm sure you get very busy around here."

He hurried down the hallway toward an office that was stuffed to the gills with books and papers and one lonely laptop in the middle of a large, antique-looking desk. "Oh, it ebbs and flows, you know. It can get a little crazy once the kids start flooding in. Right now, we're flowing with a good case of summer strep going around."

"Summer strep? Isn't strep always strep?"

He stopped at his office door and let her lead the way inside. "I suppose that's one way to look at it. We see it a little differently around here. Oh, let me get that for you."

He rushed around her, scooping a big pile of books off the chair and setting them on the floor, next to a worn, leather Gladstone bag. Undoubtedly the physician's bag that Marlee had mentioned.

Stepping into his office was like stepping back in time. The ages of the things Dr. LaSalle surrounded himself with didn't exactly match the age of the man himself.

It was quirky and fun, and if she were to stay in Haw Springs, she could envision herself bringing Archer to Dr. LaSalle. *Archer would like him*, she thought. *He would be very interested in what's in that bag.*

If she were going to stay. Which she definitely couldn't do. For many reasons.

But, boy, would it be so good to stay.

So many things she loved dearly—Marlee, her parents, Main Street, the scent of hay and the feel of warm grass under bare toes, and even handwritten signs on yarn store doors—were in Haw Springs. What, besides Archer and her job, did she really have to hang on to in Kansas City?

"So," Dr. LaSalle said, sitting at his desk. He folded his hands. "You wanted to talk about McBride Pathways?"

"Huh?" She snapped out of her daydream. "Oh. Yes. Are you familiar with the Pathways program?"

"I'm familiar with the ranch, and with the McBride brothers, yes. I've had a patient or two talk about the program. But I'm afraid that's where my knowledge ends. Regrettably, I've never been to the ranch. I've been pretty busy here. I hope you understand."

"Of course. I'm sort of new to the program myself, but from what I've seen, it is incredibly beneficial. The kids love it. They seem to make huge strides. They come back to volunteer as teenagers, and they really take it seriously. Decker…er, Mr. McBride…teaches them how to, um…tack the horses and, um…I think clean the hooves and brush them—the horses, not the hooves—and feed and water them. And ride them. They do a lot of riding. Of the horses." Morgan fought the urge to wince and call for a do-over. That little speech went nothing like the way she'd practiced it in the shower. She knew she could do better.

Dr. LaSalle grinned. "You don't know much about horses, do you?"

Morgan shrugged in defeat. "I really don't. But I'm learning. And my job isn't about the horses, anyway."

"It's not? So you're there for…?"

Morgan felt herself relax. This was the part she was practiced at and quite good at.

She pulled a McBride Pathways flyer out of her handbag and slid it across the desk. "As I'm sure you know, it costs a lot of money to get any business up and running. And I'm sure you also know that a business that requires any sort of specialty items costs even more. Horses are specialty items. Decker has been working his tail off to create a great program that's benefiting so many kids. But he relies on volunteers and grants and, well, sponsors to keep the business afloat. And that's where you come in."

He glanced at her over the flyer. "I do?"

"Yes. We need sponsors in order to continue to

offer our services to all families who need it, not just the ones who can afford it. Would you be interested in sponsoring McBride Pathways? We're looking to put up signs in the indoor arena. We will also be sure to acknowledge our sponsors on every print correspondence, of course."

Morgan didn't actually know if this was true. For all she knew, Decker hated the idea of signage in his arena and didn't do any print correspondence at all. In retrospect, she should have found out these things ahead of time. But she was a firm believer in asking for forgiveness rather than permission; what choice would Decker have if she showed up with money and sign in hand?

"Put your name in the newsletters we hand out to parents, email blasts, social media recognition?" she offered. "We could do that, too." She was 100 percent sure Decker didn't do social media. *Gonna be asking for a lot of forgiveness.*

Dr. LaSalle skimmed the pamphlet in front of him, but his expression didn't change. Getting people to part with their money was all about options, Morgan knew. She pressed on. All she needed was to get her foot in the door, and then she could sell anything to anyone.

"Or, if you don't want to sponsor, maybe you would be willing to just be a onetime donor? We're in need of those, too. You see, Dr. LaSalle, there is a bit of a myth out there that riding lessons are for rich people only. But that's not how McBride Pathways work. We like to meet people where they are. We do everything we can possibly do to make the program affordable for everyone." She could see his face softening as he continued to stare at the flyer, so she went in for the hard press. "You love children, Dr. LaSalle. That's why you're a pediatrician. And you know how hard it can be for some kids who struggle with…extra needs. With even a small donation or our lowest-tier sponsorship, you could be the person who opens an opportunity for a child. Don't you want to be that person?"

Dr. LaSalle leaned back in his chair, fingers tented under his chin, still staring at the flyer. Morgan was so close to winning him over, she could feel it. She loved the thrill of almost having a deal closed. It energized her. She couldn't wait to get back and tell Decker that she'd already made headway on her first real day out in the field.

There was a brief knock on the door frame. The receptionist leaned in. "Your nine o'clock is here." Morgan felt herself deflating. There was nothing worse for sealing a deal than a time-sensitive interruption.

Dr. LaSalle checked his watch with a start. "Thank you." He slid the pamphlet back toward

Morgan. She knew this apologetic pamphlet-slide. She knew what came next—*thank you, but no, thank you*, and, *I have to get back to work now.* "Ms. West, I'm afraid I'm just not in a position to donate a lot of money to anyone. As you could probably guess, I haven't been here very long, and I'm trying to get a clinic up and running myself."

"Yes, of course. Totally understand. But please know that your donation doesn't have to be substantial. We'll leave substantial donations to the bankers," she joked. "What is a reasonable amount to you? Even just five hundred dollars can help a child who needs to pay for his riding lessons."

"I hate to disappoint you." He stood.

She stood. "Then don't."

"I have a patient waiting. Can we follow up on email?"

"You have patients who attend McBride Pathways. I'm sure of it. And if you don't, well, then you will in the future. You never know who's looking for a new pediatrician. Especially a pediatrician who is supportive of children on the spectrum. As a parent of a child on the spectrum, I know how important it is to find resources and help from people who understand how they work."

He walked to the door, but Morgan stayed put.

She'd learned this tactic long ago, that if you just refused to leave, it made it harder for them to keep saying no. He sighed and shrugged his shoulders in defeat.

She resisted the urge to pump her fists in victory. She had him. She knew it. He would come in with some low number like five hundred dollars. And she would counter, and he would demur, and she would keep driving at him until he was up to one thousand dollars. And then five thousand dollars. And then—

She got an idea. Of course. In a place like Haw Springs, people liked to see their money go toward something.

Just as Dr. LaSalle opened his mouth to speak, she rushed toward him. "A benefit," she said. "We'd like to partner with you on a benefit. A fundraiser. Horses for Health. Um…Stables of Shots. Checkups and Gallups. Physicals and Phillies."

The receptionist appeared again. "I've checked in your 9:15," she said.

"I've really got to go." Dr. LaSalle gestured toward the waiting room. Morgan could see his stress, and she wanted to feel bad for him, but she couldn't. She was onto something big, and she just needed to get him on board. "If I get behind schedule first thing in the morning, it makes it very difficult to catch up later."

Morgan pushed on. "Think about it. School will be starting soon. People will be wanting their wellness checks and sports physicals and immunizations. We could hold an event where you could do those things on the spot. We would find a private place for you to use as an exam area. You already bring your tools with you." She indicated the bag on the floor; he quickly scooped it up, as if he'd forgotten it was there. "You don't have to give us your money, just your time. You spend a whole day working with potentially billable future patients—including new ones from Buck County and Riverside and... and probably even as far out as Spearville or Peculiar...and we ask them for a donation, plus charge a flat fee for a trail ride. After they finish with you, they go on the ride. Or, if that's not their thing, they just get time with a horse. Or they help groom one. Or...or maybe something different altogether. A carnival or a fair of some kind. Just something that makes people happily part with their money but also that benefits the community by providing health care. You get a whole bunch of new patients, and we help our students afford their lessons. In the evening, we have a benefit dinner. We'll get people from Kansas City and St. Louis to come in with their big money. I know those people, Dr. La-Salle. I can make this happen."

The more Morgan talked, the more she liked the idea. This could be big for Decker. This could be big for Haw Springs. This could be big for everyone. And she would be the one who made it happen. A temporary, part-time, unpaid ad salesperson.

"Saddle Up for Health—a Western Wellness Initiative," she stated. "The First Annual Saddle Up for Health Benefit. You could get in on the ground floor. You really should, being the pre-eminent pediatrician in Haw Springs and all."

There was a muffled noise from the waiting room that pulled his attention away just the slightest. He seemed hurried. But he also seemed to be thinking. She couldn't wait to tell Marlee about the possibility of catching Dr. LaSalle in a barn filled with twinkling lights and dancing. Her sister would be the first in line to buy a ticket.

He nodded slowly, thoughtfully, and then his nod picked up speed. "Okay," he said. "Okay. I like the idea. I'll do it. Count me in."

"Great!" Morgan tried not to gush too hard and tip her hand. *Stay cool, stay unattached, as if this is only the first of many huge sales you'll make today*, she reminded herself.

But, gosh, she was so excited.

"Great," she repeated, holding her hand out for a shake again. "We'll work up the details and get them to you as soon as possible. In the meantime, if you have any ideas, please give me a call. I've written my number on the back of the flyer."

"Okay. Sure. Definitely. I've got to go now. You can see yourself out?"

"Yes, yes, of course. Thank you for giving me your time, Dr. LaSalle. You won't regret it. This will be huge for both of us."

He shook her hand. "I hope so."

"It will be. I give you my word. You can count on me, Dr. LaSalle."

She left the office, her smile as beaming and buttery as the yellow in her sundress.

She couldn't wait to tell Decker the good news.

"A BENEFIT?" Decker said doubtfully. "What do you mean by 'benefit'?"

"Exactly what I said." Morgan was trying not to get irritated. Not that she'd expected Decker to be jumping for joy. Except, well, maybe she'd expected that a little bit. But even if he couldn't muster that level of excitement, perhaps the tiniest bit of eagerness would have been nice. Maybe some gratitude. "A benefit. A fundraiser."

Decker frowned at the computer screen, where Morgan had started to map out ideas for the event. "I don't know. Sounds needy."

"What do you mean you don't know? And you

are needy. This is going to bring in big money, Decker. Isn't that what you wanted so you can buy out David?"

"Yeah," he said, walking to the waiting area and lowering himself to the couch. "I just... Now that we're doing it, it feels like begging. My father would have never begged."

"Your father was selling beans, or...or beef, or... I don't know what he sold. But he was selling goods. You're selling services. There's a big difference."

"But he never had to just ask people for money. It doesn't feel right. Maybe David has a point. If I've got to be begging, maybe I should just sell everything and relocate somewhere smaller."

She followed him but didn't sit. She was too frustrated to sit. If, after her hard work of getting Dr. LaSalle on board, Decker decided to let his pride get in the way and shut this thing down, she would be fit to be tied. She had a feeling, though, that it wasn't his pride. It was something else, and he just didn't want to say it. "Decker, you've got the wrong idea about this. It's not begging or being needy or asking for charity. It's creating business partnerships. It's keeping your ranch afloat. *This* ranch, where your family is from. Somewhere smaller isn't McBride land." She paused. "But if you want to relocate, then fine. This benefit will get you the funds to start up at that location. Either way, you can't lose. We can call it something else, if the word *benefit* is what's bothering you."

"Everything about it is bothering me. A big, froofy event. So much pretending and small talk. It's just not me. It's not the ranch. We're real here."

"So be real. Don't pretend," Morgan said. "It'll make the small talk easier if you're just yourself."

"Doubtful."

"Trust me. I'm saying this as someone who fell in love with you instantly on a midway when you were just being yourself." Morgan stopped short, realizing too late that once again she was bringing up the past, which they'd agreed to leave behind. "Um…I mean…just…take it from me, okay?"

"What about grants?" Redness had crept up his skin. He scratched the back of his neck, leaving a temporary white line where his fingernail had just been. "There've got to be some out there. I don't have to walk around and fake smile for hours with a grant."

Morgan could see Decker's true discomfort at the idea of having to do this, and it kind of made her heart ache a little. She sat on the couch next to him. "Take it from someone who's had to pick up the pieces and pivot and, yes, sometimes even enlist help to keep moving forward. You do what you have to do to follow your dream. Asking for help to achieve your vision isn't failure. Never asking and then watching your dream die is failure. You have nothing to worry about with this benefit. If you let me really work this, you'll have plenty of funds to do whatever you want to do with Pathways."

"You hope."

"I know."

"I just wish you had talked to me before making promises," he said.

"I'm trying to help you." Morgan's limbs felt leaden. "This is my job, to get you money, remember? I told you I'm good at what I do, and part of being good is thinking of creative ways to make people open their wallets."

"I expected grants and scholarships and names on a sign, not a dog and pony show," he said.

"It's not a dog and pony show. And, by the way, Baseball, you quite literally have a dog and a pony, so bad analogy."

"I thought we couldn't call each other those names."

There was a beat of silence between them, the air heavy with so many feelings, Morgan felt swimmy and off balance. The nickname had slipped out. As much as she tried to drive away the familiarity between them, it was always there, right under the surface.

"Stop being so stubborn," she said by way of avoidance. "You're letting your pride get in the way."

"I'm not being stubborn. I'm being realistic." He pulled off his cowboy hat and ran his fingers through his waves, which Morgan tried not to notice. "Whatever you put together, I have to live with in the long run. You don't."

"What do you mean I don't?"

"I'm here forever, but you'll head back up to the city as soon as your vacation time runs out. You're temporary, Morgan. Two months from now, you won't even think about McBride Pathways. And this place will go on without you here."

For some reason that she really couldn't pinpoint, the comment struck Morgan hard. It was the truth, but at the same time, hearing it from him felt...harsh. Maybe it was because he'd gone on without her once before.

"Well, you're really good at moving on," she said.

"Not as good as you think," he said.

They stared at each other, hard, for a long time.

The door opened, and Annie stuck her head inside. She was red-faced and breathless.

"Mr. Decker?"

Decker sat forward. "What's wrong, Annie?"

"One of the students is missing."

"Missing? What do you mean 'missing'?" Decker asked.

Annie's chin crumpled, and a tear ran down her face. "We've looked everywhere. We can't find him. We've been in the barn and the indoor arena and the outdoor arena and the shed and the bathrooms."

"Who is it?" Decker asked, jumping to his feet.

"Archer," Annie said, almost mumbling it, as her eyes darted over at Morgan and then down to the floor. "I'm sorry, Miss Morgan."

But Morgan didn't hear the last part; she was already brushing past Annie and Decker and out the door.

MORGAN TOOK OFF so fast, Decker didn't even have time to formulate a plan. By the time he got outside, she had already rounded the main office building and was heading up the incline toward the street. All that was left were the two sandals she'd been wearing, abandoned on the ground. She sprinted through the grass like lightning, her yellow sundress swishing around her knees.

Of course, he thought. *She's fast. How did I forget that about her?*

His mind wanted to bring forward a memory of them racing through the field where they had their picnic, him starting all cocky and full of himself, touting that he was an athlete, so no way she could ever beat him. And then she did exactly that. By a lot. He had known, in that instant, that his heart was a goner. It had instantly scared him. He couldn't fall in love with her, and he knew it. He couldn't fall in love with anyone. Ever.

But Morgan was so intoxicating. He remembered leaning in for that first kiss, unsure if he would even be able to breathe if he got too close to her.

He forced the memory away. Now was hardly the time.

Morgan got to the top of the hill and stopped at the edge of the gravel road. She shaded her eyes and peered in one direction, and then the other, her shoulders drawing up and down with each heavy breath. She shook her head and turned back to face Decker. There was distance between them, but he could see the desperation and fear on her face.

She came back down the hill toward him.

"The barn," she said. "Maybe he's with June."

"Good thought," he said. "The kids just overlooked him when they were searching, I'm sure."

Together, they raced toward the barn, but Decker slowed, his heart sinking when he saw June coming at them through the yard. Archer was not with her. The boy hadn't left the dog's side—and vice versa—since his first day at Pathways. They were best friends. If he wasn't with her, where was he?

He knew Morgan had to be thinking the same thing. She let out an anguished little yelp and increased her speed. June yipped and jumped and nipped at Decker's elbows and heels as he tried to keep up with Morgan, like this was a big, fun game and she wanted in on it.

"Not now." He gently pushed her away. "It's not time to play, June."

Morgan was inside the barn a full ten steps before Decker was. By the time he opened the door and let his eyes adjust to the shadows, she had already turned over June's blanket and thrown open two empty stall doors.

"Archer?" Decker called, trying to catch his breath as he opened two more stalls. All the horses were outside in the pasture. There didn't appear to be even so much as a mouse stirring in the barn. "Archer?"

"That won't do any good," Morgan said.

"What do you mean? What if he's stuck somewhere and just can't get out without help?"

"He won't answer, is what I mean. You can call for him all day long. He will never answer."

"Maybe this time he will."

"Or maybe I've played a million games of hide-and-seek with this kid, and I'm telling you, not one of those times has he ever answered. I've called him for breakfast, for dinner, to hurry up, to come hold my hand, a billion things, Decker. He doesn't come when he's called. And he doesn't call back."

"But—" He'd thrown open the remaining two stall doors to no avail. Morgan had opened and was searching the tack room.

She whirled on him. "But I'm his mother. I know my child. You'll forgive me for saying this, but you don't even know me, so you surely don't know him. Just keep looking."

June pounced against the backs of Decker's legs, nearly knocking him over. "June! I said not now!" He immediately felt guilty for shouting at the dog. His frustration was with Archer's disappearance and Morgan's snapping at him and himself for being the cause of the rift between them, not the dog. "The storage room," he said. "It's full of toys."

He left Morgan to finish searching the tack room, even though he couldn't think of a single place for Archer to hide in there. He didn't want to push matters any further than he already had. It seemed he was constantly messing up with Morgan. Always saying the wrong thing or not saying anything when he should be. And now this.

To think he'd carried around a feeling all these years that Morgan was an opportunity missed. To think no other girl had ever come close to capturing him the way Morgan had. To think he'd ended up just throwing himself into his work, because who he thought was the only woman ever meant for him was gone, thanks to his own pride and baggage.

To think of everything he'd been beating himself up about, when in truth, it was entirely possible that he and Morgan were not compatible at all.

The storage room was packed with pool noodles and big, squishy balls, and cones and buckets and just about every sensory toy you could think of. He had asked Ben to assign one of the others to clean it out, but clearly that hadn't happened yet. The result was an unlocked room filled with alluring things, and plenty of dark corners to hide in.

"Archer?" Decker, unable to keep himself from calling out, kept his voice low in hopes that Morgan wouldn't hear him. "Arch? You in here, buddy?" He listened for any kind of sound like shifting or rustling around in the dark, but there was nothing.

Morgan burst into the room and immediately began shoving things around, bending to peer into holes that she'd made. She was breathing hard but was moving with an almost mechanical purpose. Decker found himself backing out of her way, lest he get run over by the search train.

June came to the open door and began whining, shifting her weight.

"We'll find him, Junie," Decker mumbled, moving out of the storage room. He patted the worried dog on his way past, then went down the line and threw open door after door, barely peeking inside any of the rooms, as they were mostly empty. Nowhere for Archer to hide. The dog's whines turned into barks. "Quiet, now. We have to be able to hear him."

Morgan appeared beside him. "What about the house?"

"Ben's?"

"And yours."

Decker shook his head. "Mine's locked up. I'm certain. I keep it locked for this very reason. I'd be shocked if Ben didn't do the same."

"Can we go see?"

"Of course," Decker said. "But let's check in with Ben on the way. Maybe he's found him."

Morgan's eyes started to look swimmy, and Decker wanted nothing more than to take her in his arms and console her. But he knew he couldn't do that. Besides, it was only seconds before she was gone again.

The kids were milling around the yard, the horses grazing in the pasture. A couple of worried parents stood by the pasture gate, glancing around, and he knew that word had gotten out.

This wasn't the first time they'd had a wanderer leave Pathways. It was rare, but it was inevitable. They had protocols in place. It didn't dawn on Decker until that moment that the fact that Annie was the one to sound the alarm meant their protocol had already broken down. Ben wasn't doing what he should have been doing.

And, in fact, Ben was nowhere to be found.

Sareena and Cindy jogged to him from the center of a group of parents.

"Any sign of him?" Sareena asked.

Decker shook his head. "Where's Ben?"

Cindy shrugged, as if she'd been wondering the same thing. "He was here, and then he wasn't. I assumed he was off looking for him, too. I don't see Scout out there, either."

Decker, hands on hips, paced in a quick circle, trying to keep the obvious from showing. Something was wrong. Way wrong. Ben wouldn't just leave unless he had good reason.

"Okay, so if Ben's with him, he's in good hands," Decker said, turning to Morgan, but she was already gone, racing toward his house. "If either one of them comes back, call my cell," Decker instructed, then realized he didn't have it on him. "I'll go get it." He turned to the parents, who were still milling around. "I'm sorry to do this, but class is canceled for today. We'll go a day longer at the end of the session to make up for it. Just…make sure you look all around your car before you back out, please? Make sure you check your back seats, too, if you left it un-locked. Annie? Annie? Where's Annie?"

"Yes?" She had been curled into a ball, alone, her back pressed against the fence. He could tell she'd been crying. "Come here, please." She did, moving slowly, her shoulders hitching. "You're not in any trouble," he said gently when she reached him. "You did everything right. But with Ben gone, I'm going to need you to be the leader, okay?"

She nodded, sniffling.

"Okay. I need you to make sure everyone whose parent isn't already here gets a chance to call their parents to go home. Use Miss Cindy's phone, okay?"

"Okay."

"And then you watch to make sure they all get into their cars and look all around and under their cars to make sure Archer's not there."

"Yes, sir."

"And if I'm still not back after everyone leaves, I need you to be Ben. That means you're in charge of everything that happens right up here. Make decisions, if you need to. I trust you. Call me if you need me. And especially call me right away if Archer shows up."

"But what about the horses?"

"The horses are fine in the pasture. You just have to make sure the people are fine, okay? We'll take care of the horses after we find Archer."

"What if we don't find him?" she asked, a tear dripping from her cheek to the ground below.

He reached out and patted her shoulder. Watching her cry was making his heart break, and he wanted to be there to console her, but he knew he had to go with Morgan. "We'll find him. He's around here somewhere, and we'll find him. You did a really good job coming to get us," he said. "I'm proud of you."

He stopped by the office and grabbed his phone, then headed for his house, which stood hidden in a cluster of dogwood and ash and cottonwood trees that had been there since the first McBrides moved in. He'd played hide-and-seek and tag around those trees more times than he could count. Even then, he'd been imagining the day that the ranch would be his.

And when he got closer and spotted Morgan through the trees, bent with her hands on her knees to catch her breath, the sunlight picking up golden streaks in her hair made wild by the wind, one strap of her sundress drooping against her arm, the years peeled back, and he was flooded

JENNIFER BROWN   123

with memories of his desire to have her here
with him.

It would be *their* ranch.

She would be chasing after *their* son. Well,
one of their sons.

If he paused right where he was, he could almost imagine that she was only taking a short
break to catch her breath before resuming a
game of tag, the delighted squeals of their children filling the air.

These were the things his father had also
wanted. Things he'd probably thought he'd had.
Yet they slipped through his fingers.

Decker had destroyed himself when he walked
away from Morgan, rationalizing that he'd rather
do the destroying than be destroyed the way his
father was. The way he and David were. He was
used to hurts that didn't heal, and he supposed
that Morgan would be yet another one that he
would just have to deal with.

She heard his feet crunch against some leftover leaves from fall. "Ben?"

He shook his head. "Also missing."

"I checked…every door…and every…window,"
she panted. "All locked, as you said." She scratched
one side of her neck, absently lifted her sundress
strap back into place and gazed across the ranch.
Now that he was close to her, he could see spots
of blood on her legs.

"You're bleeding," he said, bending to get a closer look.

She waved her hand absently. "Rosebushes."

He straightened and followed her gaze. The sun was high in the sky, making everything hot and hazy and shadowy. Coming toward them, up the slight slope from the corral to the house, was a small shadow. He looked closer. June? Not just coming toward them, but galloping toward them, at a pace that would make Tango jealous.

"Decker, there's so much space here. So many trees to hide him. Not to mention the cornfield across the highway. He could be anywhere. There isn't any water on the property, is there? Like a pond?"

"No," he said. "No ponds, and the creek has been dried up for decades."

Galloping toward them.

"We should call the police," Morgan said. "Get some help searching. I left my phone in the office."

"I have mine." He held the phone out for her to take.

Galloping.

June's just an old, lazy hound. She's happy to have someone scratch her belly for a while.

June doesn't gallop. June barely moves.

"Of course," Decker said, bolting to meet his dog. "You know where he is, don't you, Junie? You've been trying to tell me and I've been scolding you."

"What?" Morgan ran to keep up.

June saw Decker coming and stopped, panting, until he reached her. Then, without so much as a yip, she turned and ran back down the slope she'd just come up. Decker and Morgan followed her as she headed for the pasture.

He's not just in the pasture, though, Decker thought. *The kids would have seen him. Ben would have called out.*

Once upon a time, David had pressed Decker hard to wire his pasture fence.

Someone could waltz in here and steal your livelihood, he'd warned.

We put them in the barn at night.

And during the day?

During the day, we're right here. Who's going to steal a horse right out from under my nose?

Someone who came in at night and hid in the trees, waiting for a horse to come near them during the day, David had replied.

But, still, Decker had resisted. He'd been worried about the kids. What if someone forgot and accidentally touched the fence?

Someone like Archer.

Now he was glad he'd fought his brother. It kept his worry from becoming outright panic.

"Go through here," he said, ducking through the gate behind Ben's house. The gate had been left open, a sure sign that they were on the right trail. "We'll take Tango."

He could see his horse on the horizon, bent and grazing. He wasn't saddled up, but that didn't make any difference to Decker.

June knew well which horse was Decker's and went straight to Tango, standing by him and shifting her weight from foot to foot anxiously.

"Hey, boy," Decker said, approaching Tango. He ran his hand over the horse a couple of times, gave him a few quick pats, then grabbed his mane with one hand and withers with the other and kicked himself up and onto the horse. Tango, none too happy about having his lunch interrupted, chuffed. "Come on," Decker said, reaching out for Morgan. "Get behind me and hold on."

Morgan hesitated. "I don't know how," she said. "I'll keep up on foot."

"You don't have any shoes."

She shook her head impatiently. "I don't care. Let's just go."

"Have you never ridden bareback? Is that it?

You'll be okay. I learned how to ride bareback before I learned to ride with a saddle."

She let out a frustrated grunt. "I've never ridden a horse before at all, okay?"

"Easier than riding a bicycle. Let's go."

"I'm scared of them, Decker." She chewed her bottom lip as she glanced toward the trees. He could feel her fears pulling against one another. "Okay? Horses scare me. Now is not the time to have this discussion. We need to find Archer." Without waiting for his response, she started toward the tree line.

"You don't know where you're going," he warned.

"I'll figure it out. I know my son."

Decker urged Tango forward the few steps to catch up with her.

"You'll ride in front of me, then," he said. "I'll have my arms around you. It'll be okay, Morgan. This is the fastest way."

"I don't have time to learn how to ride a horse right now. I don't want to talk about it anymore. You ride, I'll keep up."

Decker was struck with how inexperienced she really was, thinking that she could keep up with Tango. She was fast, but she wasn't Tango-fast. But she wasn't stopping, and that was the important—and incredibly frustrating—thing.

"Just...hang on for a second," he said. "I've got an idea."

Stubborn, she kept walking.

He dismounted and turned toward the teens still standing at the fence, watching. He stuck two fingers in his mouth and gave a whistle. Troy, one of the older boys, turned.

"Wheels!" Decker shouted, miming a steering wheel.

After a short hesitation, Troy went running. Only a few minutes later, Annie opened the gate and Troy careened into the pasture on a red ATV. He leaned over the handlebars like he was in an action movie, his hair whisking out behind him.

Troy reached them, dismounted, and Decker got on. "Thank you. I thought y'all were leaving."

Troy simply shook his head while looking at the ground nervously. Decker knew this meant they were waiting for Archer and Ben to come back. Loyalty was a big deal at McBride Pathways, and that wasn't even something Decker tried to teach them. It just happened naturally.

Decker thumbed the throttle and took off toward Morgan, who had plunged into the woods, following June. Even over the roar of the engine, he could hear her finally begin to call Archer's name. He pulled up next to her, and this time she didn't hesitate to join him. She got on behind him and wrapped her arms around his waist, leaning into him, her body telling him to go.

He had a good idea where a curious five-year-old might end up.

He drove straight to the glade.

CHAPTER SIX

Every bump and rattle along the trail through the woods felt like an indictment. Morgan couldn't believe that she let her fears win out in as dire a situation as this. Archer needed her, and she couldn't make herself get on that horse. She was disappointed in herself.

Morgan prided herself on her fearlessness and the way she took charge of things. She wished she was born that way like her sister, but the truth was, she learned how to be that way when Cody walked out. There was no time for licking her wounds and wondering what to do. She had to hit the ground running, because Archer counted on her. Inside, she was terrified, and sure she would mess everything up. Sure that Archer would blame her for her failings and how they affected his life. But on the outside, she was confident and competent, meeting the world with balled fists and puffed chest.

In those early days, Marlee had come to Kansas City to be there with her. Marlee always seemed to know exactly what to do. She never even really needed to think before she acted. She did what needed to be done, and then she cleaned up accidental messes that might have happened in the process. *You can do this, too*, Morgan had told herself. *You've got this.*

And here she was, riding through the woods, looking for her son, thinking those same words. *You can do this. You've got this.*

But she didn't get on the horse. *Coward.*

Archer was a wanderer. But, thankfully, he wasn't a runner, looking for every instant he could find to take off. He ambled around, oblivious to danger, distracted by nearly everything that moved. He always had to inspect what captured his attention. Sure, she'd had a couple of panicked moments in the grocery store or at the library, when she'd been reading a label or a book jacket, and when she turned back, he was gone. But he was always easy to find, just a couple of aisles away, crouched and silently fiddling with something that had caught his eye. Still, in those brief seconds before she found him, Morgan was shaken to the core with the idea of him missing. Her greatest nightmare was that he wouldn't be only a few feet away, content in his own little world. That he would follow that world so closely, he wouldn't see the real world—and the real threats that it possessed—around him.

There were a billion places for an innocent, non-verbal, autistic boy to meet his end.

And now she was in that nightmare scenario. She was surrounded by those billion places.

She tried to watch for her son as they whipped through the woods, but they were going too fast. She started to tell Decker to slow down, but he seemed to know where he was going, so she leaned into the back of him, briefly pressing her forehead between his shoulder blades, choosing to trust his instinct. She could feel the warmth of his skin through his shirt and turned to rest her cheek against it instead. She was hot and sweaty, too, but at the same time she felt chilled to the bone. There was something grounding about the heat rising from his muscles.

The ATV bobbled and pitched. "Hold on tight!" Decker shouted over the engine as he slowed down to tackle the terrain. "We've got to get across this part, and then we'll be there."

She tightened her grip and leaned in harder, trusting him, while at the same time shocked at how easily she fell into trusting him, no matter what walls she tried to put up between them.

After a few rough pitches, they popped out of the woods and were in a clearing. Morgan lifted her head and marveled at how gorgeous it was. If Archer found this place, he would for sure never want to leave it. There were butterflies and birds and the sun shining down on it as if it were a spotlight. *Look*, it seemed to say. *Look at how stunning nature can be.*

Decker stopped the ATV and turned it off. The silence seemed unreal, as if they'd closed the door on the whole world. Just a whole lot of chirping, and the soft knock of something wooden butting against something else wooden as the breeze blew. And the chuff of a horse nearby. And Decker's triumphant laugh.

"I knew it!" He got off the ATV and walked to the horse, neatly tied to a tree. "Hey, there, Scout." He gave the horse a couple of pats, then turned to a tree about ten feet away. "Ben! You up there?"

Morgan scrambled off the ATV and joined him, craning her neck, trying to make sense of what this all meant. She could see that the noise she'd been hearing was a broken rope ladder blowing against the tree trunk, rhythmically tapping. Up above, nestled in the branches, was an ancient, rickety tree house. Ben's head poked through the window.

"Yes. I am here."

"Is Archer there?" Morgan asked, her chest tight with hope. If Archer wasn't up there, she wasn't sure what she would do. Maybe just curl up on the grass and cry, sure that she'd been right about her abilities when Cody left—she wasn't made for this. Not at all.

"Yes, ma'am."

Without even thinking about it, Morgan wrapped herself around Decker, squeezing his neck tightly, her face buried in his chest as she let out a flurry of relieved giggles. She felt his arms tentatively find their way around her, and she breathed in the cotton of his shirt. They swayed a little—two entwined willows in the wind. The curl of their bodies felt natural and right, the weight of his arms safe and warm.

She tore herself away and wiped the tears from her cheeks. "Is he okay?"

"Yes, ma'am. He is uninjured. I saw him go into the woods, and I know the rule is nobody leaves camp without permission. So I followed him to make sure he had gotten Decker's permission, because I knew he didn't get mine. But he wouldn't tell me. Even when I told him that I'm similar to him, so it's safe to talk to me."

Tears prickled the corners of Morgan's eyes. She'd often wondered if Archer even knew that he was a little different from the other kids at the preschool. She supposed he probably didn't yet. That she would have some time before society pointed it out to him, cruelly, time and again. Her heart swelled at the idea that there were people like Ben out there—people who would reach out to Archer, let him know that he was not alone. "He doesn't talk. But that was very kind of you."

"Yes, ma'am. I tried to get him on Scout, Decker, so we could get back to camp, but he ran away. I think he might be scared of horses."

Decker glanced at Morgan, the smallest grin tugging at the corners of his mouth, his dimples appearing. "I think it runs in the family."

Ben's face scrunched up. "I am unaware of the genetic structure of fears. Except, of course, in the instance of crows. Baby crows are born knowing which people are bad people that they should stay away from, which would suggest a genetic component. But baby humans are not born with such knowledge. It is possible that the parent crows tell the babies in some way, but it would seem unlikely that babies would understand, having no life experience. I'm not sure. I'll have to do some research and let you know. If it is genetic, then it would stand to reason that medical intervention would help him no longer fear horses."

Decker chuckled. "Okay. I'll be looking forward to hearing what your research turns up. Hey, do you think y'all can come down now? Archer's mama here is fit to be tied. I'm sure she'd like to get her hands on Archer."

"Her hands?"

"I just mean she'd probably like to give him a hug."

"With her arms," Ben corrected him.

"Yes, exactly." *Decker has the patience of a saint*, Morgan thought. By now, anyone else would be frustrated and just issuing orders for Ben to come down this instant. In fact, Morgan sort of wanted to issue that order herself. She did, in fact, want to get her hands—and arms—on her son. But it wasn't patience that kept Decker from snapping at Ben. It was love. Decker loved his old friend Ben to such a degree that he simply accepted him for who he was, and Ben accepted Decker the same way.

She wanted Archer to have that love in his life. She wanted Archer to have a friend like Decker.

She felt a swell of affection for Decker. It was hard not to love someone with such a big heart. It was hard to keep a grudge.

Ben ducked back in through the window; Morgan and Decker stared up at the tree house. After a long few moments, Ben's head popped back through the window. "I'm sorry to say that we're both afraid to come down."

"Archer has never been up in a tree before," Morgan said. "He probably didn't know what he was getting into."

"How exactly did you get up there, anyway?" Decker asked.

"Archer walked up the tree trunk using the broken rope," Ben said.

Decker glanced at Morgan as if to say, *Can you believe that?*

She gave one nod as if to say, *Yes, actually, I can*. Just because Archer had never climbed a tree before didn't mean that he couldn't. And it didn't surprise her in the least that he wanted to try.

"I climbed up on the branches," Ben said. "Which wasn't scary. But now we are very high, and it doesn't look the same from up here."

"Okay," Decker mumbled. "We'll have to help them down."

"I'll do it," Morgan said. "Fear of climbing trees is definitely not at all genetic. I grew up having to keep up with Marlee West. No easy feat." Quickly, she tied her skirt into makeshift pants the way she and Marlee used to do when they were kids, and then maneuvered herself below the tree.

Even the lowest branch required her to jump, but she got ahold of it and pulled herself up until she could get one bare foot on top of it. From there, it was as easy as climbing a ladder. She was up in moments, peering into the tree house.

"Mommy!" Archer came at her with his arms outstretched.

"Hey, baby," she said, kneeling in the front entrance of the house to take the force of his hug without toppling to the ground below. The tree house was basically a wooden box that had weathered the years somewhat ungracefully. There were hail holes in the roof, wasp nests in the peak and drifts of dead leaves in the corners. She hugged Archer with all her might, breathing in the wet puppy scent of him, his hair sweaty at the scalp, his face beet red with the flush of summer heat. "I'll bet you're thirsty," she said. "You, too, Ben."

Ben, who was still on his knees at the window, nodded. "Yes, ma'am. It is several degrees warmer in here than it is outside. Most likely, this is due to the lack of opportunity for airflow. When Decker and David built this house, they should have added another window on that side. But they were children and probably didn't know much about architecture."

Morgan chuckled. "Probably not. But I'll bet you did."

"I was interested," he said. "They were most likely only interested in playing in a tree."

Archer had let go and lounged against Morgan's lap, the way he always did—his way of being connected without being too connected. "Can I give you a hug, Ben? For going after him and keeping him safe?"

Ben tucked his arms around himself. "I'm not very good at accepting physical touch from strangers," he said. "But I can tolerate a fist bump." He held out one fist.

"Fair enough. As long as you are aware of how very grateful I am, I'll settle for a fist bump. Thank you for staying by his side."

"We are similar," he said. "When I was a little boy, I ran away a lot. It wasn't because I wanted to be away from my family, though. It was usually that there was a bug."

Morgan laughed. "Bugs can be very interesting." She bumped Ben's fist with hers and turned to peer back down the way she'd just come. Decker's upturned face stared back at her. *Now*, she said to herself, gauging the situation, *how to get you both down safely.*

"Archer," she said, pulling him to standing and looking directly into his eyes. It didn't always work, but sometimes it did, and that was all she had right now, so she might as well go for it. "I'm going to need you to do exactly as I say, okay? I promise I won't let you get hurt, but you have to trust me. You, too, Ben. I'll take him down, and then be back for you."

"Yes, ma'am," Ben said.

She scooted backward until she could gain her footing on the branch outside the door. It would have been nice if the rope hadn't been broken, but it was what it was, and she would make do. She bent, crouched and dropped to the next lowest branch, then held her hands out for Archer. For a moment, she feared he would scurry back to the corner he'd been hiding in, or maybe just ignore her altogether. It wasn't easy making Archer do something he didn't want to do. But after a pause, he raised his arms, like he was expecting to be picked up.

"Good job, buddy," she said, grabbing him under the arms and placing him on her hip, just like she was going to carry him into a grocery store. "Hang on tight around my neck, okay?" He patted her shoulder, her chest, her chin, and whined, scared, but then clamped his hands behind her neck. "Good. Don't let go, no matter what, okay?"

Morgan wasn't sure if she could get all the way to the ground with him wrapped around her like this, but she was sure going to try. She had to remain calm and steady so Archer would remain calm and steady. The last thing she needed was for him to melt down and begin flailing. If he did, they would both end up in the hospital.

Slowly, slowly, she lowered herself until she was able to step down on the next lowest branch. And then the one below that. And another.

"I've got you." Decker was standing directly beneath them, his arms upraised.

Morgan breathed a sigh of relief at how close she was to him, and lowered herself to sit on the branch she was standing on, folding Archer into her lap as she did so. She kissed his forehead

three times. "You did such a great job, buddy! I'm
so proud of you." She shimmied so that she was
straddling the branch. "Now I'm going to hand
you down to our good friend Mr. Decker, okay?"
Archer squirmed. "It's okay. He's not going to
drop you. Ready? One, two, three!"

On three, she clamped her legs as hard as she
could around the branch, feeling the roughness
of the bark bite into her skin, and lowered Archer. Her arms shook and her shoulders cried
out—when had her baby gotten so heavy?—
and just when she feared she would drop him,
Decker tapped the boy's shoe.

"Got him. You can let go."

Letting go was not something Morgan did easily, or well, but gravity was real, and her muscles
were screaming at her, so she forced her hands
to open. Archer dropped away, but she knew,
without even looking, that Decker would catch
him. She leaned against the tree trunk, taking in
great, gasping breaths—what felt like the first
breaths she'd taken since Annie burst through the
office door and told them Archer was missing.

But she only allowed herself to breathe for a
moment. She still had Ben to rescue. Sweet Ben,
who'd been by her baby's side this whole time, ignoring his own fears. Understanding what it was
like to just be so interested in something, you forgot that you'd left behind everything you knew.

She stood, her muscles quaking and her palms and the bottoms of her feet on fire, and headed back up. Ben met her on the top branch.

"You ready?" she asked.

He nodded. "Yes, ma'am. But you don't need to hold me."

Morgan laughed. "Well, that's good, because I'm pooped." She saw his face scrunch up, and she laughed again, harder. "I just mean I'm tired."

"Oh," he said. "That's a relief."

"Okay, just put your hands and feet where I put mine and follow me down. Can you do that?"

"Yes, ma'am, I think I can."

Five minutes later, they were both on the ground. Archer was spinning in the middle of the glade, as if nothing had happened, June panting on the ground beside him, looking as tired as Morgan felt.

Decker gave Ben a hearty fist bump. "Hero of the day," he said. "I'm proud of the way you handled things, Ben. Exactly like we discussed."

"Yes, sir," Ben answered, his eyes riveted to the ground. "We should do a debrief tomorrow, though, after everyone has had some time to think things over. Then we can analyze if we need to make any changes to our protocol."

"That sounds like an excellent plan," Decker said.

"Thank you so much, Ben," Morgan said. "Again."

"Yes, ma'am."

"Are you okay?" Decker asked, ducking a little to try to capture eye contact.

"Yes, sir. I'm just...pooped."

Morgan laughed, especially when she saw the look of surprise on Decker's face.

"I'm sure you are," Decker said. "I've gotta ask you. How did you get up there with the ladder broken? You weigh a lot more than Archer, so I doubt you could have climbed up it like he did."

Ben gazed at the tree house, as if even he was wondering how he'd managed to scale his way to the top. "It would appear that you are the only one who cannot climb this particular tree without falling off of the bottom limb."

Morgan wheeled on Decker. "You fell? Like, recently?"

"I was startled," Decker countered. "Ben snuck up on me."

"Tango was not secure," Ben said.

"Oh, no, were you hurt?" Morgan asked.

"Only my pride," Decker mumbled. "And I'm so happy you're bringing it up in front of Morgan, Ben. Thank you."

"He fell from the bottom branch," Ben said. "Landed on his back."

"Okay, okay," Decker said. "We all heard it the first time." He turned to Morgan. "Yes. I fell. I wasn't wearing the best shoes. You need proper footwear to climb a tree."

Morgan glanced down and held up a bleeding, bare foot. "I'm sorry? You need what?"

Laughter bubbled to the surface as she watched Decker's face redden. Ten minutes ago, she was terrified for her child's safety, and now she was laughing. More than that, she realized that laughter wasn't something she was long on ever since Cody left. It was like he'd stolen her sense of humor and packed it right along with his underwear and socks and—most maddeningly—the Roku remote. But she and Decker had never had any trouble finding things to laugh about. It was one of her favorite things about their relationship.

"Decker is correct," Ben said. "Proper footwear is ideal for any undertaking, and proper outdoor footwear is necessary for endeavors such as climbing trees. Just about the only outdoor activity appropriate for bare feet is…surfing."

"You should have been barefoot, Decker. Sounds like you surfed your way down to the ground," Morgan said. "Maybe you should stick to baseball."

Ben opened his mouth, likely to protest her use of the word *surfing*, but then smiled and nodded, proud of himself for getting the joke.

"Well, we can't all be natural athletes, Morgan. It seems there's nothing you can't do. Oh. Wait." He slowly turned to glance at Scout. "Seems there's maybe one thing you can't do."

"You sprang it on me," she protested, slapping at his arm. "I didn't have time to mentally prepare."

"It's a horse. You sit on him, and he does the rest. That's one of the things that makes horses so great. The mental preparation is all on them."

"That's what makes horses so terrifying," she countered. "They have a mind of their own. That horse could have decided he didn't want me riding on him, and he would have definitely won that argument."

"Horses cannot argue," Ben said. "They lack logic, and besides, they can't talk."

Decker, smug, pointed in Ben's direction while never losing eye contact with Morgan. "That."

Morgan rested one hand on the seat of the ATV. "This is my kind of horse. Horse*power*. How are you getting back?"

"Oh-ho! This is the thanks I get? You fist-bump everyone but me. You practically gush all over Ben. *Oh, my hero*," he said, mimicking in a high voice. "And now you kick me off of my own ATV?"

Morgan made a big display of thinking things over. "That would seem to be the case, yes."

"You're something else, you know that? Maybe you should run back to the ranch, Speedy."

Just like that, Morgan was whisked backward in time. She gasped, realizing why it seemed like she knew this glade.

"The picnic," she said, slowly scanning the expanse of grass. "We had our picnic here. We raced across the field, right over there, and I won."

Decker opened his mouth to say something, but then simply closed it again and looked down at his shoes, as if he, too, were wrestling with the past.

"After we raced, you said you were going to start calling me Speedy instead of Tweety."

Morgan almost couldn't believe that she'd forgotten about racing against Decker. It had been on the race back to the picnic blanket that things had heated up between them. She'd given him a head start, and she'd still caught up to him, yelling, *Outta the way, slowpoke! I'm gainin' on ya!*

Instead of increasing his speed, he'd turned and captured her, trying to keep her from crossing the imaginary finish line before him. But instead of tumbling away, she'd stood her ground. They'd ended up face-to-face, winded, breathing each other's breath, looking into each other's eyes. Morgan fell into those eyes. Happily. Completely. And then he'd kissed her.

And she'd let herself fall for this handsome cowboy who won her a prize just because she said he should.

If only she'd known that he hadn't fallen for her. If only she'd known he would make his lack of feelings for her abundantly clear only weeks later.

Still, the memory was good. One of her best. And, unbidden, it was followed by an image of her wrapped up in Decker's arms right here again. Breathing each other's breath. Looking into his eyes.

Kissing him.

"Um." She cleared her throat, the memory and the fantasy having bowled the voice right out of her. She was exhausted in every possible way—physically, mentally, emotionally—and just wanted to get home. Her legs felt like noodles, the palms of her hands and soles of her feet were sore, and she was getting a headache up the back of her neck. "I can drive Archer on the ATV. If that's okay with you. Or I can walk, if you'd rather."

"No, no, of course you're not going to walk." Maybe Morgan was imagining things, but Decker also seemed to be deep in thought. "We'll get back. Don't worry about us."

Quickly, as if she were trying to outpace her own memories, she hoisted Archer onto the ATV, fired it up and was gone.

CHAPTER SEVEN

AN EVENT BARN.

An event barn?

That was where this benefit was going to take place. In the event barn on the Reed property. Decker had no idea that old Ames Reed had even died, let alone that he'd gifted his estate to his niece. Who, apparently, was busily turning it into a destination wedding venue.

Destination wedding? In Buck County? Whose destination was Buck County? Most people drove out the other side of Buck County without even knowing they'd been in it.

Decker chuckled to himself.

He supposed there was nothing more outlandish about an event barn than there was about a sensory trail, and he had one of those, so who was he to judge? The old-timers of years past, who'd spilled their blood onto this land to eke out enough crops to feed their families and maybe buy a new bed for the baby, would marvel over these new ways to make money on their land.

They would be mystified. They would probably balk at Decker calling it a ranch at all. *Where's the cattle?* he could imagine his grandfather saying. *There's no ranch without cattle.*

"So, I'm supposed to go to this thing? This benefit?" David asked, turning the flyer over to inspect the back. A photo of Ben helping one of the younger students spanned the entire backside. They looked happy and thriving. Decker didn't mind it.

"It would be nice," Decker said. "That way, I'm not the only one stuffed into a suit."

"A suit? Fancy."

"At first she tried to talk me into a tux. But I put my foot down."

David laughed long and loud. "She's got big plans. I like her."

Decker made a *humph* noise.

"What's that?" David asked.

"What's what?"

"That noise you made. You don't like her?" He set the flyer down and joined his brother in the viewing area, plopping into an easy chair and resting one foot on the coffee table. "Because from an outside look, you like her an awful lot."

"Liked," Decker said, a jolt of...something... rushing through him. He was unused to this feeling of being swept away when Morgan was near, much less when she wasn't even around. "Emphasis on the past tense, D."

David let his head roll back. "Oh, come on, now. Who do you think you're fooling here? It's me. I know you, brother. Yes, you've always liked her. But you also currently like her. And, I'm guessing, you like her kid, too, because you're a big old softy. What's the big deal?"

Decker sat forward and picked up a tiny zebra that Archer had apparently left behind, trying not to let the headache that had been threatening to press in on him ever since he heard the words *event barn* come fully forward. It was Friday, the kids were gone and it had been a very long week. He was looking forward to making himself a quiet dinner and eating it on his couch while he watched a movie. Big plans. Big, big plans.

"David, do you remember what it was like after Mom left?"

"Of course."

"Do you remember how we used to sit on your bed every night and watch out the window, sure she would come back and tuck us in?"

David pressed his lips together in a straight line and slowly nodded. "I do."

"And how we would say in our prayers *Please, God, tell Mom to come back because Dad is so sad without her.*"

David had fallen silent and seemed to be studying the ties of his scrubs with great interest.

"Dad cried every night. We could hear him. Remember that? This hard-as-rocks rancher *cried*, David. And we always felt like we weren't enough. We talked about that. Like we weren't enough for Mom, and we weren't enough for Dad. We tried everything we could to be enough. We were perfect. We did our chores and kept our noses clean and worked so hard, day after day after day. And, still, we weren't enough."

"Decker, that was a long time ago." David's voice was rough and craggy. "Why are you even thinking about it, much less talking about it? Morgan isn't Mom, and you're not Dad."

"No. But I'm still me. And what if that's still not enough? I don't want to leave her wanting, you know? Regretting. And I don't want to find myself alone, praying for a woman to come back into my life. Mom never came back."

"I know that. But that wasn't about you. This ranch—ranch life in general—it just wasn't the life for her. It was too much and too little all at the same time."

"That's exactly what I'm afraid of. It's what I've always been afraid of with Morgan."

There was a long stretch of silence between them, and Decker knew that the reason his brother wasn't arguing was because he understood. He knew that feeling of falling short, and that fear that the shortcomings were actually the core of who he was. He understood the fear of letting someone down and ending up alone, working himself to the bone all day, crying all night, hoping that your kids in the bedroom next door were asleep and weren't hearing you.

Finally, David took a deep breath and slapped his palms on his legs. "Well, I, for one, think you look great in a suit. I don't see the problem." He stood. "And, for what it's worth, I think an event barn is a great idea. A moneymaker. Maybe you should consider doing that here."

"I would imagine that one event barn in Buck County will suffice," Decker said. He felt wrung out, the fight gone out of him. "Besides, I have horses in my barn. I would have to ask them if they minded sharing."

"I don't know. Scout seems like the partying type. He'd probably look okay in a suit, too."

Decker chuckled. "She."

"Ah. A gown. Even better." David stood and clapped his brother on the shoulder. "Don't forget the reason Morgan is planning this event. The benefit could be a really good thing for Pathways. If Morgan brings in her contacts from the city… I'm just saying, there might be some deep pockets there. Let her do what she does, and just try to go along with it. Don't fight it. She's doing the job you asked her to do. The job you need her to do. Trust her. Who knows—maybe you'll even have a little fun. It's not impossible."

"Yeah" was the best Decker could muster. He was suddenly very, very tired, and thinking maybe he would skip dinner and a movie altogether and head straight to bed.

"And, for what it's worth, I think you're pretty great, little brother. You're more than enough. For anyone. Like I said, Morgan's not Mom, and you're not Dad. If you like this woman, let yourself like her. It might actually be good for you. Hanging out on this ranch all alone all the time…it's unhealthy."

"I'm not alone. I've got the Pathways kids."

"They go home at the end of the day."

"I've got Ben."

"Not exactly what I was talking about, and you know it. You need someone to cuddle up with at night."

"Need I remind you that you're also single?"

"Fair enough. But we're not talking about me right now."

"Convenient."

"The woman of your dreams is standing right in front of you every day, and you're pretending she's not there. I don't have that. Unless the woman of my dreams happens to be a standard poodle with thyroid troubles." He winked, patted the door frame twice and was gone.

Alone at last, Decker sank back into his chair and closed his eyes, which always seemed a little dangerous these days. No sooner would he close his eyes than Morgan would fill his mind's eye. But not the Morgan that she was today. The easygoing, flirtatious, cheerful Morgan he'd met at the carnival would be there instead. The one who danced to Ferris wheel music and who was delighted by a cheap stuffed animal and who kissed him in the middle of the glade. The one who took his breath away and scared him half to death. That Morgan was dangerous. Fortunately, that Morgan was mostly hidden. She would peek out at him every now and then, steal his breath and go back into hiding.

The Morgan he dealt with most of the time now was harder, warier. She seemed worried, and closed off, and he was sure that there was something simmering below. A hurt that was so deep it changed her. She wouldn't even allow him to call her by the silly nickname he'd given her.

Everything about her was still beautiful and alluring and drew him to her in a way that he couldn't even describe, much less pinpoint. But she wasn't his. She wasn't Tweety anymore. She was Morgan. Archer's mom. The woman who had things to accomplish and tasks to complete. And no time for dancing.

Trust her.

Trust.

He knew it was unfair, because David was right. Morgan was not his mother. And he was not his father.

But, still, he couldn't trust her.

He couldn't trust feelings that were so big they could destroy him.

He wouldn't even allow himself to consider it.

EVERYTHING WAS COMING together exactly as Morgan had imagined it. An event barn. What a lovely concept!

And it was lovely. Natural wood and big, open spaces. An ivy wall for photo backdrops. Proper chandeliers hanging from the ceiling, and fairy lights draped everywhere. Marlee, who'd left the flower shop in the care of her assistant for the day, gasped when Atty Reed had thrown open the big double doors and flicked on the lights. Morgan smiled wide. *Exactly,* she thought. *That's how everyone's going to feel when they get here. They'll gasp.*

"There's a kitchen in the back. You can bring your own food or we can connect you with the caterer we work with," Atty said. "At the far end, you can see there's a dance floor, and we can set up for a live band or a DJ, whatever your preference. Again, if you need someone, we've got recommendations we can share with you. Restrooms are over that way. We can set up cocktail tables or rounds or rectangulars or a mix, whichever you need. And if you've got kids coming to the event, we've got baby goats out back. We can set up a petting zoo kind of thing, but that'll cost extra because we have to staff it."

Marlee gasped again and clutched Morgan's arm. "Baby goats," she squeaked. "Morgan, they've got baby goats. Who doesn't love a baby goat?"

"Exactly," Atty said.

"It's perfect." Morgan spun in slow circles, trying to take it all in. "It's exactly what we were looking for. How much down payment do you need?" She whipped out the weathered checkbook that Decker had unearthed from the bottom of a drawer. The last check that had been written from that book was four years ago, to a feed store that was no longer in business. She was grateful for the sponsors she'd already gotten on board so there was money in the account to cover the check she was about to write.

Five hundred dollars, an hour of on-site planning and roughly four hundred Marlee-gasps later, Morgan and Marlee were on the road, headed to Kansas City.

Morgan felt energized and excited. This was

the part of her job that she loved—when things were coming together as planned, and she could envision it all in her mind so clearly. Once she had a vision, she could build it out into something spectacular. The energy seemed to be contagious; Marlee practically floated above the passenger seat.

"How can you be driving so slowly with all this excitement? Put the pedal to the metal, girl!"

"This again? I'm on the highway. I'm driving the speed limit."

"That's the problem, but whatever." Marlee fiddled around on her phone a little, then turned it for Morgan to see. "Ooh, what about this color scheme? I can see the florals clearly in my mind as we speak. Sunflowers and lobelias. Yellow and blue. Hearty and delicate. A shout and a whisper."

"Wow, that sounds amazing. You should sell flowers for a living."

Marlee thrust her phone toward Morgan again. "It *is* amazing. Look!"

"I'm driving. I can't look at your phone." Morgan giggled. "What has gotten into you?"

Marlee let her hand drop back into her lap. "I don't know. I guess I just feel restless, you know? Like I'm waiting for something to happen. Something big and romantic, and ugh, I'm starting to gross myself out. Being in that wedding venue has gotten into my head."

Morgan laughed. "Romance isn't gross."

"Oh, really? Because you definitely give off ew-icky-stay-away-from-me vibes when you're around Decker."

"I do not! And, besides, that's different." There was an insistent honk, and Morgan glanced up to realize that she'd drifted into the other lane. "Do you see what you do to me? I'm starting to drive like you."

"Don't blame your bad driving on me." But Marlee seemed delighted to have the bad driving blamed on her.

"Just because I keep my distance from Decker—who is my boss, by the way—doesn't mean I think romance is gross," Morgan said. "I was married, remember?"

"How could I forget? If anyone could make romance gross, it would be Cody."

Morgan couldn't argue with that.

"And if you really thought romance wasn't gross, wouldn't you have dated again by now? She shoots, she scores." She mimed throwing a basketball through a net.

"She shoots and misses. I've dated since then," Morgan said.

"No, you haven't."

"Yes, I have! There was that guy who took me for ice cream."

"He was Archer's physical therapist. Doesn't count. However, I could definitely go for some ice cream right now."

"Well, there was what's-his-name…that one guy with the perpetually concerned forehead and the black convertible. We met in the lobby at speech therapy."

"Deep connection, Morgan. Really."

"The guy from the toddler gym. We went out, like, five times."

"So what you're saying is that without Archer, you wouldn't have dated anyone at all. That's not romance—it's convenience. And ice cream. And a black convertible, which, admittedly, is probably fun. The Decker thing was romance, and now you can't even stand to be in a room alone with him. Hence, icky-gross romance. Or should I say icky-scary romance?"

"Like I said, the Decker thing is different."

"Is it, though?"

"And I don't want to talk about it."

Marlee threw her hands up, surrender-style. "Okay, okay. I'm just saying."

"You're just saying a lot of things. We were talking about your great love showing up at the benefit to sweep you off your feet, and somehow it turned into grilling me about Decker."

They drove for a moment in silence. The traffic began to pick up as they approached the city. But the energy was apparently too much for Marlee to contain for long.

"So do you think Dr. LaSalle will be all work and no fun at this thing? Or do you think he'll spare a dance or two?"

"I think you'll have to wait in line if you want to dance with him. He's very handsome."

Marlee snapped her fingers. "Girl, I *am* the line. I don't know what you're talking about."

"So Decker is all worried about dressing up for the dinner, and at first I was thinking it would be a ritzy gala type thing, get those doctors to open up their wallets, you know, but now I'm sort of thinking that it shouldn't be overly fancy. There'll be kids there before the dinner, and we've got baby goats, and nobody opens wallets faster than a parent trying to placate their kid, right? Especially a kid who just got a shot. So why kick them out? Why not keep the kids, have a family-friendly menu and entertainment. More than just the goats. I'm kind of tossing around more of a carnival vibe. What do you think?"

Marlee was grinning at Morgan like a cat with a canary.

"What?"

"Do you even hear yourself?"

"What?" Morgan repeated.

"You're trying to re-create it."

Morgan was getting exasperated. "Re-create what?"

"Hello? A carnival vibe? Do you want him to wear a baseball cap and win you a stuffed bird, too? Give you a cute little nickname while he's at it?"

"Oh, come on," Morgan said. "That's not why I'm doing it." But a part of her wondered if maybe that was exactly why she was doing it. Maybe she was wanting to rekindle things with Decker without even realizing it.

No. That was just ludicrous. Maybe she felt butterflies around him. And maybe he'd finally opened up to her a little about his upbringing on the ranch. And maybe he'd been right there by her side every step of the way when Archer got lost. But none of that meant anything real or deep or lasting. They were friends and coworkers, and they had a little past that sometimes got her feeling nostalgic, and that was all. It wasn't love; it was…fondness.

"We're here," she said.

They'd arrived at the hospital—the one that Morgan often turned to for sponsors. Maybe Marlee was right, and Morgan's whole life, and all of her relationships, revolved around Archer's care, and she was into convenience more than anything.

Well, so be it, then.

She hoped that her prior working relationship with the hospital, and with many of the doctors whose practices were located there, would make it easier to get them on board for the event. Would parents drive their kids all the way to Haw Springs? For free immunizations, maybe. Free wellness checks? Free autism screenings? They could throw in some sports physicals for good measure. This was the time of year for those. She would head to sports medicine first.

They parked, and Morgan began to gather her things.

"Is that who I think it is?" Marlee said in an urgent, ominous voice.

Morgan glanced up and froze, her seat belt still in hand. She opened her mouth to respond but found no words would come out. She felt punched in the gut or dropped from a tall height. She had a hard time finding enough breath to make words happen.

Walking across the parking lot, crossing right in front of her car, was Cody, looking older than when she last saw him, but unmistakably him, nonetheless. She would recognize that cocky way he pushed his chest out when he walked, and the glisten of hair product that plastered his bangs straight up, as if they were trying to release themselves from his head. He was wearing that same ratty Kansas State University T-shirt that he'd had since before they were married, only now there was a new hole low on the outside of the sleeve, as if he'd caught it on something and ripped himself away. Just like he'd ripped himself away from their family, Morgan thought.

But Cody wasn't alone. He walked alongside a very pregnant woman. She looked young. Younger than Cody, for sure, and maybe even a little younger than Morgan. *Too young to have known what she was getting into*, Morgan thought. *Been there, done that.*

Morgan and Cody locked eyes. Her breath was still caught, only coming to her in tiny little sips, and her extremities felt numb. She didn't want to move, for fear that something would happen, even though she had no clue what that something might be. She didn't know what to feel—anger, indignation, jealousy? She wasn't sure if she felt any of those things. Maybe she'd spent all of her reserves of negative feelings when he'd first left and life was so hard for Archer and her. Maybe she'd already resolved this.

Cody ducked his head and began walking faster, grabbing the woman's hand as he went. The woman startled and her other hand flew up, and Morgan saw the glint and flash of a wedding ring on her finger. The woman giggled and tripped along behind him, swatting at his shoulder to slow down. She looked happy.

Married. He was married again. And here Morgan had been, trying to convince Marlee that she'd moved on because she'd gone out with what's-his-name from the toddler gym five times. How was it fair that he'd moved on to a new relationship and she obviously hadn't? She didn't love him. She wasn't holding out for him, in the hope that he would someday return to her. She wouldn't take him back even if he did return.

And why was she still thinking anything revolving around Cody would ever be fair?

Cody glanced back at Morgan and gave the smallest shake of his head—a plea? a warning?—and Morgan knew in that moment that he'd never told his new woman about the family he'd left behind. That woman undoubtedly thought she was the first to bless him with a baby. She was probably as over the moon right now as Morgan had been when they were expecting Archer.

She felt pity for the woman.

She felt pity for herself.

She also felt proud of herself.

Because she felt nothing for him.

"No way," Marlee said. "No stinking way." She reached for the door handle, but Morgan grabbed her arm to stop her.

"Don't," she said. "Let them get inside."

"But don't you want to talk to him? This is your chance. That little worm has been hiding from his responsibilities for two years. He can't hide from you here."

Morgan shook her head. "Archer and I are better off without him. Let them go."

Marlee's mouth hung open for a moment, and then she shook her head. "You're a tougher woman than I am, I can tell you that much. He doesn't deserve to just be happily going about his life."

"Trust me," Morgan said. "His life isn't happy because he's Cody, and Cody is never happy. And his day definitely won't be happy after seeing us. I saw it on his face." They watched as Cody and his wife went into the building, and then Morgan counted to ten, to give him lead time. If he dawdled inside and didn't get far enough away, then whatever happened to him was between him and Marlee. Morgan couldn't hold off her protective older sister forever. "Let's go get some sponsors," she said, opening her door.

"You sure you don't want me to stay in the car?" Marlee asked, jogging to keep up with Morgan. When Morgan was on a mission, she beelined rather than walked. "I was just along for the ride. Besides, I can't guarantee I won't throw a few punches if I run across him inside."

"No, you're part of this now," Morgan said. Suddenly she felt strong and determined and free. "And we have work to do. Forget that Cody even exists."

Because he doesn't, Morgan thought. *Not in my world, anyway.*

It's time for me to officially move on with my life. Whatever that looks like.

DECKER WASN'T EXPECTING to meet Mr. and Mrs. West. He shook hands awkwardly with Morgan's father, who had a jovial face that seemed to mask something a little more protective on the inside. Not just protective, but more like protective at all costs. Decker wondered just how much they knew about his past with Morgan.

"Nice to meet you, Mr. West."

"Yep," Mr. West said, doing nothing to ease the tension for Decker.

He squatted to greet Archer. "Hey, little guy, it's good to see you." Archer lifted his arms, signaling for Decker to pick him up. He lifted him, delighted by the natural feeling of holding him. Archer moaned and pointed toward the fence. It took Decker a second to figure out what that meant. "Oh! The horse? You want to watch the horse again?"

Archer squealed and patted Decker's shoulders. "Yes!"

This was progress. Decker wished Morgan was there to see it. She would be so excited.

He motioned for Annie, who hopped off the fence and jogged over.

"Archer would like to watch from the fence this morning. Can you make sure he gets a good view?"

"Yep." Annie spread her arms out as an invitation to Archer, but the child demurred, curling into Decker. Decker would be lying if he said that didn't make him the tiniest bit happy.

"Annie's going to run the sensory trail today, Archer. You want to watch the horses on the trail?"

"Yes!"

"Good! Maybe you can even ride one."

"Yes!" Archer crowed, but Decker knew that *yes* was just a word that Archer knew now, and when Annie would try to get him on the horse later, he would have nothing to do with it.

"Excellent," Decker said, ruffling Archer's hair. "I'll check in with you later."

He held him toward Annie, who stretched her arms out again. After a slight hesitation, Archer dived into her arms, and they walked away.

"He's in good hands," Decker told Morgan's parents. "But you're more than welcome to wait. A lot of parents do. The waiting area has coffee and tea…thanks to your daughter."

Mr. West laughed, a boom that made June's head jerk in his direction. "That sounds like Morgan. Always fussing around people, wanting to make them comfortable. She gets it from her mother."

Mrs. West made a *pooh* noise and swatted at the air. "She's just always been like that. I have nothing to do with it. She wanted us to tell you that she's out looking at the benefit venue and drumming up some sponsors in the city today."

"Oh, that's right," Decker said. "She told me she was going to do that."

"We just think it's a swell idea," Mr. West said. "We can't wait to see it all in place. She's very creative. Always has been."

"And really successful at her job," Mrs. West added. "We've never really gotten an up close look at what she does since she lives so far away. This is a real opportunity for us."

"And she's resilient," Mr. West said, giving what seemed to Decker to be a knowing look. Or maybe Decker was imagining it. "Knows how to take care of herself."

We were eighteen, Decker wanted to say, but he held back.

"You've got yourself a gem, Mr. McBride. I hope you know that," Mr. West added with a wink. Decker wasn't sure what the wink was meant to be.

"Oh, I definitely know. Morgan's special. I love having her around." Decker felt his face burning. This was ridiculous. He wasn't a teenager anymore. He could say the word *love* in regard to having someone around without it meaning anything.

And he did love having Morgan around.

"Well. You can't keep her forever," Mr. West said, and there it was—the disappearance of that jovial look, the Protective Father Who Knew Things underneath showing clear as day. "She and Archer will have to go back to the city at the end of the summer."

"As much as we hate it," Mrs. West said.

"Of course, of course," Decker said. "We'll just have to consider ourselves lucky while we have her here."

"Yes, you will," Mrs. West said, and now Decker wondered if she was actually the parent to watch out for. *Or maybe you're overthinking this like crazy, Decker, and you need to get a grip. It's not like you're meeting a new girlfriend's parents for the first time. They probably know nothing about you.*

"Junieee." Annie's voice rang through the air. June, resting by Decker's feet, jumped up and obediently raced toward the sensory trail.

"I probably should see how everything's going

down there," Decker said, pointing after the dog. "If you'll excuse me."

He left the Wests standing by the corral fence and made his way to the sensory trail. The necessity of June led him to think that maybe Annie wasn't having the easiest time of getting Archer on a horse.

As soon as the trail came into sight, he could see that he was right.

"He won't even come into the trail area," Annie complained.

Annie didn't tolerate frustration for long periods of time, so Decker knew he needed to step in before she began her own meltdown. It had been quite a while since he'd had a volunteer meltdown—especially an adult volunteer—but it had happened before, and it wasn't ideal.

"It's okay, Annie. Go ahead and work with Gunner over there instead. He looks like he's just about ready to go, and they need someone to lead."

"Okay." Annie started to walk away, then turned and came back to Archer. "You need to start riding the horse. This is not dog camp," she said. And then, checking herself, she added, "I promise it's not as scary as it looks."

"Would you like me to take over?" Ben asked, appearing out of nowhere. He bent to scratch June's ear.

"No, I think I've got this one," Decker said.

He let Archer settle in with June for a bit. As usual, the boy got on the ground and lounged his head backward so that it was touching the dog. Decker crouched next to him and gave her some good scratches. He wondered what June would do after the session, once Archer had gone. She was certainly soaking up all the extra attention.

This was the part of his job that he most loved. This was what he was good at. Introducing a child to their first horse experience. Introducing the horse with all its emotional sensitivity to a child who needed to connect and understand empathy. To help a child get past a fear. To help that child unlock a part of himself.

"Hey, Archer, do you see that horse over there? His name is Ziggy. He has brown hair, just like June, and just like you, and just like me." Archer turned his head ever so slightly to take in the horse, a curious smile on his face. "What do you say we see if Ziggy's fur feels funny compared to June's fur? Come on, now, June."

Decker didn't wait to see if Archer would be amenable to the suggestion. He just knew that if June went, Archer would likely follow. And he was right.

When they got to Ziggy, Archer started to slide down to the ground, like he always did, his head pointed toward Ziggy's hind leg.

"No, no, no, it's not safe to lie down right there. Besides, we've got to stand so we can feel Ziggy's hair," Decker said, pulling the little boy back to his feet. "Here, can I hold you again?"

Archer didn't respond. He started to have that worried look that many of the kids who'd come through the Pathways program had gotten on their faces just before a meltdown. But Decker wasn't afraid of causing some discomfort in the kids, and he certainly was capable of handling a meltdown. And so was Ziggy. Annie had done a good job choosing Ziggy for the sensory trail. Ziggy was the most experienced horse Decker had, and probably the steadiest when it came to the kids. If Archer let a wail go, Ziggy would handle it fine.

Decker picked up Archer, then reached out to pet Ziggy's neck. "Do you feel that? Ziggy's hair does feel different. June's hair is soft and fluffy, isn't it? But Ziggy's hair is bristly. And—" he reached up and tousled Archer's hair "—your hair feels kind of both bristly and soft. Feel." He took hold of Archer's hand and, feeling only the slightest pull of resistance, placed it on Ziggy's neck. Archer let out a soft giggle and kicked his legs a little, at first pulling away. But soon enough, he was patting Ziggy's neck without Decker's help at all.

Decker had done this dozens of times. He'd

held dozens of kids up to one of the horses. He'd felt them jump nervously against him and had taken more than one forehead to the chin as they hid their faces away.

So why did this time feel different? Why did this child feel different?

Because you want this. Because this is the son you always imagined, and she is the wife you always wanted. Because he belongs to Morgan, which immediately makes him special.

Archer reached toward Ziggy's saddle. Decker moved so the boy could feel the smooth leather.

"That's right. Here you go, buddy. That's what you sit on to ride the horse. Watch. I've got you, now. It's okay."

Slowly, slowly, he lifted Archer into the saddle.

"That's right. Good job. You're a natural. Look at that."

Archer sat in the saddle, stiff as a board, but smiling. One hand kept a vise grip on Decker's hand, while the other explored the saddle horn. Decker held the boy's hand proudly.

If only Morgan were here to see this, he thought. *She would be so happy.*

"Nice, Ziggy," Decker said. "He's a nice horse. He wouldn't ever hurt you. Would you like to ride him?"

"I would," he heard behind him.

Morgan stood at the fence with her sister, wearing a pair of dark blue jeans and black boots that made her legs look like they went on forever, with a pink shirt tucked in and a black blazer with the sleeves pushed up. Her hair was pulled back on the sides, with a couple of wisps dangling in her face. Decker didn't mind the view at all.

"*You* want to ride?" he asked. "You got a fever or something?"

She chuckled. "I do. A fever for a benefit that is coming together beautifully. You're going to make so much money, Decker McBride, you'll be able to keep this ranch afloat for a decade." She came through the gate. "Okay, maybe that's an exaggeration. But you'll stay open for another year at least. That will give us a chance to brainstorm the next benefit. Make it even bigger and better."

"We? Next?" He couldn't help the hopefulness that bloomed in his chest.

He swore he saw her cheeks pinken with a blush. "You know what I mean. I wouldn't mind coming back to help out, if you wanted to make it an annual thing."

"You should have seen her in action," Marlee said, still standing on the other side of the gate. "So impressive. I've never seen anything like it. She just walked in there and started schmoozing like a politician. Those doctors were putty in her hands."

"I'm sure they were," Decker said, his eyes unable to unlock from Morgan's. *We? Next?* he wanted to repeat. *Annual thing?*

Morgan finally broke the gaze, looking down at her feet, a small grin on her face. "She's exaggerating."

"I am not exaggerating. You walked in like you owned the place, and I was kind of convinced that you actually would own it by the time we left. They couldn't say no."

"Some of them said no."

"Two. And they both said they'd need to think about it. Which is not no. They'll come around. Oh, and one doctor asked her on a date."

Decker stayed silent. He didn't love the idea of Morgan going on a date with a doctor, even while knowing that he had no right to expect her not to.

"He asked if we could meet after his office hours to talk about it," Morgan explained, looking as pained as Decker felt. *Or maybe you're imagining that she looks pained, because you want her to look pained.*

"Oh, yeah. 'Talk about it,'" Marlee said, making air quotes with her fingers.

"You saw how packed his waiting room was. Our timing was terrible."

"Yet he let you come back to his office right away. No wait for Morgan West. He was positively giggly around you."

"We've been working together for years," Morgan insisted.

"And has he always looked at you with hearts in his eyes, or is that new?"

"Okay, okay," Morgan said, her cheeks lit up like a Christmas tree now. "You're blowing it way out of proportion. Are you seeing this, Mar? Who is this big, brave boy up on top of this horse?"

Her entire face lit up as she came toward Archer. *She glows*, Decker thought. *She positively glows when she's around her son.* He wanted to have early-morning coffee alongside that glow. He wanted to watch the sunset to see if her glow outshone it. He wanted that glow in his life all the time. He wanted it so much, it hurt.

"Archer! You're on a horse!" she exclaimed, clapping her hands as she made her way toward her son.

"He's a natural. Took right to him. Sits in that saddle like a pro." Decker knew he needed to gather himself. He didn't know what was wrong with him—he was getting too sentimental. He needed to pull it back, remember that he broke her heart and it would never be in the cards for them to be together.

Archer reached for her, and she took him into her arms.

Decker knew he should step away, make room for her. But he couldn't make his feet move. He wanted to be in her orbit, just like those doctors had wanted. He had no idea why there was a jealous lump in his throat, but there was, and he couldn't deny it.

"Thanks for going with me, Mar. You can go back and rescue your assistant now."

"Ah. I've said too much and I'm being dismissed."

"Yes, and yes," Morgan said.

"Always happy to clear a room. It's my special skill." Marlee took a bow and headed toward the parking lot.

"Your parents are in the office," Decker said. "If you want to say hi."

Marlee turned and walked backward. "I have an assistant to rescue. Apparently. I'll say hi to them at home. See you there, Morgan. Unless you decide to run away with your doctor boyfriend."

"Goodbye," Morgan said.

Alone, Decker could feel Morgan's proximity even stronger. "She's a jokester, huh?" he asked, trying to neutralize the air between them. He didn't want his jealousy to show. He didn't want his jealousy, period.

"She's something, all right," Morgan said. "So am I getting on this horse, or what?"

Decker let out a breath he hadn't realized he was holding and felt himself relax. "Sure. But I thought you were—" he paused, glanced at Archer "—s-c-a-r-e-d."

"I am," she said. "But I saw how you got him up there. You were really good with him. You'll keep me safe, too, right?"

"I would never let anything happen to you." The words were out before he could stop himself. Her eyes softened; he swallowed and looked away.

"Besides," she said, "I want Archer to see me do it." She smiled at her son, bouncing him up and down a little. He giggled. "Mommy's turn, right, Arch?"

She put the boy down, and he beelined for June, flopping down on the ground again. Another little boy—Thomas—approached June and sat down next to her, too. Decker saw Archer's eyes flick to the boy defensively, but he didn't protest.

"What do I do?" Morgan asked, facing Decker, looking determined and beautiful.

"Um," he said, trying to clear his mind. A lot had happened in just a few minutes, and he definitely wasn't thinking clearly. "Yeah. Um. Okay, so the first thing you need to do is step up on this mounting block." He gestured to the little red staircase at his feet. The only person at Pathways allowed to mount their horse without a block besides Decker was Ben.

She gave a quick nod and reached out to grab his hand as she stepped up onto the first, then second and third steps.

He tried not to feel the lightning that tried to zap through him. He pushed past it. "Okay, so you don't want to leave the reins too slack, just in case he should take off on you."

She froze. "Take off?"

"He won't. It's Ziggy. But you always have to assume that he could. So you gather up the reins like this, and then with your left hand, hold them and grab the mane as well."

Her hand started to follow, but stopped, nervousness radiating off her. "I don't want to pull his hair."

"You need to relax," he said with a smile. He took her hand and placed it lightly on Ziggy's mane. "He doesn't mind, I promise."

She nodded and sank her fingers into the horse's mane, tentatively at first, and then with more confidence.

"Okay, good. Now you're going to put your left foot in the stirrup. Yep, just like that. And your right hand on the saddle. And swing yourself up and over."

She nodded again, swallowed nervously, then easily launched herself onto the horse's saddle. She laughed triumphantly, her hands gripping the saddle horn for dear life. "I'm up," she said. "Look, Archer! See? The horse is nice!" She gasped, and then stage-whispered, "Decker! Do you see what I'm seeing?"

Archer had sat up like Thomas and together they were lining leaves of grass along June's outstretched body.

"He's playing with someone," Morgan said. "I can't believe it. I've never seen him do that before. He's always playing alone, or maybe alongside someone, but never with."

Decker was too taken by the look on Morgan's face—jubilant and fresh and almost a little tearful—to tear his gaze away to look at Archer. "It's the ranch" was all he could manage to say.

"Can we ride?" she asked.

"Huh? I mean, yeah. You can ride the trail if you feel like you're ready."

She glanced down at the horse, and then around at the trail. "I was hoping you could ride with me?"

"Oh. No. We can't do that."

"Why not?"

"Ziggy's not built for that," he said. "We're too heavy. And, besides, you can't ride double in a saddle. We'd have to ride bareback." *And, most*

importantly, the thought of being that close to
you makes every alarm bell in my head go off.
Especially the way I'm feeling right now. I might
just take you into my arms and let the years melt
away. Ask for a do-over.

"And you can't possibly make an exception," she challenged, skepticism lacing her voice. "Even for a short ride."

"That's correct. I can walk with you while you ride Ziggy, though, if that'll make you feel better. I'll be with you the whole time. I'll just be on foot, is all."

"Walking with me, like I'm one of the kids? No, thank you." She took her feet out of the stirrups as if she were going to attempt to dismount, but after a few awkward movements that were clearly not going to work, she gave a perplexed look and slipped her feet in again.

"What's the big deal? Everyone is a beginner at some point."

"The big deal is that I think it's something else that's keeping you from riding with me." She leaned back and started to cross her right foot over the horse's neck.

"Nope, don't do it that way," Decker said, reaching out to stop her leg.

She put her leg down and leaned forward instead but didn't seem to know what to do from there. "I think you don't want to ride with me because it's *me*." Frustrated with her lack of progress, she sat up again. "How do I get off of this thing?"

Decker suppressed a grin. "Do you want me to help you?"

"No. Yes."

"Okay, so hold on here and here." He moved her hands to the horse's mane and the pommel. "Now slip your right foot out of the stirrup. Yep, just like that. And you're going to swing that leg over the back of the horse. Go slow. I've got you. Yep, and now take your left foot out of the stirrup, and…" He held her around the waist as she slid down from the horse. She turned and brushed her hair back from her face. She was close. Too close. His heart thumped. He took two steps back.

"For goodness' sake, Decker. I was asking you to ride on a horse with me, not take me to the altar."

Even she looked shocked that she'd said it aloud.

"I'm sorry," she said. "I was excited. It's been a good day. I just wanted to celebrate."

"It's okay," Decker said. "I understand."

"No, it's not…" She paused, clearly frustrated. "You go ahead and work with Archer. And… what's the other boy's name?"

"Thomas."

"You've done amazing things, so you work with Archer and Thomas. That's what you're here for. I'll go inside and work on the benefit. That's what I'm here for."

He watched as she walked away. It was hard for him to tell what she was feeling.

But he knew what he was feeling, and it was a mixture of emotions too complicated to separate.

He only knew that he had to push them aside. He had a job to do.

And a past to ignore.

And he knew, with absolute certainty, that if he got on a horse behind her—if he let himself pull in that close—he would be a goner.

CHAPTER EIGHT

RUSH HOUR AT The Dreamy Bean was pretty calm compared to the rush shifts at the coffeehouses Morgan frequented in the city. Still, Ellory was a one-woman show at The Dreamy Bean, so she was moving fast. She scurried around on her platform Mary Janes, whirring machines into life, clinking spoons on the sides of cups and spraying clouds of foam on top of drinks for the half dozen people who waited.

"Do you need help back there?" Morgan asked, leaning over the counter.

"Do you know how to run an espresso machine?" Ellory asked.

"No, but I can spray whipped cream like nobody's business."

"Hired," Ellory said. "And thank you."

Morgan pushed through the waiter's door that separated the lobby from the kitchen, grabbing a rainbow-covered apron and tying it around herself on the way. She went straight to the sink and

washed her hands, then stood awkwardly behind
Ellory, waiting for instructions.

Ellory handed her a to-go cup. "Lid and warmer,
please," she said, then raised her voice. "Janice?"

A woman stepped forward, and Morgan pushed
the cup into her hand.

"Can you steam some milk?" Ellory asked.

"Sure!" Morgan had watched enough baristas
to kind of know, and Ellory was probably just
being nice by letting her help anyway, so it was
probably the easiest task in the kitchen. Chances
were, Morgan was actually making things harder
for Ellory with just her presence.

That seemed to be a theme for her these days.
Her presence felt too big, too unwieldy. After
her little moment on the horse yesterday, Decker
had steered clear for the rest of the day, always
in another building, another field, another barn.
Working, cleaning, hiding.

Or at least she assumed he was hiding.

After all, hiding was something he did quite
well, wasn't it? Probably came naturally to him
at this point, especially when he was hiding from
her.

Still, she didn't need to push him like that. She
had no idea what had gotten into her.

Except she kind of did.

Marlee wasn't wrong. The doctors had always
given Morgan a lot of attention. And in the past,

she ate it up. Considered encouraging their advances. Maybe proposing a date herself. She'd always been too busy with Archer to actually make anything happen, but the feeling, the desire, was there. Until now.

Being around all of those handsome doctors had only made her think about Decker, the tan on the back of his neck, the way he held his body upright and solid when he ran, the way he looked in a tight white T-shirt, grimy from chores. The way he interacted with the kids.

When she and Marlee had arrived at the ranch and she'd seen him holding Archer, her heart had melted. He was gentle and soft, and Archer clung to him like it was the most natural thing on the face of the earth. Like they'd always been in each other's lives. Morgan had no idea if Archer missed Cody or not—he'd never expressed missing Cody, but that may have been because he couldn't—but she knew joy on her son's face, and she definitely saw joy there yesterday as he patted the horse's neck, and even more joy as he sat atop the horse for the first time.

She saw joy on Decker's face, too.

And then Archer had made a friend. An actual friend!

Something about it all felt so right.

"Whip and nutmeg, please," Ellory said, setting a to-go cup in front of Morgan. And then another. "This one just needs a lid." And a third, empty one. "Three squirts of caramel syrup."

Morgan jumped to life—even though she knew the tasks Ellory was giving her were easy, she found herself concentrating hard, wanting to get it right. After all, if she messed up a drink at the end, Ellory would have to start all over again.

They got into a rhythm, Ellory putting Morgan on the register for a second wave of rush. Morgan was good at customer service, and she didn't mind that her most difficult task was trying to get a pastry into a paper bag using tongs instead of her fingers.

Finally, the rush ended. Ellory wiped down the counter as Morgan took off her rainbow apron.

"You are a lifesaver, my friend," Ellory said. "Thank you. Your order's on me."

"Actually, I was ordering for two, so I'll go ahead and buy. You can pick up my iced matcha next time I'm in here. That looked delicious."

She smiled. "New recipe. It's amazing, if I do say so myself. And they've been flying off the shelf." She folded the wet rag and draped it over the side of a little sink. "But you're not going to distract me that easily. Uh-uh. Spill."

"Spill what?"

"You said you're ordering for two. You're not...?" She pointed at Morgan's belly.

Morgan followed where she was pointing, and then laughed uproariously. "Oh! No! Not that. The other one is for Decker."

Ellory, arms crossed, raised one eyebrow. "Keep going."

"It's not what you think," Morgan said.

"I think it's Saturday and you're going to see your employer when you don't have to. Bright and early. With treats."

"Yeah, I guess when you put it that way, it sounds...friendly."

"*Friendly* is one way to put it, sure."

"It's not like that. I owe him an apology. I sort of gave him a hard time yesterday after he was doing something really sweet for Archer."

"Tension is high between you two."

"Um, yes, you could say that again."

"But you know," Ellory said, picking up two cups to start Morgan's order, "*tension* is sometimes another word for *passion*."

Morgan felt her cheeks burn. "Maybe once upon a time," she mumbled. "But not anymore."

"And why not?"

"You know why. The...cowboy story?" Morgan had, during her last visit to the Bean, told Ellory all about her romantic past with an unnamed cowboy.

Ellory, who was scooping coffee into a filter,

whirled around. "Decker McBride is the cow-boy crush?"

Morgan nodded. "And my first kiss."

"And now you're back and he's teaching your little boy while you keep his business alive. It's so romantic."

"Trust me, it's anything but romantic. It's somewhat volatile and extremely frustrating."

"It doesn't have to be." She handed Morgan two pastry bags. "Take him the raspberry Danish. They're fresh and amazing, if I do say so myself. If you have feelings for him still, just tell him."

"That sounds a lot easier than it is. I don't know how I feel. I definitely don't know how he feels. And there's Archer to think about. And... I don't know. I guess I'm once bitten, twice shy."

"Well, you know a surefire way to find out how he feels, right?"

"What?"

"Ask him." She pushed the coffees into a tray and slid it toward Morgan.

Twenty minutes later, Morgan stood on Deck-er's front porch, Ellory's words ringing in her ears. *Ask him.*

Forget that plan. Now that she was here, part of her wanted to turn on her heel and go back. Leave the treats on the porch and text him an apology. There was no way she was going to ask him about his feelings. No. Way.

But part of her wanted to see him. She couldn't ignore that.

Before she could change her mind about being there, she knocked on the door. Maybe he wasn't awake yet. Or maybe he was out in the pasture or in the barn or—who knew—maybe fixing the rope ladder on that infernal tree house far across the property. She'd just about convinced herself that it was true, when the door opened, a freshly showered Decker standing on the other side.

His eyebrows went up. "Morgan," he said. "What's wrong?"

Her words were caught in her throat. He was scrubbed and pink, the wispy curls on the back of his neck weighted down and dripping into the collar of his white T-shirt, which was pristine and gleaming and clinging to the muscles of his chest. His jeans were crisp and his socks were white, and he smelled like soap and aftershave.

She held up the drink container and willed herself to stop staring and just speak. "Peace offering," she said. "Can I come in?"

"Sure, of course," he said, backing up to let her pass. "But why a peace offering?"

"The horse thing yesterday," she said. "I shouldn't have pressed you like that. I was excited."

"Oh. Don't worry about that. I understood."

She had never been inside his house before. She wasn't sure what she expected, but it almost felt like somewhere she'd been before. It was cozy without being stifling. It was clean without being obsessive. It was modern and masculine and comfortable.

"Have a seat." He ushered her into the living room and gestured to the couch. She sat and leaned forward to slide the drinks onto the coffee table, which was covered with books. She picked one up.

"World War II. Are you a history buff?"

"Oh, you know," he said. "I wouldn't really say a buff. Just keeps me busy. Sometimes TV gets boring, and the house gets quiet."

She set the book back on the table and picked up another one. "Lenny Dykstra?"

He nodded. "His nickname was Nails. Played for the Mets and the Phillies. And then went to prison. That's a memoir. It's pretty good, if you want to borrow it."

"Maybe," she said noncommittally, then picked up another. "Ooh, a baseball almanac." She gave him a playful side-eye. "How good do you think you are?"

He brought the dimples out to play. Morgan felt a tingle run its course throughout her body, but for some reason, she didn't fight it. There was something about sitting in his living room with him that just felt right. "Pretty good."

"Okay..." She riffled through some pages.

"Which player had the most base hits in the 1970s?"

"Oh, come on. That's too easy."

"Don't bluff. Who?"

He leaned in close and whispered, "You caught me. I guess I'll take a wild stab. Pete Rose?"

She snapped the book shut. "You peeked."

"No, I did not! Ask me another—I'll prove it."

"Okay, who had the most base hits in the 1920s?"

"Rogers Hornsby. Come on. I thought you were going to challenge me. I had those kinds of facts memorized by the time I was eight."

"Okay." She flipped a few more pages. "Okay. Who were the St. Louis Browns before they were the St. Louis Browns?"

"Oh, gosh, I guess you stumped me," he said. "I have no idea. Maybe the, um…Milwaukee Brewers…who played for one year, 1902, in Lloyd Street Park, for 48 wins and 89 losses? That's just a wild guess, though." He winked.

Morgan studied the book, then crowed, "Wrong!"

"No, I'm not."

"Yes, you are. They played in 1901, not 1902. You clearly know nothing about baseball. I'm thinking you need a new nickname. Maybe Horseyman." Was she flirting? It felt like flirting. She didn't mean to be flirting. It was just happening. But she didn't feel embarrassed or

bad or like she needed to take it back at all. She
let it sit there, wondering if he would bristle.
But he didn't.

"Ah, yes. Horseyman. Has a certain ring to
it. And I'll call you Miss Clean. Instead of...
the other name. Ooh, wait. Maybe I'll just call
you that—The Other Name. The Artist Formerly
Known as Tweety? The Tweety Who Shall Not
Be Named? That's the one. Has a certain ring
to it, don't you think?"

She set the book on the table and pulled the
two coffees out of the holder, handed one to him.
"You can say it. Tweety is a much better nickname than any of those. Miss Clean makes me
sound like a clean-freak old lady."

He raised one eyebrow knowingly as he took
a sip of the coffee.

"Ha ha," she said, slapping at his shoulder.
"You're not funny. Have a Danish. Ellory's a
baking whiz."

He took a pastry bag from her, pulled out the
Danish and took a big bite. He groaned with delight, and Morgan felt that groan all the way to
her toes. She hadn't remembered him making a
similar groaning noise after they'd kissed, but
now that she heard it again, she realized that
he had.

"Good, huh?" she asked, trying to find her

voice. Her throat felt dry. She took a sip of her coffee.

He nodded, studied the bag. "The Dreamy Bean. Is that the one owned by the vintage girl?"

Morgan giggled. "I'm not sure what a vintage girl is, but yes. Ellory is the adorable blonde who wears a lot of vintage clothing."

"She can bake, that's for sure."

"Well, she's single, if you're looking," Morgan said, and although it was a joke, it fell flat as it came out of her mouth. She didn't want to think about Decker and Ellory together. She hated the idea, in fact. A lot.

"I'm not," he said, just as flatly. He took another bite, then said around it, "And, if I was, she's not my type."

"Oh, really? And what is your type?" Okay, this was definitely flirting. And she couldn't— or maybe just didn't want to—stop herself.

Morgan knew she was treading on dangerous ground here. She knew she was setting herself up for opening old wounds.

He dropped the remaining pastry back into the bag and swallowed. "Don't have one."

Ouch. She didn't expect that to sting, but it did. She'd had her hopes up without even realizing it.

"That's not true. Everybody has a type. Come on. Are you afraid? Are you embarrassed?" she teased, but he was no longer playing along, and her words dried up.

"Why are you here, exactly?" he asked. "I appreciate the treats, but, um…I don't understand."

Morgan tried not to feel unwanted. A part of her felt the urge to get up and leave, scurry away from this discomfort. "I'm here to apologize," she said, her voice raspy and uncertain.

"For what?"

"I told you, for pouting about the horse. You were trying to help me. And you were definitely helping Archer. And I ruined it. And I'm sorry."

He tilted his head as he gazed at her. She found it impossible to guess what he was thinking. She took a nervous gulp of her drink. She still hadn't touched her Danish. She wasn't hungry, what with her stomach all tied up in knots and all.

"You don't need to be sorry about anything," he said. "If anyone needs to be sorry, it's me. And, trust me, I am. Every single day. You have no idea."

Morgan felt her chest grow warm. She'd been waiting to hear those words for so long. A part of her had hoped that he was miserable without her, so that she could feel vindicated when he finally admitted that he'd made a mistake in breaking up with her. But instead of feeling vengeful victory, she simply felt closeness.

"You want to see something spectacular?" he said, completely surprising her.

"Yeah. Okay. Sure."

"Let me get my boots." He grabbed his Danish and took off for another room, groaning again as he took another bite.

Morgan got up, all nervous energy, and paced the room. There were framed aerial photos of half a dozen baseball stadiums hung on the wall by the window. A cluster of close-up photos of leaves on the wall opposite. A small shelf stuffed with old Elmer Kelton paperbacks. A basket of fireplace tools on the hearth. Family photos lined the mantel.

Decker in a Little League uniform, holding a baseball bat and peering into the sun ever so seriously. David kneeling in the grass with a black puppy in his arms, beaming, showing off two missing teeth. Decker, David and their dad holding fishing poles. The siblings and their dad in nearly identical graduation photos. The siblings and their dad standing in front of an arch, with a sign across the top reading Triple Mac Ranch.

She heard the sound of Decker's boots and turned to see him standing behind her, already wearing his black cowboy hat.

"Triple Mac?" she asked, pointing at the photo.

"Three McBride Men," he said absently, fiddling with the fit of his hat. "David, Decker and Douglas—that's my dad."

"You changed the name of the ranch."

He nodded. "After my dad died, yeah. I wanted to open Pathways, and Triple Mac sounded like macaroni and cheese to me. I always hated it. Even though that was his way of letting us know that it was going to be our ranch someday. I felt guilty about it at first, but then I realized he wouldn't have cared. He would have just been proud that one of us wanted to keep it in the family. It's not a working ranch the way he envisioned, I'm positive of that, but it's a working ranch and it's still ours. Triple Mac or Pathways. I still have the sign in the barn, though. Couldn't bring myself to get rid of it. Come with me."

He led Morgan out of the house and across the yard. As they approached the barn, she could hear snorting and whinnying of horses inside. He led her inside and went straight to Tango's stall.

"Morgan, this is Tango. Tango, Morgan."

Tango stuck his head out of the stall and Morgan stroked his nose. It was soft, and she could feel his breath on the underside of her arm. It tickled. She felt a dangerous thrill run through her. Tango was enormous compared to Ziggy. "Nice to meet you, Tango," she said. "Formally and all."

"Give me five minutes to get him ready, and we're going to take a ride."

"A what?" she asked, taking two steps backward. "He's a lot bigger than Ziggy." But Decker grabbed her hand and pulled her back to the stall door before she could get away.

"Don't be a chicken. Tango's a perfect gentleman."

"Tango is like a thousand feet off the ground, and might I remind you, if he doesn't want me on his back, he will get me off his back. I could break my neck on that thing."

Decker winced playfully. "Don't let him hear you call him *that thing*. He'll throw you for sure."

Morgan moved away again, but Decker caught her hand a second time, lacing his fingers through hers as she pulled their arms taut. Morgan couldn't help smiling. She loved the feeling of his hand in hers. She loved the way they played together. *Yes, this is definitely flirting, and I'm not the only one doing it.*

She loved everything about this moment, even if her stomach was flipping at the thought of getting on the horse.

"I'm kidding, I'm kidding," he said. "I'm going to ride with you. It's a short distance, and we won't go faster than a walk. Now, stop arguing and help me get him ready before we lose all the morning sun."

Morgan did trust him, but she was struggling to hear his instructions. All she could hear were the words *ride with you*. Now that it was an actual possibility, she didn't know if she could handle being that close to Decker McBride again.

But she knew that she wanted to try.

GETTING MORGAN ON Tango was one of the hardest things Decker ever had to do. It wasn't so much of a physical challenge as it was a mental one, and his belly hurt from laughing. It was hard to help someone onto a horse when you were doubled over just trying to breathe.

"Stop making fun of me," Morgan whined, but there was a smile in her voice, too. "I'm scared. I can't help it."

"Just grab his mane like I showed you before."

"There's no saddle. How am I supposed to pull myself up with no saddle? How am I supposed to sit?"

"On your backside. And you have a mounting block. You can practically step over him."

She placed her hand on Tango, who decided to be a comedian and give a loud snort. She jumped back with a yelp.

"When I try, he does that," she complained. "I don't think he wants me to ride."

"He's probably telling you to hurry it up already."

"Well, he can wait. I'm not asking him to do something he's terrified of, am I?" She aimed this last at Tango, who snorted again, drawing a little *eep* from Morgan, and more laughter out of Decker. Tango had to be the world's best horse.

"I don't know. If I were Tango, I would feel a little uncertain about carrying your nervous Nellie self around."

"I am not a nervous Nellie. I am aware and realistic."

"If you say so, Nellie. It's okay. You don't have to ride him. I'm sure we can dig up a tricycle for you. One that doesn't do the scary snort. Want me to get the pony?"

"Kind of. But no. I can do this." She made another attempt to throw a leg over the horse, and once again bailed at the last minute, toppling herself off the block. She landed on a small cushion of hay. "I don't know why you insist on thinking you're funny."

"Okay, okay," Decker said between guffaws. He reached down and grabbed her around the waist, pulled her to a standing position. "I'll get up first so you can see how it's done. Watch carefully."

Decker didn't need the mounting block. He hadn't used one since he was a kid. Swinging himself up onto a horse was as natural as throwing a baseball or brushing his teeth or...or kissing Morgan. But he used it anyway, the ease of which making him want to start laughing all over again.

"Show-off," she mumbled.

He dismounted. "Your turn."

She stared at him warily, irritated, for a long moment, as if she were trying to decide if she even wanted to do this anymore. He guessed she probably didn't. Not really. But she seemed to have a point to make. She took his hand and climbed the mounting block steps to the top. "Don't do anything mean."

"I'm not going to do anything mean. The last thing I want is for you to get hurt."

She cocked her head to the side and gave him a *Really?* look. He supposed he could own that. He considered acknowledging it—just putting it all out there and hashing it out right now—but they were having fun. She had brought him breakfast. And he wanted to take her to the ridge. He wanted to see how the early-morning sun played in the sparkle of her eyes, wanted to see it softly light her cheekbones, dance down the highlights of her hair, rest in the shallows of her collarbone.

He knew that getting on a horse with her was dangerous. But he also knew that he was already sliding down the path to danger. He didn't want to fall for her all over again, but he was drawn to her, and no amount of self-protection seemed to be working. He could distance himself all he wanted. He would still feel her presence, even if she were on the other side of the ranch.

"You can trust me. I'm not going to let anything happen to you. Tango is very patient. I've got you. Now, grab his mane and swing your right leg up."

She chewed the inside of her cheek, thinking it over, and then grabbed Tango's mane once again. Only this time, she seemed more determined than afraid.

"Good," Decker said, coaching her. "Now put your hand here…right…and pull yourself up. Think up, not over."

At first, she seemed unsure which muscles to use, and which motion would most propel her the direction she wanted to go. She made a couple of false starts, but then got the determined crease between her eyebrows that he hadn't even realized he'd noticed about her until now.

Morgan was no giant, by any stretch, but she was athletic and nimble. Once she made her mind up that this was happening, there was nothing that would stop her from getting on the horse.

It was almost as if her fear of backing down overrode her fear of the horse.

She produced a hair tie from her pocket and

swept her hair into a messy ponytail, then squared her shoulders, took a breath and lifted herself up onto Tango's back, as if she'd been doing it all her life.

Decker was dazzled by watching her in motion, and he found himself not wanting to move, or even breathe, with her so close to him. It was like having a butterfly land on him—he wanted to stay as still as possible so he didn't frighten her away.

"I did it!" He felt her smile all the way down to his bones, and had to resist the urge to place his hand over his heart to keep it inside his chest. Her smile faded. "But there's no way you can get on him with me up here."

"I think I might be able to manage," he said, easily climbing atop Tango. "I've ridden a horse once or twice."

She turned to face him. "You are such an insufferable show-off."

He grinned. "I'm just good, Morgan."

"Nothing show-offy about that statement. Let's get this thing on the road. Oops! Sorry, not thing." She leaned forward and patted Tango. "Let's get this majestic beast on the road. Better, Tango?" She sat up straight again.

Decker found himself staring at the back of her neck, which looked soft and warm, and he had an almost uncontrollable urge to just rest his forehead there, feel her warmth radiate through him. He wanted to wrap his arms around her waist and pull her close to him, hold her in the way that he'd dreamed of, ever since she got into her car and gave a shy wave goodbye all those years ago.

She giggled and turned her head again, and now her face was only inches from his. He could smell coffee on her breath. Apparently, he was leaning in, even while telling himself that he couldn't—as if she were a magnet and he were helpless against her pull.

Decker was speechless. He couldn't tear his eyes away, even though he knew that what was showing in them was a hunger for things he couldn't have.

"Are you okay?" she asked. "Did I do something wrong?"

Finally, he snapped out of it. "No." He cleared his throat. "No, you did everything just fine. Really great. Now you and Archer are both riders."

"So let's ride," she said brightly. She was helping him out of the awkward situation. He knew this. *Or maybe she's feeling the pull, too, and is trying to force herself to ignore that it's happening.*

Or maybe I'm being hopeful when I have no right to be.

He cleared his throat again and instructed her on how to use the reins. Satisfied that she had the horse under as much control as she could, he eased Tango out of the barn and into the early-morning sunlight.

Suddenly, given his feelings of being so close to her, the trek seemed too romantic, a date that he'd fantasized about but had never had. Just the two of them, riding out into the early-morning sun, full of coffee and pastries and love. When he'd imagined this moment, he hadn't put anyone's face to the image. That would have been too real. But now that he was here with Morgan, he realized she was the only one who made sense. And that was unnerving. He wasn't ready for this. He would never be ready for this. Because on the heels of every fantasy was a very real memory. He would rather never have her than have her and lose her.

It felt like a bad idea. But it was a bad idea that he couldn't talk himself out of. He couldn't admit these feelings to her. He kept pushing Tango forward, ignoring the inner warnings to simply take her for a shorter ride across the pasture and back.

But he wanted to give her this ride. It was his favorite ride on his favorite horse to his favorite spot on the ranch ever since he was a little boy. It was his spot. His secret. The place he went to grieve, to think, to fantasize, to be the most him that he could be. Sharing it with her was a gift, maybe the greatest gift he had to give.

At first, Morgan sat stiff and tense, her muscles constantly at the ready for when Tango— in her mind—ultimately decided that he didn't want a passenger and would just toss her to the moon. But after a few minutes, she started to relax, allowing her body to move with the rocking motion of the horse, rather than against it. Decker felt her lean into him a little, and again fought the urge to just envelop her into his arms.

He directed her to guide Tango east. Buck County was situated on top of one of the hills that formed the valley that cradled Haw Springs below. There was a spot on the east border of the McBride property that just happened to have full view of the town. Decker slipped off Tango to give him a break while climbing the hill, and walked beside them, answering Morgan's questions and pointing out landmarks from his childhood.

Morgan drew in a breath when they reached the overlook.

"It's gorgeous," she said. "I can see all the way to my parents' house."

"I know. It's my little secret. The best view in Buck County." He pointed. "There's Main Street."

"Oh! And Marlee's flower shop!"

"Your sister owns that place?"

"She opened it a few years ago. It's been stressful and a ton of work, and she seems to go through assistants like nobody's business. But she swears it's not because she's a mean boss." Morgan laughed. "Oh, hey, there's The Dreamy Bean. I worked there this morning. Did I tell you that?"

"Second job? Isn't this supposed to be your summer break? How many jobs do you have when you're not on break?" He, too, was starting to relax. To enjoy Morgan as a friend and forget about all the complications between them.

"I was just helping out," she said. "I can't stay still for too long. Life's too short to just stand around on the sidelines, you know? Besides, I really like Ellory. She's…different. She's kind."

"Hopefully kind isn't all that different."

"It isn't…and it is. You know what I mean?"

"That's because you live in the city," Decker said. "People are less kind in the city."

"I don't know," she said. "People can be kind anywhere and they can be unkind anywhere. There are plenty of kind people in the city. And plenty of unkind people in the country."

"I suppose that's true. I've run into some kind people in the city, too."

"You get into the city much?" she asked.

"Now and then."

Morgan gazed down at her lap, and then said, staring straight ahead, "If you come to the city every now and then…how come…you've never looked me up?"

There it was. The question he knew she'd been wanting to ask. The question that he wished he knew a good answer to. The question he'd been avoiding examining, not only since she'd been back, but for the entire decade leading up to her coming back.

"I didn't think you would want to see me. But I did watch for you when you were in town."

She made a skeptical noise.

He pointed again, shifting his finger to where she'd been pointing to earlier. "The house is robin's-egg blue with white trim. They got rid of the swing set about a year after you moved out. The trampoline followed six months later. Your mom planted those bright red azaleas the summer after that. You came home by yourself your first Christmas, but after that, you had a man with you. You looked happy and settled. I stopped watching after that."

"I wasn't," she said. "I mean, at first I was. But then I wasn't. Or, at least, he wasn't. And then he made my life miserable. Cody Parker is not the kind of guy who suffers his misery alone.

I think he's the reason the phrase *misery loves company* was ever coined."

"I'm sorry," Decker said.

"It's my own fault. I knew Cody was short-tempered when I married him. I actually knew it in college, before we ever got engaged. He was known for it on campus. But everyone thought it was funny, you know? *Oh, there goes Cody Parker, off to ruin someone's day, ha ha ha,*" she mimicked. "Only it's not funny when it's your day that he's ruining."

"Did he hurt you?" Decker asked, feeling tension build inside of him. He was able to keep his feelings for Morgan at bay, but he wasn't sure if he could keep his feelings at bay if he knew that this man had put his hands on her.

She shook her head. "Not like that, no. But he tore me down all the time. And he tore Archer down. He had no patience for Archer's differences."

Decker's hackles went down, but only slightly. He was already connected to Archer in a way he hadn't expected. The child was light and love and innocence. How could anyone tear him down?

"I can't imagine," he said, although the truth was he didn't want to imagine. He couldn't allow himself to imagine. If he imagined too much, he would imagine himself finding Cody Parker and inviting Cody to try to tear *him* down.

"Surely you can imagine having your heart broken, though, right? I mean…you've dated."

He gazed into her eyes. "I've dated. But my heart has been broken only once," he said. "A long time ago."

She frowned. "You can't mean us."

He gave a slow nod, every part of him screaming that he shouldn't get into this conversation. That this was too close, too much. He'd spent a decade forgetting about Morgan West. But his mouth didn't follow the orders of his brain, and the walls around his well-protected heart began to crumble. "I can. I do."

"But you did the breaking, not me." He might have expected chilly anger or indignation from her, just as he'd been getting from her since she came back to Haw Springs, but instead it was only confusion in her voice. "Decker, I had fallen in love with you. It was you I wanted to come back for."

"It was complicated, Morgan."

"How complicated can it be? I was in love with you, and you sure seemed to be falling in love with me."

"I was."

"But then you broke up with me, with no explanation. And then you just disappeared."

It was the word *disappeared* that had him. That was how he'd always thought of his mother.

She'd *disappeared*. Somehow *disappeared* was easier to swallow than *left*. Disappearing was something that happened to you, not something you wanted to do.

"I know" was all he said.

"You know." Now, here was the anger he'd grown accustomed to. "Well, that's really great to hear. You know you disappeared and that things were complicated. That clears up everything. Thank you for being so open and honest about your feelings. Thank you for helping me understand the greatest heartbreak of my life."

"Morgan, it's not like that. I was so in love with you, it scared me. I envisioned a future with you that I didn't think I could ever have. I left you…before you could leave me."

"You had no reason to think that I would have left you."

"But I had every reason to think that it would destroy me if you did."

"So you chose to destroy yourself. And destroy me in the process."

He gave a slow nod.

"And what about now?" she asked. "I know you can feel it the same way that I do. So what about now?"

"Morgan…"

Now I think you could destroy me even more, because I would lose Archer, too.

"Let's go back," she said, not waiting for the rest of his answer, turning to face forward again. Decker could feel Tango begin to shift his weight in agitation.

She squeezed her legs around Tango like she'd been born on a horse and knew exactly what to do.

Ironically, it was that part of Morgan—the intuitive, intelligent, bold Morgan—that made him fall in love with her in the first place. She'd been through a decade of triumphs and hurts and had come out exactly who she was when she went in, only stronger.

It was that same girl—intuitive, intelligent, bold—that was making him fall in love with her again.

And the same girl who made love look too risky to try.

CHAPTER NINE

"HE'S IMPOSSIBLE. Set in his ways. Clams up at the slightest discomfort." Morgan tossed a can of peas into the shopping cart. It rattled off the side. She winced; she'd thrown it too hard, as if she were lobbing it at her frustration.

"Are you sure you're not just out of sorts because you saw Cody?" her mother asked, turning a loaf of bread over to read the label.

Morgan stopped. "Marlee told you?"

"Well, it was sort of a big deal," she said. "She couldn't believe you didn't confront him. At least demand some child support out of him."

"I very much doubt he had thirty thousand dollars in his pocket, Mom. What would have been the point of that?"

"Not to let him get away with it." Her mom put the loaf of bread in the cart, making sure to place it out of Archer's reach. She'd learned the hard way that Archer just loved to poke his finger through the plastic bread bag, making all the bread stale before anyone ever got a single slice. "He shouldn't, you know. It's not right. He should help you."

"I'm not letting him get away with it." Morgan tossed three cans of pasta sauce into the cart, a new favorite that Aunt Marlee had introduced into Archer's diet. Morgan was glad to be past the peanut butter phase, but it wasn't like red pasta sauce was much better in the mess department. *Couldn't you have gotten him addicted to broccoli?* she'd asked her sister while hosing him down one evening. "It's not up to me to get child support out of him. It's up to the state."

"But the state isn't doing anything."

"Right, so I am doing what I can. I'm working hard to raise Archer on my own. I don't need Cody."

Her mom stopped and turned. She cupped Morgan's cheek—one of the most comforting feelings in the world to Morgan. Something about her mother's touch instantly calmed her, no matter how upset she was. "Honey, you're doing a terrific job. Nobody is questioning that at all. It's that you deserve help, and Cody owes it to you. It's just not right that he gets away with it. Your sister would have given him what-for on your behalf if you didn't want to."

"It's not that I didn't want to, Mom. I've imagined giving him what-for since the day he left.

It's that he was with someone. I think she's his wife. Or fiancée at least."

Her mother nodded and stretched her hand out in front of her. "And pregnant out to here, from what I understand. So he'll get away with it again."

"Maybe. Or maybe not. But she looked happy. Maybe they were there for an ultrasound or something. I couldn't just destroy that day for her. Regardless of what he's done, she doesn't deserve a special day like that ruined. And if he's changed…I don't want to take that away from her, either. What's done is done. It's time to move on."

"That's very kind of you, Morgan." They turned to the next aisle. "I don't know if I could do the same."

Morgan laughed. "Trust me, nobody is more surprised by this reaction than I am. You have no idea how many times I've fantasized about what I would say to Cody Parker if I ever saw him again. Eventually, I'll get mine. I feel strongly about that. In the meantime, I do what I have to do. Like put together a benefit for the most stubborn man on earth."

"You know, if you'd like Archer to finish the session, but you don't want to fuss with that boss of yours anymore, your father and I would be happy to pay the balance. We have a little saved away."

Morgan's stomach clenched. "What? No." She realized she sounded desperate and worked to steady her voice. "I've made so many plans. I can't just walk away from it now. I'll be able to handle working with him a little more. It'll be fine."

Her mother squinted at her, scrutinizing her. Morgan felt the scrutiny all the way to her toes. "I think I understand," she finally said.

"Understand what?"

"Your sister said something about this man being someone you knew before you left."

"Marlee has the biggest mouth on the face of the earth," Morgan mumbled.

"So it's true. He's very handsome. I remember you being heartbroken over someone your freshman year of college. Was it him?"

Morgan thought she had been able to keep Decker a secret from her parents all those years ago. She knew if she told them she was racing off to meet a boy at the carnival midway for the second and third nights in a row, they never would've let her go. And then she was on her own in college. She only told her roommate and her sister about Decker. Apparently, she had been more transparent than she realized.

"It's ancient history."

"But sometimes history can repeat itself."

"Not this time," Morgan said. "For sure."

They finished their shopping and took the groceries home. Morgan helped her mom put them away, then gave Archer a packet of applesauce and turned on one of his favorite TV shows.

Her brain still felt muddled by her conversation with Decker, her mother's intuition getting the best of her and the words *sometimes history can repeat itself.*

But this time it can't, she thought. *Because it's not just* my *heart on the line. I can't let someone else hurt Archer the way Cody did.* But she knew that wasn't the full truth of it. She'd felt so comfortable and so connected with Decker, sitting on that horse on the ridge overlooking the valley. Riding with the warmth of his chest so close to her back. It was a feeling that she belonged there. Not just that morning, but always. Like it was the only place she truly belonged. Like she would never find another place where she belonged more.

Like, if Decker had gotten down off that horse, dropped to a knee and produced a ring, she would have said *yes* without hesitation, because it was somehow preordained, and she could see the future so vividly.

She would have quit her job in the city, moved back to Haw Springs and been perfectly and completely happy.

Which was ridiculous. Because Decker Mc-Bride was never going to love her the way she loved him.

He'd had his heart broken once, he said. *He'd* had *his* heart broken? The very thought of it made Morgan roll her eyes in disgust. How dare he act like the victim?

How dare he not see the future in such vivid detail as she did?

How dare he not love her back?

No, she wouldn't quit. That would give him too much satisfaction. Plus she believed in the cause now. She wanted to bring in money for the ranch, because as frustrating as that man was, he was earnest about wanting to help kids like Archer succeed. He loved them.

Curse him and his complicated feelings, she thought, as she got out her binder full of plans and opened it.

She and he may be permanently over—not that they'd ever really begun—but she wasn't going anywhere until the last penny had been dropped into the donation bucket.

She sat at the kitchen table, making notes and organizing. She planned to hit the ground running in the morning.

Forget their past. Forget their future.

She had work to do today.

DECKER FELT RIDICULOUS. The man staring back at him was about as ill-suited as it got.

The dressing room door was flung open. David stood on the other side, his phone in his hand and a grin on his face.

"What are you doing? Absolutely not," Decker said, grabbing the phone out of his brother's hand.

"You look like a magazine model," David said, sticking his fingers in Decker's hair and messing it up. "I like it. A whole new direction for you. Cowboy spy. Double-O Horseshoe. It's got a ring."

"That's it—I'm not doing it." Decker started to loosen the bow tie that was practically strangling him to death.

"No one ever asked you to do it," David reminded him. "This was your own stubborn idea."

"Morgan mentioned it."

"And she changed her mind. You don't need a tux to go to a carnival."

Truth be told, Decker felt like wearing the tux would be an olive branch. Her chilliness toward him had reached an all-time freeze since their conversation on the ridge. He didn't know how to reach her, and part of him thought maybe he just shouldn't. Just let it lie. The benefit marked the end of the session. She would be leaving in a week, and he would maybe never see her again.

Or maybe she would be back next summer. And the summer after that. And the one after that.

The thought of continuing to see her intermittently gutted him more than the thought of never seeing her again. Out of sight, out of mind, and all that. He knew that true love didn't really work that way, but it sort of did, and he could handle the thought of her being gone forever better than the idea of counting down the days until she reappeared.

When this summer was done and over with, he would either need to figure out a way to get her to stay permanently, or figure out a way to say goodbye that was truly goodbye without hurting her again.

And without hurting yourself? Well. That would be impossible.

"I'm not wearing a tux," David said.

"Your date is okay with that?"

"I don't have a date. I'm going solo."

"Really? You don't have a line of admirers just dying to become a veterinarian's wife?"

David grinned. "I didn't say that. I just said I'm not taking any of them to the benefit."

"Ha ha, big brother. Very funny."

"Nah," David said. "There's no line. And I haven't had time to date anyone recently. Been too busy. I have a lot of things I want to get into place before I look at commitments."

"Well, all I know is I can't go to this benefit in flannel and jeans. It's my ranch."

"Our ranch."

"Our ranch that you want out of." He handed David's phone back to him.

"Fair enough. But maybe just…" David reached to a rack behind him and produced a blue-checkered sport coat. He held it up against Decker. "This. And jeans. And your snakeskin boots."

Decker faced the mirror, holding the jacket up against himself. It was a nice look. And he would definitely feel more like himself in his jeans and boots, while also not feeling like himself at all.

"She'll love it," David said.

Decker hung the jacket on the wall and continued loosening his tie until he was finally able to pull it out of his collar. He took a deep breath. "This isn't about her."

"Right." Another photo.

"Would you stop that?" He tried to swipe the phone back, but David whisked it out of his way.

"You are wound tight, little brother. What's gotten into you? If it's not about her, I mean…" He arched an eyebrow that said he knew very well that it was 100 percent about her. He squeezed into the dressing room and sat on the bench. Decker's shoulders slumped. Looked like he wasn't going to be getting dressed anytime soon. "Did something happen?"

"No. Nothing happened. Nothing has happened between us since we were eighteen years old."

"Ah. So that's what's happened. Nothing."

"Yes. No. Not in the way you mean it."

"All I know is she's mopey and you're angry, and all of a sudden, she's riding horses with Archer, like she was born on a horse. And I know she wouldn't be on a horse unless you okayed it, so you must have taught her how to ride. I know that something happened between you, and it didn't go well."

Sometimes David was more in tune with Decker than Decker ever wanted to admit. He said nothing.

"I see," David said. "But the benefit is coming up, so you'd both better get over it and put on your smiley faces like the best friends that you are, right? And if that means you wear a tux, it means you wear a tux. I get it."

"We're not best friends."

David raised his eyebrows. "That's not what it looks like to the rest of the world. But you've both put way too much work into this Hail Mary benefit—you can't afford to unravel now. Literally can't afford it."

Decker began to unbutton his tux shirt. Truth

be told, he kind of liked the shirt. It was white and crisp against his sun-drenched skin. "Thank you for the reminder that you're going to sell this ranch if we don't bring in enough money."

"I've been thinking. Why do you want to hang on to this land with all its bad history, anyway? Dad should've sold it the moment Mom walked out on him. Heck, his dad should have sold it. It's been generation after generation of hard work and poverty, nobody ever really getting anywhere."

"Dad's hard work and poverty put you through vet school."

"I put myself through vet school. Decker, I know you have strong feelings about the ranch, but please, you have to understand that I have strong feelings, too. I've worked so hard for so long. I want to get somewhere. If we sell the ranch, I'll be able to do what's important to me, too. Right now, it's all about what's important to you."

"It's just about what's important," Decker said. "Period."

David nodded. "I don't argue with that. But you can still do what's important on a smaller patch of land. We can both have what we want, little brother. It doesn't have to be you versus me. It can be us versus the world. Just like it always was."

Decker didn't have anything to say to that. Part of him knew David was right. He was being selfish, out of pride or sentimentality, or... He wasn't really sure what, exactly. He only knew that he was holding his brother back.

"Can you leave, please? We can talk about this later. I don't have time right now to worry about the future."

David stood and backed out of the dressing room. "Okay, okay, I just want you to think about it."

"I'm thinking."

"And, seriously, Decker. Don't go with the tux."

"Right. Gotcha."

He shut the door and latched it so nobody else could barge in on him. But he couldn't shut the door on his thoughts. Right now, it seemed that no matter what move he made, it would be the wrong one.

CHAPTER TEN

THE BARN WAS beyond magical. Marlee had really outdone herself with the flowers and the decor.

"You should go into wedding planning," Morgan told her. "You've got a knack."

Marlee paused, mid-hustle, to admire the interior of the barn alongside her sister. "It's nothing," she said, but she was beaming. Morgan knew it was definitely not nothing. It had taken hours of work, and her sister was proud of herself and her accomplishments. As she should be. "But weddings…bah. No, thanks."

"What do you mean 'bah'? Weddings are where the money is."

"They're also where the insufferable lovers are. Don't get me wrong. I support marriage in theory. I just always feel uncomfortable around it. Too much icky, squishy, *moo-moo-moo*."

Morgan burst out laughing. "*Moo-moo-moo*? What is that?"

Marlee turned toward her sister, her lips pooched out in a kissy face. *"Moo-moo-moo."*

Morgan was practically doubled over with laughter. She mimicked her sister. *"Moo-moo-moo."*

They were maybe a little loopy. They'd been working long days for two weeks now and had enjoyed very little self-care, especially sleep. This was par for the course for Morgan anytime she had a big event coming up, but Marlee was accustomed to a much slower, Haw Springs lifestyle.

Marlee scrunched up her face, sticking her lips out like a fish. *"Moo-moo-moo,* oh, Decker."

And, just like that, Morgan's laughter was gone. "Anyway. I need to get back to work," she said, the words rustily creaking their way out of her mouth. "It looks really awesome in here, Mar. You did an amazing job. Truly." She turned and began walking toward the kitchen.

"Oh, Morgan, come on. I was teasing." Marlee followed her sister. "Don't be mad. It was a joke."

"I'm not mad," Morgan said. "I'm just focused. I have hors d'oeuvres to check on. You know what happens if you leave Mom and Dad to their own devices." She tried to keep her voice light, but even she could hear how wooden she must've sounded to her sister. Morgan couldn't help it. Being a woman in the corporate world, she was accustomed to having to fight to prove her worth.

She'd worked way too hard in her life, and way too hard on this benefit to have it belittled as some sort of romantic fling. Besides, she and Decker were barely speaking, much less kissing.

Still, Marlee had also worked hard. And she'd done an amazing job. Marlee had been there for her since day one. She had given so much of herself—she deserved grace. Morgan was grateful. She stopped, spun to face her sister and gave her a quick peck on the cheek. "I'm not mad. Thank you for all of your help. Really. The flowers are absolutely gorgeous. You're going to get tons of customers out of this. People will be coming to you from as far away as Rayville."

Relief washed over Marlee's face. "If nothing else, maybe I'll have a lock on the Haw Springs prom crowd."

Morgan chuckled. "Hey, now, that's a sizable crowd."

"And everyone gets their flowers from the supermarket."

"We used to," Morgan said. "Remember? That sparkly ribbon was the height of sophistication. You really knew your date liked you if you got the sparkly ribbon. Especially the iridescent sparkly ribbon."

"Now we know it was actually that your date's mom liked you. Or at least liked her son enough to shell out the extra ten bucks." Marlee used her finger to tip up the end of her nose. "But it doesn't matter. We were trendsetters. Now everyone is sparkly."

Morgan swept her arm wide. "We're still trend-setters. You just watch. The yellow and blue color palette is going to be all the rage." She held up one pinkie. *"Moo-moo-moo."*

Archer, who had been quietly playing with his animal figurines, began echoing his mother. He held up a giraffe. *"Moo-moo-moo!"*

Marlee and Morgan sagged against each other with laughter.

"What was it Grandma Jo used to say? 'Little pitchers have big ears'?"

"And little Archers love to echo," Morgan added. "I'm going to work on the hors d'oeuvres."

"I'll help you," Marlee said. "But I think you should call them horse d'oeuvres."

"Horse d'oeuvres! Yes! See what I mean? You're a natural at the party-planning stuff."

Calling the snacks any iteration of hors d'oeuvres was pushing it, really. Hors d'oeuvres sounded finicky and delicate and fancy. Liver mousse and goat cheese with apricots and bacon-wrapped seafood—those were hors d'oeuvres. Everything in Morgan's kitchen was either carnival-themed or horse-themed. Or, in some cases, both. Trail mix with popcorn. Carrots and apples and hot dogs. Cookies decorated to look like friendly little horse faces. Cotton candy and candy apples and a food truck parked out front that specialized in loaded curly french fries.

The doctors began to stream in with their nurses and clipboards and tubs of supplies. Morgan met them at the door to show them to their respective stations so they could unload and get comfortable before patients arrived. She'd managed to talk partitions and tables and mobile curtains out of a supply company, as long as she plied the medical staff with logo'd pens and pads of paper and pamphlets. One thing Morgan had learned early on in her career—everyone was for sale.

Except for Decker, she'd thought many times while doing her wheeling and dealing. *Decker has no price. He would rather starve than sell himself.*

And if she didn't make this benefit a success, he may do just that.

The barn had been split in half. The party half, and the clinic half. There was an immunization station, two sports physical stations, an ENT station and two well-check stations. Tucked in the back—where brides usually dressed for their big day at the barn—was a sensory room, where a doctor who specialized in treating children on the spectrum waited in the quiet.

And then there was Dr. LaSalle, who came in

with no entourage and no equipment, other than his trusty Gladstone bag. His lab coat was covered with rainbow-colored llamas, and a massive bag of lollipops was tucked under one arm.

Morgan held back a chuckle. Dr. LaSalle was different, all right, and she guessed his station—which was a simple medical advice station—would remain full all day.

"The babies are all cleaned up and ready for their spotlight." Morgan turned to find Atty Reed, whose flannel shirt definitely smelled a little like wet goat. "They're gonna be hungry, too, so the early birds will get to feed them."

"Thank you," Morgan said. "That'll be a huge hit." Smell notwithstanding, the goats were adorable, and Morgan knew the kids were going to go crazy over them. Fifty cents for a handful of feed was going to go a long way.

Atty crossed her arms and surveyed the room. "I've gotta admit, when you said medical clinic and carnival, the two images just didn't make sense to me. And a bunch of doctors with needles definitely didn't scream *party time*. I thought you were a little crazy."

Morgan chuckled. "I may be a little crazy. I've certainly thought that about myself a time or two."

"But it's crazy in a good way," Atty said. "Because this really works. There's a band and fun food and games outside. I wouldn't mind getting a shot if I got to ride that giant slide you had brought in."

"That's my hope," Morgan said.

Atty gave one more look around, nodding. "You're gonna rake in the money, that's for sure."

"I need to," Morgan said.

The truth was, putting on this kind of benefit wasn't cheap. And not everyone was as eager to strike a deal as the partition company. Not everyone was willing to volunteer their time, like the doctors. She'd paid some hefty deposits and was counting on a stellar turnout to be able to pay the other half and still have enough left over to save the ranch.

"I'll be in my office if you need anything," Atty said.

"I hope you'll come out and grab a bite," Morgan said. "Enter the raffle. Maybe even ride that slide."

"Oh, honey, I already rode the slide," Atty said. "They needed a test driver."

"And?"

Atty smiled, a rare occurrence. "And it's fast and it's fun and I'd pay a dollar to do it again for sure."

She walked away, leaving Morgan to survey the barn by herself. She tried to do so without a critical eye. *Don't see the things that didn't turn*

*out the way you planned. Just see things as the
kids will see them.*

A slow smile crept across her face.

Marlee wasn't the only one who'd outdone herself. They both had.

"Ice," she said, interrupting her own thoughts
and jumping into action. "I forgot to fill the ice tub."

She bustled off to find a bucket that she could use
to transport ice from the machine in the kitchen to
the metal trough parked outside by the food truck.
A table awaited; Marlee was dutifully lining it with
sodas and waters. Later, after the clinic, they would
introduce some adult beverages to the mix.

"Ah. Ice. I was just about to come in for a
bucket," Marlee said.

Morgan dumped the ice into the trough. "It'll
take both of us."

Marlee glanced up, over Morgan's shoulder,
and did a double take. "Um. Let me get the next
one." She took the empty bucket from Morgan
and hustled to the kitchen.

Morgan looked where Marlee's attention had
just been grabbed, and saw David walking across
the lawn, cleaned and pressed in a sport coat and
a crisp new pair of jeans.

Behind him, Decker.

Wearing a tux jacket, white shirt and bow tie,
with worn, perfect-fit jeans, boots and hat.

Looking…breathtakingly handsome.

DECKER DIDN'T KNOW what he was expecting, but he wasn't expecting this.

From where he stood, the inside of the barn looked like a dream. Through the open doors, he could see what seemed like whole fields' worth of flowers and sunny centerpieces on rustic runners stretched across blue gingham tablecloths.

Outside was a full-on small-town carnival. There was a tall slide waiting for kids to grab a burlap sack and sail down. There was a small fleet of carnival games—ring toss, duck pond and balloon pop. And baseball. Of course there was a baseball toss. He would have expected no less. There was a cotton candy machine and a food truck and a pen full of baby goats.

And a drink station. Where Morgan stood, staring back at him.

His breath caught.

Morgan had never screamed *cowgirl* to him. She was always meant for the city, even when the city was only the city limits of Haw Springs. He'd never seen her in a western hat. Or boots. Until today.

She wore a long, blue, ruffle-and-lace patchwork dress with brown hat and boots, her skin glowing with the sun, almost radiating its own shine. Her brown hair spilled down her back in loose waves. When she glanced up at him and smiled, he swore his heart stopped.

In that moment, he saw it all very clearly. As clearly as if it had actually happened, and this was purely a memory. Morgan, sitting on the tailgate of his truck, boots discarded to the side, her bare feet dangling down, toes pointing to the ground after a long day's work. Archer, sitting in her lap, leaning his head back against her chest the way he loved to do. June napping next to them, as content as she'd ever been, every so often barely peeping through one eye to oversee his work.

And him, baling hay or cleaning Tango's shoes or fixing the fence, or any number of routine tasks that he must do, only it didn't feel routine because he had Morgan right there. He had Archer right there.

He had a family.

"You look…" Morgan trailed off as he approached her.

"Stubborn?" David interjected. "I told him not to go with the tux."

Decker lifted open his unbuttoned jacket. "I didn't. I went with the tux jacket."

"And shirt. And tie."

"Well, if I just wore the jacket with nothing under it, then I would look silly. Come on, now."

Morgan's eyebrows rose. She barely concealed a little smile.

David pulled a soda out of the ice and raised it as if toasting his brother. "Ladies and gentlemen, McBride Pathways has officially procured a stubborn, old mule."

Decker knew that his brother was going for a laugh, but Morgan simply stood there, a soda can in each hand, staring at him. It was like déjà vu, the two of them alone in a bustling crowd, speaking volumes without saying a single word.

David cleared his throat uncomfortably, and then tipped his can to Morgan. "This sure is impressive. A toast to Morgan West for going above and beyond."

This seemed to finally drag Morgan's attention away. She tipped one of the cans she was holding in response, then stuffed it deep into the ice. "To McBride Pathways. May she live forever."

"Yeah?"

"The goal tonight is to give Pathways so many resources, it can't fail."

"Wow. Big goal."

Morgan offered a thin smile. "It's a big program. More than that, it's an important program. And this is an important benefit."

David gazed around. From where they were standing, they could see all the way into the makeshift clinic, where the medical staff had begun milling around, talking with each other. "That, I can't argue. My hat's off to you."

She bowed her head just slightly, her hand

reaching to the top of her hat, reminding Decker a little of Ben. "Thank you."

David took a drink and then looked back and forth between Morgan and Decker. "I think I'll mingle."

"Don't do anything I wouldn't do," Decker said.

"Like wear a tux?" David teased.

"Especially not that. You think that being the only one is a bad thing."

"Touché, little brother." David lifted his can one more time, then turned and disappeared into the building. Decker heard him call out a greeting to someone inside.

"He knows everyone," Decker said. "Thank you for what you said, by the way. About Pathways being important. David's a great guy. The best, really. He's just nervous about the future."

"He needn't be. Not when it comes to the ranch, anyway. I've got that covered, just like I said I would." Even when she was frustrated with him, Morgan had his back. *Just like a wife would*, he caught himself thinking, and quickly chased the thought away. Tonight was going to be a test, for sure.

"He wants out. I don't know if I've told you that."

Morgan went back to filling the ice trough with cans. "I figured."

"He's going to sell. I'm just hoping the benefit raises enough for me to buy him out. I don't suppose you want to buy his half if we come up short." He was joking, but could tell by the pause in her actions, the tension that drew her shoulders up, that she didn't find it funny.

"You suppose correctly." She went back to work. "Maybe you'll find an investor while you're here. Dr. Maher in there specializes in children on the spectrum. And Dr. Fisher has two autistic children of her own. I don't know how deep their pockets are, but I know they're definitely deeper than mine."

"If you're this successful all the time, you've got to be doing okay."

She shoved a can far into the ice, with a little more vigor than she'd had while placing the others. She turned to face him, leaning against the trough. Her face looked hot and flushed.

"I'm a single mother raising a special-needs child on one income," she said. "*Okay* is about as far as it goes. Remember me, the one who couldn't afford Pathways without striking a deal?"

"I do," he said.

Marlee, who had gone inside mumbling about finding more drinks, stuck her head outside. "Morgan? Do you know how to hook up the sound system?"

"Of course. I'll be right there."

Marlee lingered. "Looking very formal in that tux, Decker. What do you think of all this?"

"I think your sister is amazing," he responded.

"Me, too," she said. "So amazing, she's going to come hook up the sound system, since people will be arriving in about twenty minutes."

Morgan jumped away from the ice bucket. "Twenty? Oh, my gosh, time flew. Excuse me, Decker."

"Of course."

Morgan pushed past Marlee, but Marlee didn't follow her inside.

"Between you and me?" she said, after Morgan had gone. "I think you should ask her to dance tonight."

"That so?" he asked. "How come?"

She cocked her head as if she couldn't decide if he was being dense by accident or on purpose. "Because she'll say yes, dummy," she said.

"We don't... Our relationship... Everything is strictly business," he said.

Marlee threw her head back and laughed. "Right. You keep on telling yourself that, and she'll keep on telling herself that, and maybe someday it will be true. But probably not. You really don't see it? Open your eyes, then. Because literally everyone around you can see it. Maybe, you know...just talk to her. For real. Stop giving her vague answers and just be up-front. My little sister is very understanding. And very forgiving. I mean, look what she's done for your ranch. I think she deserves a heart-to-heart." She started to go back through the door, then paused. "By the way? The tux?" She gave a thumbs-up and an approving nod that drew a laugh out of Decker.

"Thanks," he said.

Now alone, he pulled a soda out of the ice and popped the top, then slowly turned, surveying the hustle and bustle of the event in its final stages of preparation. He heard the boom of music coming on midsong, which then quickly turned down to a *thump thump* that was the perfect backdrop for the celebratory feel of the event. The band would play the good stuff later, but for now, it was all children's dance party songs. Of course she figured it out. And quickly. Because that was who she was.

Marlee was right. Morgan deserved better than he was giving her.

He saw Ben lumbering up from the parking lot, making a beeline for him. He was dressed in khakis and a polo shirt, his face beet red from the heat. He walked toward the lot to meet Ben halfway.

"You look great, buddy," he said.

"It's hot," Ben answered. He wiped sweat from his forehead with the back of one arm dramatically. "T-shirts aren't as hot, because the fabric can breathe, which is a weird way of saying that air can get through, because of course fabric doesn't have lungs like people do, so actual breathing is not what is happening when someone says fabric breathes. This fabric does not breathe."

"Remember high school graduation? You were in a whole suit that night."

"That was also very hot," Ben said. "And not breathing whatsoever. Please don't remind me of that until I cool off a little."

"Fair enough," Decker said. "Are you excited for tonight?"

Ben shrugged. "It'll be okay. I'm not very good at games, and I don't like slides because they go too fast."

Decker balked. "What? I've seen you barely hanging on to Scout when she's in a full-on gallop."

"Scout will slow down if I ask her to. A slide will not do that, because it has not been trained. You can't train a slide. I think I might ask Annie to dance tonight, though. Do you think she will say yes to that?"

Decker paused and gave Ben a big clap on the back. "Annie, huh? I kind of suspected you felt that way about her. It's about time you did something about it."

Ben shrugged, looking very uncomfortable.

"How long has this been going on?" Decker asked.

"I have not asked her to dance before."

"No, I mean, how long have you and Annie liked each other?"

"We have been friends since she started volunteering at Pathways." *Not what I meant*, Decker thought, but he decided to let it go. "Annie is like me. She also has autism spectrum disorder. We have a lot of other things in common, too. For example, even though Sugar is her favorite horse, she also likes Scout and thinks she's the smartest horse. And sometimes I even let her ride Scout when I don't feel like riding. And she knows a lot about geography and space and the animated television show *The Land Before Time*, which aired for two seasons in 2007 and 2008. And she likes cookies-and-cream Pop-Tarts, which are inarguably the best Pop-Tarts."

"Wow, you guys must get a lot of talking done on the trail," Decker said.

"We sometimes text, too," Ben said.

"Well, what do you know. A little romance blooming right under my nose."

Ben paused. Decker walked on for a couple of steps, then turned back to see his friend trying to puzzle something out.

"Wouldn't the only thing right under your nose be your lips? Because you don't have a mustache. If you had one of those, that would, technically, be right under your nose."

Decker laughed. "Don't ever change, my friend." Ben looked down at his clothes, and Decker knew that, once again, he'd confounded his friend, who undoubtedly thought Decker had meant not to ever change out of his clothes. Decker began walking again, and Ben caught up. "Don't ever stop liking *The Land Before Time* and cookies-and-cream Pop-Tarts."

"I do not believe that I can willfully change what is pleasing to my taste buds," Ben said. "But I've never researched that. I will get back to you after I've had some time to look into it."

"Thanks," Decker said. "And also, ask Annie to dance. I definitely think she'll say yes."

"Okay." Ben still sounded uncertain. "Will you ask Morgan to dance?"

You, too, Ben? Decker wanted to ask. First David, then Marlee and now Ben. Maybe what Marlee was saying was true. Maybe there was something radiating off them that everyone around them could see, even if he couldn't see it himself.

Even if he was pretty sure Morgan wouldn't allow herself to see it.

Seeing it would be too real. Seeing it would be too painful.

Seeing it would be pointless.

"Maybe," he said, squeezing Ben's shoulder as they walked.

CHAPTER ELEVEN

THE CLINIC COULDN'T have gone better.

Word had gotten around as far away as Independence that the expensive specialists were going to be providing free care for a day, and so families loaded up their minivans and drove the two hours from Independence and Raytown and Lee's Summit and Blue Springs all the way to Buck County. At one point, there was a line of families that stretched out the door and all the way into the parking lot.

One of the doctors had to call in two administrative assistants from the city to come down and help check people in.

Every child who saw Dr. LaSalle walked away with a balloon animal, until he ran out of balloons.

Multitalented, Morgan thought.

Their donation bucket filled, not once, not twice, but four times. Cash was stacking up in the kitchen, so much so that Marlee left and came back with a handful of cash bags that she swiped from her flower shop. Even then, when they emptied the cash boxes at the concession stands and the games, they found themselves having to cram the money inside the bags, until Morgan gave up and began stuffing it into a bag she'd unearthed from the tack room *just in case*. Ben called it a pommel bag, said it belonged to Sugar and seemed very uncomfortable with the idea of Morgan using it for something it wasn't meant to be used for. He kept returning to the kitchen, eyeing it, until Morgan promised him that she would return it to the tack room as soon as the event was over.

Sure, it was mostly ones and fives, but there were some twenties in there, too, and some of the local Haw Springs businesses dropped hefty checks into the kitty. It looked like a lot of money, which was all it took to keep everyone in good spirits. Eventually, Morgan had to ask Sareena to guard the kitchen, which she happily did, thrilled to be part of the team.

The evening was winding down, the horse d'oeuvres were gone, the cotton candy machine was out of sugar, the lights were turned off, the owner was cleaning up. The hot dogs were half-price, as they tried to unload the already cooked supply. They were out of potato chips and out of soda—only water was left, and the baby goats, sufficiently petted and bellies full, had begun curling up on the ground for a snooze.

Morgan grabbed a bottle of water and sank into a rocking chair on the west porch, her hat in her lap, her boots discarded in the bride's room. She was exhausted. Right now, all she wanted to do was watch the sky turn orange and red and purple as the sun called it a day. She was ready to call it a day, too, and be proud of their success.

"This seat taken?"

Decker gestured at the rocking chair next to her.

"Into sunsets?" she asked, nodding toward the chair to indicate that he could take it. There was something familiar and comfortable and inevitable about having him here with her. Like she'd seen it in a dream.

"Very," he said. "This is a good one. And it's a good spot to watch. Front-row seat."

Morgan took a sip of her water and drew in a long breath of sweet evening air. This was the kind of air that just didn't exist in the city. For a long time, she told herself that she didn't need this kind of air, that she preferred city air. But now that she was back in it, she couldn't deny that this was exactly what she wanted. And needed. The part of her that wanted to come home permanently was speaking louder and louder, and the part that felt loyal to her job and life in the city was fading away.

"Sometimes, when I see a sunset that is this beautiful, I think about all of the sunsets in my lifetime that I've missed." She turned to face him. "Do you know what I mean? I'm so busy all the time, always rushing to do the next thing, and then the next and the next, I just bustle right past sunset after sunset after sunset. It's sad—I don't even think about sunsets. I've constructed a life that does not include sunsets. We all have."

"Not all of us," he said.

Morgan gazed silently at the sky for a long, quiet moment. She tried to imagine herself making time for sunsets in the evenings. Inviting Archer to join her, so he could come to appreciate them, too. So that he wouldn't look back at all the sunsets he'd missed and feel sad for what he was doing in his life.

As if he were dialing into her thoughts, Decker said, "Archer sure seemed to have fun today."

"Time of his life," Morgan agreed, thinking about her son, laughing and squealing as he rode down the slide with Marlee. Pulling his hands to his chest, delighted by, while also afraid of, Buster, the most aggressive baby goat. Playing a chasing game with Thomas, their cheeks red and sticky with cotton candy. He'd had more new experiences today than he'd had in the past six months combined. "It was really good for him. And good for me to see him like that."

"Where'd he go?"

"My parents took him home. Mom wanted

to get a meal into him and make sure he had time to wind down before bed. He'll probably be sound asleep long before I get there. I still have all those partitions to tear down."

"I'll help."

She waved him away. "You don't have to do that."

"Of course I do. This is a benefit for my ranch. And I'll get the kids to help."

Morgan took in a quick breath. "Oh! Speaking of! Did you see Ben and Annie dancing a little while ago? It was so sweet. He literally tipped his hat and bowed at the end of the song."

Decker grinned. "Turns out, Ben is a hopeless romantic."

"She was looking pretty starry-eyed, too," Morgan said. "I think she doesn't know what hit her."

"John Wayne reincarnated is what hit her," Decker said, and they both laughed.

The shadows were growing longer and longer. The sun sank down behind the trees. The moon was already visible above.

"Morgan, I want to tell you something," Decker said. "I think you deserve to know."

His voice was so somber and serious, Morgan's heart gave a little thump in her chest. "What's wrong?"

He held up a hand. "Nothing. It's not like that.

I…believe I owe you an explanation. I've owed it to you for a long time now."

Understanding dawned on Morgan, and now the feeling in her chest was overpowered by a familiar ache. *Not tonight. Not after such success.* Not while she was on cloud nine, so proud of herself and her accomplishments. She jumped up so fast, her chair rocked on its own.

"The slide's about to close down, and I haven't gotten to ride it all day," she said. "Why should the kids get all the fun? Come on." She reached down and grabbed his hand, but he didn't move.

"Please," he said, stroking the back of her hand softly. "You deserve this."

She sank back into her chair, steeling herself. "Okay. Tell me."

"When I was ten, my mom left. It was a total shock to all of us, but especially to my dad. He thought she was all in. There was no real explanation, except that ranch life was hard, and she didn't want it anymore."

Morgan stared into her lap, imagining what that must have felt like to Decker. Her family had been so happy, her parents so in love, she had no way of knowing what he'd gone through. But it broke her heart to even think of it.

"But she didn't just leave him—she left all of us. And the ranch wasn't the only life she didn't want anymore. We were part of that life. She

didn't want us. It was hard to swallow. Sometimes still is. So I built walls, Morgan. You
know? Even as a little kid. I couldn't understand
how she could just walk away from all of us. It
seemed so cruel."

"It *was* cruel," Morgan said. She gave his hand
a squeeze.

"I told myself that I would never let this ranch
go, because my dad worked so hard to keep it in
the family. He lost his wife over it, had to raise
two kids all by himself, and I can't stand the
thought that he'd gone through all that just for
us to let the ranch go. But I also told myself that
I would never fall in love and would never get
married. Because, in my mind, you can't trust
that. I didn't want to put myself through that
kind of hurt again, and I didn't want to take the
chance of putting my children through that hurt."

Morgan nodded. Understanding was sinking
in, and while the anger over him not telling her
this years ago was still there, smoldering under
the surface, the outward anger was starting to
fade a little.

He held her hand between both of his. "And
then you came along and messed up everything,"
he said. "I fell in love with you instantly. And
it scared me to death. But since you were from
Haw Springs, I figured…well, maybe you would
be open to this life. Maybe you wouldn't cut and

run, like my mom did. But then you went away to college, and you were in the city, and you were getting a taste of that life, and you were loving it."

"I hated being away from you, though," Morgan said.

"You started talking about your dreams of what you would want to do after you graduated from college, working for a big ad agency in the city. I lost you before I ever really had you. I knew I would never leave the ranch. And I knew you wanted a life that was far away from the ranch. Breaking up with you was the only thing that made sense."

"We could have worked it out. I would have at least tried."

Decker gave a sad smile. "You have a job in the city. You're good at it. What I was afraid would happen…happened. You stayed there."

But you never gave me a chance to make the choice, Morgan thought. But she couldn't say it out loud. It would seem like pouring salt on a wound that he was holding open for her to see. She couldn't do that to him.

"For what it's worth," he said, "I figured you would get over me long before I would get over you. But I didn't think about your hurt, only mine. And I'm sorry for that. I hope you'll someday forgive me."

She gave his hand another squeeze. "Forgiven."

She was almost surprised to find that she meant it. She may not have agreed with the way he handled things, but she understood. And she forgave him.

She laced her fingers through his, stood and tugged on his arm again.

"Let's leave all that stuff in the past, okay? Focus on the present." She widened her eyes, pulled harder and mouthed *the slide*.

He chuckled and let himself be pulled to standing. "Okay, okay. The slide. Let's go."

Morgan jogged toward the slide, giggles slipping out of her mouth. She felt lighter than she'd felt in a long time. The grass was cool and soft under her bare toes, and a tiny breeze had kicked up, raising goose bumps as it danced across her sweat-softened skin. Decker trotted along behind her, his boots thumping the ground.

Was this frolicking? she wondered. It had a frolicky feel.

They each grabbed a burlap sack at the bottom of the slide and trekked up the long staircase to the top.

"I get the left side," Morgan said.

"That's the fast side," the worker at the top of the slide said. "Practically launched those kids into outer space all day long."

Morgan grinned at Decker. She'd been watching the kids; she already knew this.

"No way," Decker argued. "That's cheating, putting me on the slow side."

"You say that like it's a race or something," Morgan said, batting her eyes innocently as she sat on the sack, wrapping her skirt around her legs.

"Everything is a race, Tweety." Decker's eyes flickered with orneriness as he jumped on his sack, propelling himself down the slide like a shot.

"Hey!" Morgan cried, pushing herself to follow him. "But when it's a race against me, you always lose!"

The slide had two humps, and it was during the first one that she caught up with him, and the second one that she surpassed him. She landed in a heap at the bottom, laughing, out of breath. Within seconds, he was sitting next to her.

"You…are such…a cheater," she said.

He raised his eyebrows and spread his hands across his chest innocently. "Me? I didn't ask for the fast side. That would have been cheating. I simply slid down a slide. A victim, really, of someone else's cheating ways. I had the slow side. You heard it with your own ears."

"Uh-huh, nice try, Baseball. You didn't just slide down a slide. You called go before I was ready, and you launched yourself like you were in the Olympics."

"That makes it sound like I took advantage of a situation just to win an arbitrary race that wasn't even a race."

She flipped the hat off his head. "It sure does, doesn't it?"

"No," he said, catching his hat in midflight and stuffing it back down onto his head. "Taking advantage of a situation just to win an arbitrary race that isn't a race looks much more like this. Rematch!" He was on his feet before Morgan could even register his words. He snatched her burlap and tossed it in the opposite direction of the stairs, then raced up, two at a time. "Let's see who gets the fast side this time, Tweety!"

"Cheater!" she shouted, as she scrambled for her tossed bag. But she was giggling as she said it. She followed him, pushing herself to take the steps two at a time, just like he was, but she knew she would never catch him.

Unless, of course, she got creative.

Without even thinking about what she was doing, she took advantage of the slowness on the humps of the right-hand slide. Decker was at the top as she reached the topmost hump. She quickly stepped over onto the left slide and hopped onto the right, ignoring the shouts of the worker at the top, plopped down on her burlap and propelled herself forward.

She reached the bottom milliseconds before Decker did.

"Who's the cheater now, huh?" Decker was shouting from the slide all the way down. "Who's cheating?"

"Yeah, but who won? Twice!" she said as he landed with a thump next to her.

"You're done!" the man at the top of the slide shouted. "Both of you. Don't come back up here."

Decker let out a laugh to the sky. "And who got us kicked off the slide, huh?"

"Drastic times call for drastic measures. I have no regrets."

"Uh-huh, and it's all fun and games until someone breaks a tooth on the megaslide."

Morgan bared her teeth at him. "Do I look like I have a broken tooth? No. Because I'm a champion."

He brushed strands of hair off her forehead, giving her goose bumps once again. Making her feel like her heart would never slow down. They locked eyes, and it got way too serious for Morgan's taste. Must have felt the same to Decker, because he suddenly stood and offered her his hand.

"Come on, Champ. I'll buy you a half-price hot dog to celebrate your victory."

She let herself be pulled up, the burlap discarded under her bare feet. "Ooh, big spender, you sure know how to make a lady feel special."

"I try," he said. "If you don't rub it in too much, I'll even buy you one of those Twix bars over there."

"Wow." She was no longer behind him, being pulled along, but was walking beside him. Still, she didn't let go of his hand. It felt too good—warm, strong, safe—against hers. She wondered if he felt the same. He must have, because he made no move to break the connection, either. "Dinner *and* dessert. I didn't realize I'd won such a coveted race."

They stopped at the hot dog booth and Decker bought two dogs, two waters and two Twix bars. They found a nearby table that had been recently abandoned. It was still covered with garbage from the people before. But Morgan didn't care. She hadn't realized how hungry she was until she started eating.

"I can't help noticing," she said around a mouthful of hot dog. She swigged a huge gulp of water. "That you're also enjoying the winner's meal. Don't you think that kind of defeats the purpose of a winner's meal?"

"Mmm, no." He chewed, swallowed. "This isn't the winner's meal. This is the cheater's meal. I said I would celebrate your victory, but I never said you won fair and square."

"That's okay," she said. "We both know what really happened. You may not be able to admit it, but I am the superior megaslider. Maybe the best there's ever been."

He laughed, shoving the last of his hot dog into his mouth. "That ego, though."

"Hey, it's that ego, which is self-confidence, by the way, that has kept me afloat when I should have been drowning. And it just brought tons of money into your ranch. Let's not forget that."

"Well, watching you today has been impressive, to say the least. You're good, Morgan. I'd like to think that I gave you the initial boost, though."

"Ha!" She took a bite of her hot dog. "And how exactly did you do that?"

"You conned me out of a stuffed bird. I was your first foray into sales."

"Conned. Okay. It wasn't difficult, you know. You wanted to be 'conned.'" She made air quotes with her fingers. "Besides, being dumped isn't exactly a confidence booster, is it? You gaveth, and then you tooketh away. Pretty cruel, Baseball."

Decker pressed his lips together in a thin line and nodded, like he was contemplating the issue. He swallowed his food. "So we joke about it now?"

"Forgiven, but never forgotten, and all that."

"Healthy."

"I try."

"Well, then, I guess I need to tell you one more thing."

"It's good. Really. You don't have to." She wadded up her napkin. Her food threatened to lodge itself in her throat, which wanted to tighten up the way it always seemed to do when Decker came around.

"No, I need to tell you this," he said. "I should have told you ten years ago."

"Decker…"

He held up a hand. "Just hear me out."

She sighed. "Okay. Fine. Let's get it out. What should you have told me ten years ago?"

"I…" He took off his hat, scratched the top of his head, replaced the hat. Stared at his lap, clearly wrestling with something weighty. "I… don't know how to tell you."

"Just say it."

"Okay." He took a deep, steadying breath, then, on the air out, said, "I lied to you."

"Okay?" It came out a question, but Morgan knew. Secretly, she'd known all along. He'd dumped her because he'd found someone else. Now she really didn't want to hear it. She wasn't sure how she would feel; she only knew that she would feel less happy than she did sliding down the slide, and that seemed like a tragic way to end the evening.

"I don't know how to... I guess I'll just come out with it." He met her eyes and very seriously said, "I lied about seeing *Twister*. I've watched it at least twenty times."

HE HAD TO duck from the flurry of playful swats that Morgan delivered.

"You liar! I can't believe you! Do you see what I have to put up with? It's a wonder that I'm sane at all."

"Oh, you poor baby," he said, laughing and dodging her hands. "How will you ever survive this injustice? And the sanity thing is debatable, don't you think?" He stopped trying to dodge, and instead grabbed her wrists, stopping her midswat. "I'm very sorry," he said somberly. "I hope you can forgive me for this great injustice. For all of them, really. I mean it."

She wrenched her hands free. "I'll have to think about it." She aimed a pouty stare into her lap.

Lately, Decker had begun to think that maybe David's idea was the best idea—sell the ranch altogether. Let go of the hurt and the bad memories and the history that nobody but him cared about. Say goodbye to his mother and her cruel

departure once and for all. Say goodbye to all
of it. Just start over, with a clean and fresh slate.

Only instead of buying a smaller plot of land
and rebuilding an abbreviated version of Pathways, maybe he should go an entirely different
direction. Move into town, buy a house, open a
small tack store or… He didn't know what, exactly. His possibilities had always seemed so limited by his own desires. He always thought he
knew what he wanted and what he intended to
do with his life.

But it wasn't working out that way. He wanted
his ranch. He wanted his dream. But he also
wanted Morgan. It was hard enough to keep her
out of his mind when she wasn't here. But he'd
built a life based on that fact. She wasn't here, so
clearly it would never have worked out for them.

But she was back, so now what? Was it some
kind of sign? Was he wrong all along? Surely it
wasn't a coincidence that she'd walked through
his door at the precise moment that he needed
to make a decision about his future.

No, that was a ridiculous thought. Coincidences
were coincidences, and she would be heading
back to the city soon enough. She would take
his heart with her, and he would be left with an
empty, aching chest if he wasn't careful. Time
had healed this wound before, but he wasn't sure
if it would again.

"Y'all've been a great audience," he heard from inside the barn, and it was only then that he noticed that the music had momentarily stopped. "We've just got a couple more, so come on out to the dance floor and show your support of a great cause!"

There was a smattering of applause and a couple of hoots.

"We haven't seen McBride Pathways up here on the floor, have we?" There was more applause and some cheers. He and Morgan glanced at each other. The air felt electric around them. "Well, if y'all are still here, we'd love to get ya dancing. Celebrate the good work you do." Now the cheers had grown loud; there were more people still here than Decker had realized. "You hear the crowd. Come on out!" A guitar started up, and they launched into "Why Don't We Just Dance."

After Morgan had gone off to school, Decker had missed her with an ache that was so intense, he sometimes felt it in the core of himself, thudding along with his heartbeat. *So this is what is meant by being heartsick*, he remembered thinking.

He'd felt that same relentless thud in his belly once before. In his young experience, it was a thud that never went away.

In those lonely moments, Decker became painfully aware of the things he and Morgan never had a chance to do.

And tonight, he became painfully aware of just one: they never had a chance to share a dance.

For a moment, he didn't think he would have to ask at all. Maybe they would both just stand and head into the barn, wordlessly. But Morgan, suddenly shy, glanced down at her lap.

Decker knew he shouldn't do this. Every warning bell was going off in his head. *Dance with her, and you'll do something rash*, his brain screamed. *You can't fall for this girl, because she will leave again. Soon!* But the pull to her was too great. He ignored the warning bells. He'd already fallen.

If he could only have her in his arms for these few minutes, it would be better than not having her in his arms at all.

"They're waiting for you," Morgan said. "You're the man of the night."

"I think you're the one we should be celebrating," he said. "You did all of this yourself."

"I had help," she said.

They simply gazed at each other for a moment, and Decker knew that the choice was no longer his. It had already been made.

He stood and held out one hand. She took it, smiling, and they walked into the barn together.

CHAPTER TWELVE

THE DANCE FLOOR was packed. While things were winding down outside, the party seemed to be reaching a climax inside. David was at the edge of the floor, dancing alone. He saw Decker and Morgan come through the door, stuck two fingers in his mouth and began whistling. Like a wave, the crowd caught on, the cheers raising the roof.

Decker took Morgan's hand and lifted it, pointing to her, making her feel warm with self-consciousness and pride.

The band didn't miss a beat, but they seemed to level up the intensity a notch. Soon, Decker and Morgan were jumping and bobbing with the crowd, falling into the line dance, which Morgan knew, but Decker did not. She grabbed his hand and shimmied hip to hip to help him follow along, but they mostly just bumped hips and stepped on each other and laughed until the song was over.

Morgan ended spectacularly, by tripping over

Decker's boot and flying forward. Had it not been for him catching her around the waist, she might have gone sprawling right in the middle of the dance floor. She was breathless with laughter as he pulled her upright, holding her close.

And just like that, the laughter was stolen right out of her throat. Only this time it wasn't replaced with the bitterness she'd grown so used to. And she didn't sense the familiar closed-off tentativeness radiating off him, either. They stayed frozen in place, Morgan breathing in the leather scent of him and feeling the tension of his forearms on her back, noting the way his eyes scanned the whole of her face, lingering on her mouth. She felt his longing in the way he held her, steady and sure and completely still, as if he were afraid that she'd fly away if he so much as moved a muscle. She didn't want him to let her go. She was happy here. Content.

"Whoo! There they are!" The lead singer had given up the microphone and a familiar voice took over, busting into the moment like a hand grenade. Decker's arm slid away from Morgan's waist as they both got their footing and faced the stage. Marlee stood at the microphone, glowing and sweaty from dancing, and so filled with energy it spilled over into every word. She held up one arm in victory, then elongated a pointer finger in Morgan's direction. "Ladies and gentlemen, that right there is Decker McBride, owner of the McBride Pathways program, and my little sister, the inimitable Morgan West, who put this fundraiser together! Let's give them a round of applause!" There was a swell of whoops and hollers, and half a dozen hands patting Decker and Morgan on their backs. Marlee waved her hands around to quiet the crowd. "Aaand," she said, "I'm proud to announce that we raised over ten thousand dollars for McBride Pathways tonight!"

The crowd went crazy, and now Morgan felt jolts and jostles against her shoulders and back, the pats finding more exuberance as Marlee talked. She could hardly believe her ears. *Ten thousand!* It was more than she could have hoped for.

"Come on up here, you two!" Marlee said.

Morgan felt herself propelled toward the stage, people stepping aside to let her and Decker through. She knew that Decker was probably hating every minute of this attention, but for ten thousand dollars, even he couldn't argue that he probably ought to say thank you.

She was first to the microphone, which Marlee gave her while simultaneously squeezing her so hard around the neck, Morgan felt choked. Marlee pulled away and stood to the side, clapping. Morgan tried to hand Decker the microphone, but he demurred. *You first*, he mouthed.

"Thank you," she said, then paused for the crowd to quiet. "Thank you. This project has been very close to my heart. Decker and I actually go way back." Someone whistled a catcall and the air bubbled with giggles. "No, not like that." But she could see Decker nodding in a knowing way toward his brother, who was undoubtedly the whistler. "Okay, maybe a little like that." She pulled the microphone away from her mouth and laughed, embarrassed, but not in a bad way. *So this is what it should feel like when he and I are together*, she thought. "Anyway. My son, Archer, is on the autism spectrum. I'm sure y'all saw him earlier, dancing right in the middle of the floor like it was *Saturday Night Fever*?" More laughs. "Yeah. He's great. Um, but he struggles sometimes. And he has more struggles ahead of him, I'm sure." Morgan felt a wave of emotion come at her out of nowhere. She'd been so busy dodging Decker and fighting over the past, she'd not allowed herself to really absorb the changes in Archer. He loved a dog and made a friend and rode a horse. These were huge things. She had to take a deep breath to keep from getting emotional. "But he has changed this summer, since being part of the Pathways program. He made a best friend—the hound dog, June. But he's also made friends with another child, which is unusual for Archer. And he has learned to tune in to the feelings of his horse. He's learned to face his fears and try things that make him uncomfortable, which is really important in life." She pointed at Decker and wiggled the microphone in the air, to more laughter. "He's bonded with Decker. It's been so touching to watch. I'm so proud of my little boy. And I'm proud of this man right here. I'm proud of Pathways, and that I got to be a little part of it. This program isn't just helpful to families like mine. It's a godsend. Decker McBride is a godsend. And you all did a good thing tonight, supporting him. Your donations are going to make a big difference in the life of a child, I can promise you that. Thank you."

She handed the microphone to Decker so she could clap along with the audience. His face was red. His shyness was adorable. "Thank you," he said. "I owe everything to y'all. And to Morgan." He turned to face Morgan, his tone growing serious. "I don't know what I would have done without you this summer. I'm so glad you came back. Now what do I need to do to get you to stay?" The audience chuckled, and Morgan could hear Marlee behind her cheering, but there was something beneath Decker's shy grin that made Morgan's cheeks burn so hard she could feel it in her toes. It was more than she could handle. She broke the spell by tearing her gaze away from him, turning to the audience and rubbing her fingers together. *Money*, she mouthed, and again there were cheers and laughter.

"Anyway, we are going to help a lot of kids who need it, thanks to y'all. I'm grateful. Thank you, everyone, and have a great night."

He handed the microphone back to the lead singer, practically chucking it away as if it was on fire, then grabbed Morgan's hand again and led her off the stage. But the crowd wasn't letting them go anywhere.

"How about we'll end the night with an oldie but goodie in honor of these two old friends?" the lead singer said into the microphone. "Everybody grab your honey and pull them in close. This is Merle Haggard's 'My Favorite Memory.'"

The lights dropped low as the music started. Morgan faced Decker. She felt alive and electric. Everything about this day had gone perfectly, and her barriers had been broken down. She didn't even realize she was holding both of Decker's hands in hers.

The singer's voice cut through the air, a line about meeting for the first time.

Decker grinned at her, lazy and lopsided and happy and full of dimples. She knew that he was thinking the same thing she was thinking—the song was perfect. He lifted his eyebrows in a silent question, and she nodded. He let go of one of her hands and slipped his arm around her waist. She placed her hand on his shoulder and swayed with the music, enveloped by him. She felt like she was in the safest place in the world.

The barn fell away. The people. The band. Her sister. David. Everyone faded into a pinprick, and it was just the two of them, holding each other and swaying. She allowed herself to close her eyes and let her forehead drop to his shoulder. She breathed him in, all the memories of those few days together at the carnival swirling around them. She no longer felt as though she was dancing, but more that she was floating on time. Or maybe between time. In a space where everything was right between them, which made everything…right.

In this moment, she realized that the hurt no longer mattered. The past was just the past. Their hearts still beat together easily and eagerly. For the first time in maybe as long as she could remember, Morgan let down her guard, stopped trying to control her world. She became limp in his arms, turning her head so that her cheek rested on his chest.

Decker pulled her in closer, more of a hug than a dance, and Morgan turned her face up to his. He was looking down at her, their faces close. She realized that today was really the first time they'd really touched like this since the picnic when they'd shared their first kiss, and in this moment, she was positive that they were about to share another.

It was what she wanted more than anything. And she could see it in his face, feel it in the way his hand gripped hers, the way his arm cradled her, that he wanted it, too. She didn't care who was watching or what it might mean. She wanted him to kiss her. She wanted to acknowledge that what was between them was always there, and always would be.

"Don't ever leave." For a moment, she thought maybe he was singing along to the song, but the words didn't match.

She smiled. "I don't want to, but eventually my feet will get tired."

He stopped swaying. "I mean it, Morgan. Stay."

Morgan froze. "What?"

"Don't go back to Kansas City. Come home for good. Stay with me. Let me make everything up to you. Let me love you the way I have loved you all this time."

She shook her head. "Decker...I..."

They didn't even realize the song was over and the music had stopped, until the crowd gave another hearty cheer.

Overwhelmed and mortified, Morgan quickly pulled away from Decker, dropping his hand, stepping out of his reach, breaking the spell.

All eyes were on them. She couldn't think. She felt dizzy.

Marlee pushed in between them and grabbed each of their hands, holding them up high for one last cheer from the crowd.

Morgan pasted a smile on her face, even though her entire body was buzzing with adrenaline and embarrassment and something she couldn't quite put her finger on. Longing? Possibility?

Marlee dropped their arms, then turned and hugged her sister. "Rescuing you," she said into Morgan's ear.

So she had seen. And had stepped in on purpose.

Good. Because Morgan needed a minute. To think. To process. To protect herself.

Did she need to protect herself? She was no longer sure.

The band said their goodbyes and started putting their gear away, as people began to file out the door.

Atty appeared and turned the lights back on. The room was bathed in an unfriendly fluorescent light that said, *Time to go home.*

Marlee let go and turned to hug Decker, giving Morgan a chance to slip away.

"I've got to…" Morgan said to no one, then scurried away to the kitchen, where she joined in packing up the leftover snacks. She didn't look to see where Decker went, but by the time she was finished, he was gone.

"WELL, THAT LOOKED SERIOUS," David said, startling Decker, who hadn't heard his brother let himself in. David sat at the kitchen table, a cup of coffee and an empty plate streaked with doughnut glaze in front of him. He nodded to a Dreamy Bean box on the counter. "Breakfast?"

"You've got to stop just letting yourself in whenever you feel like it," Decker said, grabbing a doughnut out of the box and heading to the cabinet for a plate and cup. He dropped the doughnut on the plate and poured himself a cup of coffee.

"I brought you doughnuts and made you coffee. What kind of thank-you is this?"

"Thank you," Decker said. "But next time, maybe the doorbell. Or a text at least?"

"Will do, will do. But I had to know. So give me the scoop."

Decker bit into the doughnut. It was airy and sweet and vanilla-y and nearly dripping with glaze. "What scoop?"

"Come on—don't play dumb with me. I saw you two last night. Everyone at the benefit saw you. Did you rekindle things? They sure looked rekindled."

Decker did not want to have this conversation.

Mostly because he didn't have any answers. His arms still felt the weight of her, his chest felt the warmth of her forehead. His T-shirt still smelled like her perfume. Everything had changed. And nothing had.

He'd put it all out there. Made himself vulnerable. Asked her to stay, without even realizing that he was going to do it.

And she'd run away.

Too late, he'd thought. *You're too late, you stubborn mule.*

After the dance, Decker had helped stack the chairs and fold up the tablecloths and empty the trash cans. He'd walked the perimeter of the barn, picking up missed garbage, and then he waited at his truck for Morgan to appear. He wanted another dance.

He wanted another chance.

He wanted to talk to her, at the very least.

But in the time that he'd waited, reality set in on him again. He convinced himself that, to her, it was only a dance, that it meant nothing more, and that any Morgan-related plans he might have been mulling over were ill-advised at best. He'd hurt her too deeply. He'd been so stuck in his past, he'd held her back. He couldn't just step in now and demand that he get what he wanted.

And wasn't he guilty of that here on the ranch, too? Wasn't it unfair of him to ignore his brother's needs so he could stay rooted in the past? McBride Ranch was not the future. Morgan was not the future. He was going to have to let go. Of Morgan. Of the ranch.

He was going to have to build a different future.

And he needed to stop holding David back, and let him build his future, too.

They'd raised a pretty penny at the benefit. He would be able to make a down payment on another, smaller ranch. A ranch without memories. A ranch that had never known Morgan West existed.

"Well…?" David prodded.

Decker pulled out a chair and sat across from his brother. David had been looking out for him since the day their mom walked out. He would be a fool to not take his brother's advice now. He turned up his palms. "Well, nothing."

"Oh, come on, man! Why are you doing this to yourself?"

"Doing what?"

"You know what. Anyone with eyeballs could see that you two still love each other."

"And anyone with a brain would understand that it's just not meant to be. She's going back to Kansas City, and I'm staying here. Case closed. Done."

David was silent for a long while, then shifted

so that he was facing the table. "That's very sad. If I found the love of my life, I wouldn't choose a patch of land over her, that's for sure."

"Speaking of," Decker said, wanting to change the subject. He was tired of having to explain himself. "I'm not going to fight you on this anymore. We're going to sell."

David's eyes bugged. "You're kidding, right?"

Decker took a huge bite of doughnut and shook his head solemnly.

"Well, I'll be." David took off his baseball cap, smoothed his hair and put it back on. "You're sure about this? What changed your mind?"

"It's just time to let some things go," Decker said. "The money we raised last night, along with my portion of the profit from selling, will help me get Pathways up and running elsewhere."

David didn't look as pleased as Decker thought he might have. "I didn't expect this."

Decker took another bite. "Surprise," he said, the doughnut landing hard in the pit of his stomach.

"What about Dad?" David said softly.

"Dad's gone," Decker said.

"I know that. But…well, I know you always felt so indebted to him. You always said you were going to make him proud by making this ranch more than it ever was."

"I failed," Decker said simply, but he could

feel all of his roiling feelings begin to bubble up inside of him.

"You didn't fail, Decker," David said. "I'm sorry if I ever made you feel that way."

"This isn't about you, or anything that you said or did. You're fine. This is about me and my own missed chances. If I don't start making things happen now, my whole life will be about missed chances. But I won't let you get caught up in missed chances because of me. As soon as we find a buyer, you're free."

"Thank you, little brother," David said. "I know this is hard for you, and I know you're doing it for me. I'll call the Realtor. I just… Are you sure you're okay?"

"If I'm not, I'm sure I will be. I've got to tell Ben, though. He'll take it hard, no matter what I promise him. He's not good with change."

Leaving the only house he ever knew would be difficult for Decker. He knew that. Calling a new place home and breaking in his horses on new, much smaller pastures and rebuilding the Pathways trails would be difficult.

But this—breaking the news to Ben—would be the most difficult duty of all. Telling Ben that he would have to get used to a new ranch, if Decker could find something small enough here in Buck County that was still big enough to house a hand. At worst, he would have to tell

Ben that he could very well be out of a job, and at least temporarily out of a home. Would maybe even have to get used to a new town altogether. Someplace like Riverside or Glenstone or even as far out as Sidley. Ben wasn't going to take the news well at all. And Decker was just going to have to accept that.

"I should probably go do that," he said, and before David could argue, he pushed himself away from the table and strode out.

He knew exactly where Ben would be at this time of morning. Ben never wavered from his routine, not even by a minute. The only time he'd ever missed a day of work was when he was laid up with the flu. And, even then, he'd met Decker at the barn to tell him he wasn't going to meet him at the barn that day.

As expected, Ben was grooming Scout in the stables. He glanced up when Decker's boots hit the concrete floor.

"It's early."

Decker chuckled. Ben would never let him get away with anything. "True, true. Good morning, Ben."

"Good morning. Why are you working already?"

"Couldn't sleep. Got something on my mind that I need to share. My brother brought breakfast. Doughnuts. I put them in the office, if you'd like one."

"Maybe after I'm done brushing Scout. I'm afraid I'll get tiny horse hairs stuck to my fingers if I eat a doughnut while grooming."

"That seems like a fair notion. They'll be there all day. The doughnuts and the horses."

"Thank you."

Decker waited for Ben to stop brushing, and then helped him put away the grooming equipment and lead Scout back into her stall. After she was settled, he turned to Ben.

"Do you have a minute to talk?"

"I have many minutes that I can allot to talking. However, I would like to complete my chores before the students get here, so I don't want to spend too much time on talking. That's how you end up with fewer minutes for chores."

"This won't take long, and I'll help with the chores," Decker said, leading Ben to a stack of hay bales that offered natural stair steps to sit on. Ben sat dutifully next to him. He was reminded of all the times Ben sat dutifully on the team bench during practices and games, watching him, cheering him on, logging his stats so they could go over them together later. Decker felt blessed to have a lifelong friend like Ben, and he felt terrible for what he was about to do to him. "I just need to tell you that I'm putting the ranch up for sale."

Decker could feel Ben still beside him, could feel his shock, but he didn't say anything, so Decker plowed on.

"This ranch is too big, and it carries too many hard memories for me. And David needs the money. We can do all the work of Pathways on a different ranch. A smaller one."

Ben frowned at the ground, which Decker knew meant that he was thinking hard about the situation.

"Will the smaller ranch have a house?"

"Yes, of course," Decker said. "And a cottage for you as well, just like the one you have here."

"Will that one have a shelf above my stove for the black pepper?"

"It'll have whatever shelves you want it to have," Decker said. "If it doesn't, we'll build them after we move in."

Ben processed some more, then screwed up his forehead tight. "Who are you selling it to?"

Decker shrugged. "Whoever wants to buy it, I suppose."

"What if Morgan wants to buy it? Then will you stay?"

Decker felt a flash of exasperation. Why did everyone think they knew something about him and Morgan? "It was just a dance," he said aloud, although he wasn't really talking to Ben as much as he was talking to the universe in general.

"Will she move to the new ranch with us?"

"No," Decker said, unable to keep his exasperation from coming through loud and clear. "She and I had a little flirting going on when we were young, and we danced one dance last night. But that was it. That's all it's ever been. Some flirting and one dance. We were never going to end up together. Okay? I can live my life without her. I've done it this long, and I've been just fine."

The words burned their way out of his mouth. *Lies*, his brain argued. *Lies, lies, lies.*

"Okay," Ben said, stung.

Decker sighed. "Listen, Ben. I just wanted you to know that things are going to change. But we will be okay. And you can go look for somewhere else to work and live, and it won't upset me. I'll totally understand. But if you decide to go with me, there will be a place for you."

He clapped Ben on the back and got up, done talking. Maybe for the whole day.

Just as he rounded the corner, he saw Morgan standing, frozen with a bag clutched to her chest.

He didn't need her to say a word to know that she'd just overheard the entire conversation. What had he said about her? He'd already forgotten. Had he said he could live his life without her?

He was pretty sure he had.

Actually, given the tears glistening in her eyes, he was positive that he had.

He reached for her. "Listen, I didn't mean…" He couldn't continue. He wasn't sure what he did mean anymore. Especially when it came to her.

Her chin wobbled, even as she lifted it to keep herself together. "I thought we could go make the deposit together, but, um…maybe it's best if you make it yourself," she said, holding the bag out to him. Her voice was rough, husky. "Seeing as today is the last day of the session, I'm going to spend most of it finalizing paperwork and, um…" She swallowed. "And, um, cleaning out my things. I won't leave you with a mess."

"Morgan," he said plaintively, "can we talk about last night?"

"I'm sure we both have a lot of work to get done." She turned quickly on her heel and walked out of the barn, leaving Decker to hold the heavy bag of cash and listen to the soft sniffles of Ben behind him.

CHAPTER THIRTEEN

I CAN LIVE my life without her.

Every time the words echoed through Morgan's ears, they stung anew. Last night, he'd asked her to stay, and now he was saying she could go, and he would be *just fine*.

She'd been so bowled over by his request to stay, she hadn't been able to speak. But she'd thought of nothing else since the dance. *Stay. Let me love you.*

The idea was terrifying. And it was comforting. It was everything she wanted. And it was everything she'd told herself she didn't want, didn't need.

No matter how hard she tried to fend him off, she had to admit to herself that it felt so good, swaying in his arms. Laughing with him on the slide. Learning about his past, his family. Understanding him better. Working with him. Watching him hold Archer up to pet the horse. Riding with him. Looking over the ridge with him.

She could imagine this life being her best life. In some ways, she always had imagined that.

But she worried that Decker asking her to stay was too soon. They'd only really known each other again for a short time. How could she be sure staying with him was the right move for her and Archer?

All night long she went back and forth. Stay or go?

When she'd overheard what he said to Ben, she'd gotten her answer. *Go. He won't miss you.*

It hurt. Decker McBride had to be the most confusing man on earth. But it was reality, and reality was something she could work with.

She spent the morning ruminating while she cleaned out cabinets and drawers, giving the place one last spruce up before what she knew would be her final departure. He may not want to admit it, but he needed her. She believed that wholeheartedly. And she'd stepped up to meet his need. If nothing else, she was leaving Pathways a better place.

Students and their parents began to trickle in. Morgan got busy putting on a pot of coffee and opening a container of leftover cupcakes from the benefit the night before. She felt a jolt on the backs of her legs, then little sticky hands wrap around her calves.

"Hey, buddy!" she said, reaching back to ruf-

fle Archer's hair. He'd been busily eating pancakes when she'd left that morning, so engrossed
in his TV show that she couldn't even get him
to look up when she said goodbye.

Marlee came in after him. "Ooh, breakfast,"
she said. "Don't mind if I do." She plucked a
cupcake off the tray.

Archer had run back to the door.

"Zee! Zee!"

"He's been saying that all morning." Marlee
took a bite of cupcake. "I have no idea what it
means. I've tried everything."

"Zee! Zee!"

"Zee," Morgan whispered, racking her brain
for anything that might be condensed into that
one syllable. "Zee. Oh! Ziggy? Are you saying
'Ziggy'?"

She had seen one of the older kids riding Ziggy
earlier. They'd left him to graze in the pasture when
they were finished, and he was visible through the
front window.

Archer did a little hop that Morgan knew to be
confirmation that she'd guessed correctly.

"Do you want to see the horses?" Marlee asked,
and Archer did another little joyful hop.

Morgan's heart swelled. To think it was just a
few weeks ago that Archer had been too terrified
to even touch the horses; now he was a rider, excited about riding. That had been Decker's doing.

He did a lot of good at Pathways, there was no doubt about that. And even though she felt stung to the core by Decker, she still believed in the project. She believed that she'd done a good thing here this summer, and that many children would benefit from her hard work. She was proud of herself, and she was proud of Decker.

And she was sad that he was selling the ranch.

Morgan knew that this land was important to Decker, and not just because of Pathways. There was a generational connection. He felt born from this land, rather than on it. If he sold it—if he moved away—would he feel in some way orphaned? She guessed he would.

And why exactly do I even care? she thought. *He doesn't care what happens to me. Why should I care what happens to him?*

Because I do. I care about him, and I know he cares about me. Regardless of what he says.

Marlee finished her cupcake in three bites and brushed her hands off. "Okay, little buddy," she said. "Let's get you on Ziggy."

Morgan followed them outside. It was already oppressively hot, and the sun was still low in the morning sky. By lunchtime, nobody would be outside, unless water was somehow involved. It was the kind of summer day where you couldn't eat an ice cream cone or Popsicle fast enough—

the sun would devour it before you could, even if you were eating with all your concentration.

It was the kind of weather that reminded Morgan that summer was coming to an end. School would be starting soon, and Archer would need to be there. This would be his last year of preschool. Kindergarten was just around the corner, and he had so much progress to make yet.

The older kids had begun to stream out of the barn, greeting the younger kids with carefully scripted high fives and awkward hugs. A tween named Stephanie edged her way to Archer, and she stood shoulder to shoulder with him, her eyes planted squarely on the ground between them.

"Good morning, Archer," she said. "Are you ready to ride today?"

"Are we allowed to request a horse?" Marlee asked. "He's been asking about Ziggy all morning."

Stephanie nodded and left to retrieve Ziggy from the pasture.

"What would we do without Aunt Marlee, Archer?" Morgan asked, reaching down to run her fingers through her son's curls. "Aunt Marlee is much better than Mommy at getting what she wants."

"Hmm," Marlee said. "This stuff's easy. You

just ask. But did you see what Aunt Marlee didn't get last night? A dance with Dr. LaSalle."

"Well, there's always next time."

"What next time? Like I'm hanging out with pediatricians a lot in my spare time? It's not like I can stop by to have him look into my nonexistent child's ears. I'm afraid I'm just going to have to give up." She picked up Archer and balanced him on one hip. He looked huge perched on his tiny aunt's hip. "And you're going back to yucky old Kansas City without me," she continued. "Which is definitely not what I want."

Thomas barreled into the little clearing, nearly crashing into Marlee, and Archer wiggled to be let down. Popping his thumb out of his mouth, he gave chase, circling around legs and trees after Thomas, giggling his little head off. June sneezed and shook her head, jilted.

"I know, Junie," Morgan said. "Me, too. We might as well get used to it. He's growing up."

Morgan could have stayed and watched all day while Archer played with his peers and rode his horse through the sensory trail. She could have happily and proudly just grabbed a lawn chair, propped her chin on her palm and gazed at her little boy all day while idly running her fingers through June's fur.

But she'd started to feel the ache of loss pushing in on her, and she knew she needed to get back to work or she would begin to get emotional. She was going to miss this place.

"Everything okay?" Marlee asked, following her into the main building.

"Mmm-hmm, fine. Why do you ask?"

"Well, for one thing, you've rearranged the magazines on that table, like, four times since I got here, and nobody else has touched them."

Morgan had been stacking the magazines, but instead she let them drop on the coffee table in a heap.

"It's going to be hard, leaving you."

"Then don't. Just stay. Who's going to care?"

"Me," Morgan said. "I care. I have a job and a, well, a life in Kansas City."

"And a whole lot of loneliness. Don't pretend that you love it up there. You've thrived here this summer, Morgan. Why not have that all the time?"

"I thrive in KC," Morgan said icily.

"Of course you do. I'm not saying that you don't." Marlee reached over and rubbed Morgan's back. "What's going on with you?"

Morgan sagged into a chair, miserable. "I don't know. I don't want to leave."

"Then don't. You can sell your house. Stay with Mom and Dad until you find someplace else to live. Or you two can stay with me. You'll just have a lot less space. But that's okay. We'll make it work."

"And what am I supposed to do about my job?"

Marlee twirled around with her palms up, as if this answered everything. "You have a job. I'm sure after all the fundraising you've done, he'll be more than happy to pay you."

"Oh, no. Not here. No way."

"What? Why not? You told me just last night that you were loving it here."

"I was loving it more than…other people were loving it. That's for sure."

"Other pe— Do you mean Decker? You've got to be joking, right? He's gaga for you. Everyone could see it on his face last night. Let me tell you, there were more than a few sour faces in that crowd, realizing that they didn't stand a chance with him, if you know what I mean."

"I messed everything up, Marlee."

"You? How?"

"He asked me to stay. Last night. He said he loved me and asked me not to go."

"You're kidding. I thought it was just getting kind of heated between you two. That's why I stepped in. I figured you didn't want a crowd watching, if you were going to rekindle things. Or not rekindle things."

Morgan shook her head miserably. "Nope. You

were rescuing me from answering him when he asked me to stay. I didn't know what to say. It's been a lot of years, and I've been burned by him before, and I have to think of Archer, and I'm just…"

"Scared," Marlee said.

"Yeah. I needed time to think."

"So tell him you had to mull it all over and now you've changed your mind."

"I overheard him this morning," Morgan said. But she realized that if she continued, if she told Marlee what she'd overheard him saying about her, she might actually cry. And there was no way that she was going to let Decker McBride, after all these years, make her cry.

"And?"

"And…it doesn't matter. I'm going home."

"Morgan, it's okay to change your mind. You could end up here. On this ranch. Permanently."

"He's selling the ranch and using the benefit money to start up Pathways at a smaller ranch."

"Selling?"

"We were trying to avoid it, but apparently we didn't make enough money. I don't know. I only overheard him. I haven't talked to him myself."

"You know what you should do?" Marlee asked, fire in her eyes. Morgan knew that when her sister got like this, she was a steamroller, and everyone and everything better get out of her path. "You should buy it."

Morgan barked out a laugh. "Me? Yeah, I don't think so."

"Why not?"

"Well, for one thing, there's this little issue of money. I don't know how much he's asking, but I know that no matter how much it is, it's out of my budget."

"Ask Dad for the money."

"No, Marlee."

"Ask Mom, then. Ask me. I'll help you. I've got some savings. Surely you've got some savings, too."

"Marlee. Stop. I'm not going to buy it. I don't need to remind you that I don't get any child support from Cody. Remember how you had to work out a deal for Archer to come to Pathways for free? I've got a decent job. It doesn't pay a ton, but I'm good at it and there's room to grow. I don't want to give that all up for a *maybe we can make this work*."

"Maybe he'll sell it to you at a discount because he's in love with you."

"He's not. And even at a discount…I don't think you know how expensive even one single horse is, much less five."

Morgan walked over to her sister and wrapped her up in her arms. She loved how protective

Marlee was of her. She was always 100 percent on Morgan's side, no matter the circumstances. Morgan could confess that she'd murdered some-one, and Marlee would have asked what they did to deserve it.

"I love you, sis. I'll visit more often. I prom-ise."

But it would be a visit only, there was no doubt about that. Because, even though she missed her family terribly, and even though the summer had been the most satisfying summer she could remember in a long time, she knew one thing for certain.

She needed to go home. She needed to leave Haw Springs, Buck County, McBride Pathways—and especially Decker McBride—behind. For good.

She needed to get back to her life. Even if that life made her ache for this one.

When Morgan left McBride Pathways, she tried to slip away at the end of the evening unno-ticed. But as soon as she walked out the back door of the main building, she heard Decker's voice. He was leaning against the trunk of the tree she had parked her car under. He had one foot propped on the tree behind him, and his hat was pushed low over his eyes. Even as angry as she was with him, Morgan couldn't help appreciating how handsome he was, the ease with which he leaned against the tree, as if he and the tree were one.

"Thank you for everything you've done here," he said. "You really are something."

She stopped, considered just continuing on into her car and leaving, but decided she was going to have the decency to at least say good-bye. "Thank you for helping Archer. I'm sure he'll never forget June and Ziggy and Thomas. And you." She opened her car door and pushed the box full of her things onto the back seat. Her movements felt stiff, mechanical. Her voice felt like ice cubes.

He pushed away from the tree, one finger nudging his hat back so he could see her better. His hair was ringed with sweat, adding extra bounce to the curls around his ears. "You know I'm doing this for David, right?"

"Are you sure?" she countered. "Feels a little like you're doing it because I didn't give you an answer you wanted to hear last night. You love this ranch, Decker. It's in your soul. Letting it go will be like letting yourself go."

He reached out and gently took her hand. "Morgan, I fell for you the first time you spoke to me," he said. "And I tried to reason with myself—*maybe she's too good to be true. It was just the romance of the moment. She'll lose interest when she goes off to college.* I told myself all those things, but it wasn't turning out to be true, and it scared the heck out of me. I was a kid and had these huge feelings, and I was sure that you were going to decide you wanted nothing to do with ranch life or with me. I let you go to spare us both the pain of losing each other down the line."

Morgan allowed her fingers to curl over his. "You never gave me a chance," she practically whispered. "You took that away from me."

He swallowed, stared hard into her eyes. "I've held on to this ranch because I think I've been holding on to a dream that someday my mom would come back, ask for forgiveness. And at the same time, I was pushing every other dream away. But she's not coming back. It wouldn't make any difference now if she did. My dad's gone, and my brother needs the money. And I think more than that, he needs to let the bad memories go. To free himself of the past. He deserves that. So I'm selling for him. I'll rebuild. The ranch and myself. And I'll take care of Ben. I'm not leaving him high and dry. I'm just letting go of land.

"The benefit you put on is allowing Pathways to flourish, just in a different location. I wouldn't have been able to do this without you. I would have had to shut down and wait for a buyer before I could even think of next steps. So thank you."

He pulled her other hand into his. "I'm not a bad man, Morgan. I need you to understand that. Even if you walk away from here hating me—and I wouldn't blame you if you did—I don't want you to walk away thinking I'm a bad person."

A tear slipped down her cheek. At this point, she didn't know what she thought she was walking away from. "How can this feel so right between us if it's not?"

He gave her hands a soft squeeze, let them go, leaned in and gave her a peck on the cheek. "Goodbye, Morgan."

MORGAN SLIPPED BACK into regular life without missing a beat. That was what she was best at— hitting the ground running. She supposed she had Cody to thank for that. When you got left high and dry, you didn't have time to mull over your choices. You only had time to act.

Which was why, even though she was back to regular life, something was just...off. Her job was okay money and good security, but she wasn't passionate about it. She hadn't realized that until she'd been using her skills for something she was passionate about. Everything at work just seemed dull and boring and a little bit stressful in comparison. Always watching to make sure she hadn't taxed a relationship with a customer. Keeping meticulous records. Schmoozing. Making sure the boss saw her working hard and never saw her slacking off.

Never getting to see Archer make a new stride, her only time with him the few short hours between when she picked him up from after-school care and bedtime, during which time they endured what seemed like an endless battle of wills. *Yes, you will eat those chicken nuggets. Yes, you will take a bath. Yes, you will brush your teeth. No, you won't wear your cowboy boots to bed.*

Archer asked about Zee nearly every single day. At first, it gutted Morgan. Made her feel guilty, like she had ripped Archer away from something he obviously cared about greatly. With him being nonverbal, it was impossible for her to know just how much anguish he was in over something at any given time. And when she didn't know, she imagined. And she never imagined lightly.

I've probably ruined him forever.

I've created pain for my son.

I've given him something he loved, and now I'm withholding that very thing from him.

The only good thing about focusing on Archer's pain was that it diverted her attention away from her own.

Every so often, she would be flattened by a memory or a curiosity. Had Decker worn cowboy boots to bed when he was a little boy? What was he doing right now? Was Pathways still up and running? She checked the website incessantly, until one evening, she saw what she was looking for and dreading at the same time.

FOR SALE.

All caps, across the top of the website. Along with the following:

McBride Pathways will be opening at a different location in the near future. Please revisit for more details as we have them. Our next session will be at our new location.

Morgan's heart ached. This was not what Decker wanted. She was sure of it.

She'd given a lot of thought to what had happened with Decker and David and their mother. She'd given a lot of thought to that kiss on her cheek. And the look of pain on his face when he said, *I'm not a bad man, Morgan.*

She knew that. She supposed a part of her knew that about him from the day he'd told her it wasn't working out between them. If she'd thought he was a bad man, it would have been so much easier to let him go. She wouldn't have thought and wondered for all these years. She wouldn't have felt so injured by the loss.

But the funny thing was, now that she understood the reason behind the way he acted, she didn't feel any less injured. He wasn't a bad man, and she couldn't let him go.

She was so engrossed in her thoughts, she didn't even hear the footsteps following her in the garage attached to her office building downtown. She didn't see the shadow elongating in the fluorescent lights next to her, either.

It wasn't until someone said her name and grabbed her shoulder that she whirled around with a scream, dropping her purse on the garage floor.

She felt like she was gazing into the past.

"Cody!" She jerked her shoulder out from under his grasp and bent to pick up her spilled handbag. *Speaking of bad men*, she thought angrily. "Are you crazy? Don't ever touch me like that again."

He threw up his hands and had the gall to act offended by her reaction. "I didn't expect you to be so jumpy. Jeez."

She scooped everything back into her purse and stood. "I'm not jumpy. You can't just sneak up on people in a parking garage and grab them without them knowing you're even there. It's common sense."

"Sorry! Sorry! Sue me. Whatever. I can tell you haven't changed. Still so entitled. Everyone treat Princess Morgan with kid gloves."

"What are you even doing here?" she asked.

"Looking for you," he said. "I had to follow you from your house to figure out where you worked, and then I had to wait here all day because I had no idea what kind of hours you worked." He looked around the parking garage. "Fancy. You must be living the life."

She rolled her eyes. "Yeah, I'm the other half now. Wait—you followed me from my house? Do you know how creepy that is?"

"I needed to talk to you."

She held up her phone. "You could have texted. My phone number hasn't changed. I should call the police and report stalking." She held her phone to her ear and channeled her inner Marlee. "Oh, and I'm being stalked by the man who owes me thirty thousand dollars in child support, so while you're hauling him in, go ahead and toss him in deadbeat-dad jail."

"I'm not stalking you. I just need to talk to you. Put the phone down."

"I purposely didn't speak to you when I saw you at the hospital. Go live your life. I'm not going to mess with it." She turned toward her car, surprised to find that she was shaking with adrenaline. So many times she'd wondered and rehearsed how she would respond, what she would say, when she finally got to be face-to-face with Cody again. It was nothing like this, and she never anticipated nerves to get to her.

"Wait, Morgan. I know." He scooted ahead of her and turned around. "Just hear me out."

"Does she know that you have abandoned a child already? Does she know about me at all? Was she there when you were served divorce papers when my lawyer finally found you using a private detective?"

"Not exactly."

Of course not, Morgan thought. *I wouldn't have expected any less from him.* But, still, she found herself shocked and offended that she didn't even exist in his history, and even more offended for Archer.

"Well, for her sake, I hope that baby comes out totally perfect. Because we know how you handle imperfection. Get out of my way. You have nothing to say to me that I actually care to hear." She tried to walk around him, but he moved into her path.

"I know! I know. I'm a horrible dad. A horrible person. I'm trying to be better. Can you… can you just stop, please, and listen? I want to give you this."

He produced a bulging envelope out of his jacket pocket and held it out to her. She stared at it, blinking. What kind of crazy antic was he up to now? She didn't even want to touch anything that he might hand to her.

He wiggled the envelope. "Take it."

Hesitantly, she took it. She could tell before even looking that it was packed with money. She opened the top of the envelope and peeked. She could hardly believe what she was seeing. Hundred-dollar bill after hundred-dollar bill.

"It's not all of it, but it's pretty close," Cody said. "Within a couple hundred, anyway. I'll get that to you as soon as I can."

Morgan couldn't tear her eyes away from the money. It began to distort as her eyes began to swim with tears. If he'd only known how hard this had been. How much she'd needed that money two years ago. She might have been able to stay in her old house. She maybe would have held out for a job she was passionate about.

She might have even moved home.

And he was saving money the whole time she and Archer were scraping by to survive.

"I want to start over, Morgan." She flicked a panicked look at him, and he held his hands up again, as if to stop her. "Not with you. With Deana. And our little girl. I…I want to relinquish my rights to Archer."

Morgan blinked. "Your rights?"

"My parenting rights. I have a lawyer drafting up the paperwork right now, and you'll be hearing from him soon, but I wanted to get things fair and square first."

"Fair and square," she repeated. "You think anything about this is fair or square? You're delusional. Everything you've done has been unfair. You're abandoning him completely, and you somehow think that's fair. I was right. You are crazy."

"I just need you to not talk to me if, you know...if we should ever see you out and about again."

Morgan resisted the urge to laugh out loud. She'd already done that. He was the one making contact now. All he had to do was go away, which he'd already done two years ago. This was so very Cody. Had to have control, always. Had to be the one steering the narrative.

"I know you deserve better than this," he said.

"*Archer* deserves better than this," she corrected him. "He deserves a dad who loves and cares about him. And don't you dare even attempt to claim either one of those things."

"I know." At least he had the decency to hang his head, even if Morgan very much doubted that his remorse was at all sincere. "At least this way, maybe he can have that. With...you know...with someone else."

Morgan tucked the envelope into her handbag. It stuck out the top like a prize won at a carnival.

She had begun to absorb what all of this meant for her. And for Archer. Her anger was starting to dissipate, but the last thing she wanted was for Cody to see her happy. He didn't even deserve that much.

"I'll be waiting for the paperwork," she said. "But let's get this clear. You're in no position to demand anything from me. Giving us the money that you owe doesn't mean we owe you anything."

"I know, I know."

"And I truly hope nobody treats your daughter the way you treated me. But, since I know you will, just tell Deana that when you dump her, she can come to my house for a sympathetic ear. You obviously know where it is. Goodbye, Cody."

She hurried to her car and shut the door. If he had said anything more, she didn't hear him. As far as she was concerned, Cody was simply a voice from the past. A bad memory that she was eager to let go of.

She waited until she was out of the garage before she let out an excited little shriek. "Call Marlee!" she shouted at her phone.

"Hey, do you remember the ranch hand who worked for Decker?" Morgan asked as soon as her sister picked up.

"Ben? Yeah. Why?"

"Do you think you could get me in touch with him? Without Decker knowing?"

"I suppose so. They've put the place up for sale, but I bet he's still living there."

"Give him my number. I have a business proposition for him."

"A business proposition?"

Morgan pulled the envelope out of her purse and set it on her lap. She wanted to feel the heft of it. The reality of it.

The possibility that it represented. She held it against her heart. Everything looked different now. Everything.

"Sis, you will never believe what just happened."

"Ooh, tell me."

CHAPTER FOURTEEN

MORGAN HAD BEEN a flurry of activity since Cody cornered her in the parking garage. She had so many phone calls to make, plans to get in order, secrets to keep.

And a job…to quit.

The deal hadn't been made yet—not exactly—but she knew Decker would take her offer. He had to. She didn't have any other options. She hoped that her complete dismantling of her life would push him into saying yes. Plus she had Ben as leverage. If Decker turned her down, he would have to turn them both down.

She walked into her boss's office bright and early on a Monday morning.

"Hey, Stan," she said. "Can we talk?"

The man who'd taken a chance on a desperate, young, single mother, and who had been so kind to her, looked up from his desk. "Uh-oh, it's never good when someone starts like that." He chuckled, but then noticed that Morgan wasn't chuckling with him, and dropped his pen. "Oh. It's not good. Have a seat."

She was surprised by the tears that sprang to her eyes as she sank into the seat across from his desk. Dear, dear Stan. She felt like a traitor, leaving him. "It's not." Her voice was thick and rough.

"You're not going to one of our competitors, I hope?"

"No." She plucked a tissue out of the box on his desk. "I'm going home. To Haw Springs."

"You just got back from Haw Springs. Everything's okay?"

"Yes. My parents are there, and my sister."

"And?"

She let out a breathy laugh. She could never hide anything from Stan. "And...I'm buying a ranch. Well, a third of one, anyway."

This time Stan let out the laugh. "You? You're buying a ranch."

"What's so unbelievable about that? I just spent a whole summer on a ranch. Maybe I'm a natural. Born to ride horses and...muck stalls and...do other ranch things. You don't know."

"Other ranch things? Sounds official. Do you remember that time the wasp got into your office?"

"How could I forget? I was traumatized. I heard phantom buzzing in there for weeks afterward."

"Exactly. You don't even do a singular bug, but you're a natural on a ranch? I thought you were going to call 9-1-1 on that wasp."

"It was very aggressive. I needed backup."

They both chuckled. It was a little obvious that she wasn't buying a ranch to satisfy her passion for the great outdoors.

"So, tell me. What exactly is on this ranch?"

She could feel herself blushing. She didn't want to trivialize her feelings for Decker by blushing like a teenager, but she couldn't help herself. "Horses?"

"Ah," Stan said. "It's not a what. It's a who. So you had a really great summer, huh?"

"I knew him before. I can't explain it. And I don't even know for sure if it will work out."

"But you have to find out."

She nodded, the tears starting anew. "I don't think I can go the rest of my life without knowing for sure."

"Then you have to go."

"I'm sorry."

He rolled his chair away from his desk and came around to her, arms outstretched. She stood and folded herself into them, grateful. She hadn't realized it until that moment, but Stan really had been a stand-in for her father while she tried to pick up the pieces after Cody left. "You should never be sorry about love. And if you get there and decide that you actually can live the rest of your life without him, and there are far too many wasps involved in ranch life, you always have a place here. I'll make sure of it."

"Thank you, Stan. Really. You've always been so good to me. You have no idea how much this means to me."

He let go and stepped back. "I think I do. I've been married to the same woman for thirty-five years. I know all about *can't live without*, trust me. But you, Morgan West, are quite good at what you do. So we would be fools not to take you back anytime you ask." He walked back around his desk and sat. "How much longer do we have you?"

"I meet with the Realtor this evening. I should know more after that. But I'm guessing two or three weeks. Just long enough to pack."

He smiled. "Then we will be grateful for the next two or three weeks."

And I will be grateful for you forever.

She felt giddy as she drove out of Kansas City a few hours later, her destination Haw Springs. Her actual destination: her future.

When she picked up Archer from preschool, there was much excitement, because he'd learned a new word. When Morgan discovered that the word was *horse*, she laughed out loud. The timing couldn't have been more perfect. *Yes, let's*

go see the horses, she said brightly, and con-
tinued smiling as he zoomed around the room
with glee.

Ten minutes into the three-hour car ride, he
was sound asleep, which was going to make bedtime in a few hours interesting, but Morgan was
so focused on the destination, she didn't care.

She was doing the right thing. She was sure
of it. Never surer of anything in her life.

"Is it true?" her mother asked as she met Morgan at the car. She pulled Archer, still asleep, out
of his car seat. He stirred and wrapped his arms
around his grandmother's neck. "Marlee says
you're doing it. You're coming home. Is it true?"

Morgan, beaming, nodded. "If everything goes
the way I want it to, yes."

"Oh, my goodness, oh, my goodness, oh, my
goodness," her mother said, hugging Archer tight.
"It's what I've wanted for years."

"Me, too, Mom," Morgan said. "I just didn't
know it until I spent the summer here. I belong
here."

And she did. She knew that even if Decker
denied her proposal and didn't want anything
to do with her, she was still meant to be here.
She was meant to be in a place where the coffee
shop owner invited her to throw on an apron and
help out, and where her sister arranged beautiful
sunflower centerpieces for a party, and where

Archer could ride horses and commune with a hound dog if he wanted to. Where she could lean on her dad's shoulder and vent frustrations while grocery shopping with her mother.

Haw Springs was home, and she never should have left.

"Come in for some dinner," her mother said. "We've got Salisbury steaks."

Morgan checked the time. She was early. Her appointment wasn't for another forty-five minutes, so she turned off her car.

"Okay. Salisbury steak sounds great."

Her dad was already at the table, napkin tucked into the collar of his shirt, just like always. When Morgan was young, it used to mortify her for people to see him like that. But now it made her smile. Her dad was like a big kid about a lot of things, which made him fun to be around. Archer was going to thrive with his grandpa's influence in his life.

"Dad, did you do the napkin thing when you took Mom out on your first date?" she asked, settling into "her spot"—the chair she'd occupied at the family table for as long as she could remember.

"Of course not," he said. "She was so sophisticated, I had to wait until the second date."

"Not true," her mom said. "I wasn't sophisticated at all. And he only waited until dessert."

"It was ice cream," he said defensively. "It drips. What, did you want to walk around with a man wearing choco-crunch all down the front of him?"

"Of course not," Mom said. "I wasn't complaining. I was correcting."

Morgan's dad leaned toward Morgan and stage-whispered, "*Correcting* is a softer word for *complaining.*"

"Oh, pooh," her mom said, swiping a napkin at his shoulder. She settled into her spot at the opposite end of the table. "Pass the potatoes before they get gluey."

Morgan allowed herself a moment to imagine her and Decker having this kind of banter over the dinner table. It seemed like a dream, yet at the same time like something that could happen. And she wanted it so badly, she began to feel nervous. What if he had changed his mind?

She had to try, no matter what.

"So, Morgan," her mom said, tucking into her plate while Morgan scooped some potatoes onto Archer's plate. He was sleepy and on the edge of cranky, and mashed potatoes weren't really a texture he tolerated, but she was determined to offer them to him just the same. *You never know when their tastes will change*, she used to tell Cody when he would get frustrated. *Give him time.* "Where will you stay? When you move home, I mean?"

"Marlee has some extra space." Morgan cut up half a steak on Archer's plate. He groaned disapprovingly. It was obviously going to be pancakes for dinner for him again, but first, this. "She said we can stay with her until we find something."

"Well, and of course you can stay here, too. We'll help with Archer."

"Thanks, Mom. I'll take all the help I can get. I wish I'd had it when Cody left."

"You've always had it. You just had to come accept it," her dad said. "Sort of like that rancher over there, yeah?"

Morgan stopped chewing. She hadn't planned on mentioning Decker until things were more... settled.

"Marlee," she seethed.

Her dad shook his head. "Your sister didn't need to say a word. I guessed. And you just confirmed."

"Well, I mean, you'd have to be blind not to see how the man looked at you," her mom said.

"And how you looked at him," her dad added.

"It's the same way your dad looked at me. Puppy-dog eyes. Everything I did delighted him. Everything I said. He couldn't keep his eyes off of me. We saw that in Mr. McBride every time we showed up."

"And that time we talked to him," her dad added. "He was like a lovesick tweenager."

Morgan giggled. "It's just *tween*—you don't need to put the *ager* at the end of it."

"Fine, he was like a lovesick tween," her dad said. "Wouldn't look us in the eye, got all sweaty and nervous."

"Really?" Morgan wasn't hungry anymore. Butterflies were whirling around her stomach, and she wanted time to speed up so she could get to Decker before she lost her courage. She wanted to see the puppy-dog eyes for herself. Really see them. And believe them.

Archer, cranky now, complained loudly and tossed his fork on the floor. He started to grab the edge of his plate, but Morgan whisked it away before it, too, ended up on the floor.

"Okay, okay," she said. "Pancakes it is."

"You enjoy your dinner," her mom said, jumping up. "I've got some in the freezer."

Archer wolfed down the pancakes, and his mood seemed to improve. But after only a few minutes of playing, he was lying on the couch, sucking his thumb and watching a cartoon, glassy-eyed. Morgan scooped him up and carried him to the back bedroom where they'd stayed all summer. She changed his clothes and tucked him into bed. It was barely 6:00 p.m. She was going to regret this in the morning.

But, right now, she couldn't think about morning. She couldn't think about anything but what was about to happen. The butterflies had begun to make her palms sweat. It was time to go make this right.

She kissed her mom and dad goodbye, hopped into her car and drove toward McBride Pathways, practicing her spiel out loud the entire way.

"Decker, I know you're going to have reservations about this, and nobody would blame you. No, that sounds too bleak. *Decker, if you sell the ranch to Ben and me, I will make sure the ranch thrives, like our love for each other.* Ew, no. That's so cheesy. *Decker, I want to become your business partner and your life partner.* Good grief, no—that sounds like a business merger. Ugh."

When she pulled into the driveway, Ben was already there, standing by the Realtor's car. She was pointing out something on the horizon, and he wasn't even following her finger. Morgan laughed. There was no way the Realtor was telling him something about the ranch that he didn't already know. He looked nervous, but it was so good to see him again. She practically jumped out of her car.

"Hi, you must be Morgan. I'm Tempe, the agent you've been working with."

Morgan took her hand and shook. "Yes, so

nice to meet you." She reached out and gave Ben
a side hug before he could protest. She felt him
tense beneath her arm, but she didn't care. "Hey,
there, business partner. Are you ready for this?"

She could see Ben toss the words around in
his head, looking for a reason that they, seman-
tically, didn't make sense. But he either couldn't
find any, or he was just as anxious to get to
Decker as she was. He simply nodded, no argument required.

"Let's go, then. Mr. McBride is waiting for
us in the main office. From our phone conversation, it sounds like I don't really need to give
you the tour of the property." Tempe raised her
eyebrows questioningly.

Morgan giggled. "I'm thinking we don't need
one, no. But Ben could give *you* a tour if you'd
like," she said.

"I have not prepared a tour," Ben said. "But I
suppose I could improvise, if necessary."

"Oh, not necessary." The Realtor waved him
away. "I've got on heels, anyway."

Morgan, anticipating Ben's confusion, whispered, "Her high-heel shoes aren't great for walking on uneven ground. They'll probably push
right through the dirt."

"Oh. Yes," Ben agreed. "Thank you, ma'am."

Morgan smiled. She had a feeling this was
going to be a great partnership. She stopped

walking, holding all of them up. "One thing, though, Ben. If we're going to be business partners, you don't have to call me 'ma'am.' 'Morgan' is fine. It's perfectly respectful."

"Yes, ma'am. I mean, Morgan."

She patted his shoulder. "It's a work in progress, but I'll take it."

"Right, then," Tempe said. "Are we ready?" She didn't wait for an answer, but closed the distance to the door, grabbed the handle and pulled it open.

Here we go, Morgan thought, her stomach balled in knots. She took a deep breath and let it out, feeling the unfamiliar weight of her heart on her sleeve. *Do-or-die time.*

She stepped through the door.

Decker, standing at the desk, looked up. Recognition crossed his face, quickly followed by confusion and incredulity.

"Tweety?" he said softly.

She gave a shy wave, the butterflies in her stomach bursting forward and filling the room. "Hey, there, Baseball."

WHAT WAS IT Yogi Berra called it? *Déjà vu all over again*?

That was exactly what Decker felt when he saw the door open and Morgan step through. At first, he thought maybe his wishes and desires had become so strong he was simply hallucinating. Willing her into existence. Like the Ghost of Christmas Yet to Come, she was here to show him where the mistakes of today would land him tomorrow.

But she talked.

She was really there.

"What are you doing here?" he asked, taking in the others who had followed her through the door. Ben and...his Realtor? "What's going on?"

Morgan shrugged. "We're making an offer."

The pieces were starting to fall into place, and while it made the puzzle complete, the picture still didn't make sense. "What do you mean 'making an off—' Wait. You're the interested buyer I'm supposed to meet with?"

"Very interested," Tempe said.

Morgan was beaming, and he had to concentrate hard not to get distracted by her beauty. "I'm one of them, yes." She gestured to Ben, who ducked his head and tipped his hat to Decker in that formal way he had of doing when he wanted to be serious and ultra polite.

"Ben? You?"

Ben, eyes to the floor, nodded. "Yes, sir."

"How?"

"I've been saving my paychecks this whole time."

David burst through the door. "Sorry I'm late.

Got caught up with a basset hound. Ate a sock."
He looked at Tempe. "They'll eat anything. What
did I miss? You tell him yet?"

Decker held back a laugh. "You knew, too?"

David spread his hands. "I was sworn to se-
crecy."

"Well, I'll be."

"We only want to buy David's half. We have
enough for a down payment," Morgan said. "And
we're willing to take out loans to cover the rest.
We've discussed everything in great detail. We
have a whole plan."

The Realtor stepped to the desk. "Here's the
amount that will buy David out." She pulled a
paper out of the folder she was holding. "He's
agreeable to this arrangement. It's very reasonable."

"I never wanted you to lose the ranch, little
brother. You know that."

Decker stared at the paper. He could hardly
believe his eyes. David was being more than
fair, but at the same time, it was a lot of money.

"Of course, the horses would remain yours,"
the Realtor said.

"Except Scout," Ben interjected. "I would like
to buy Scout."

Decker let out a laugh. "She's all yours. I'll
sell her to you for a dollar."

Ben rarely showed a lot of emotion, but the

smile on his face was wide and undeniable. His hands balled into fists that he shook at his sides. *Victory*.

"What about your job?" Decker asked Morgan.

"I'm going freelance," she said. "I've already got two customers. Marlee and Ellory. I'm hoping to make the ranch my third. Commission based, of course. I've already got tons of ideas. Maybe a local celebrity baseball game. Do you know anything about baseball?"

"Oh. I know everything about baseball."

"Technically, I'm not sure that it's possible to know everything about a subject," Ben said. "I will have to research and get back to you on that, though. If it's possible, I would like to know everything about some subjects."

Morgan and Decker both chuckled, their eyes locked, so much more than just a business transaction flowing between them.

Decker felt a tumbling sensation sweep over him. Like a wave had washed in and tried to carry him away, and he was only staying upright by sheer luck alone, his toes digging into sand that was constantly shifting, moving, seeping out from under him.

So this is what it feels like, he thought. It was wonderful and terrifying and slightly nauseating, but in the best possible way.

Just let yourself go with it, McBride. Let yourself fall in love with her.

Let yourself take that chance.

"So…do we want to go over details?" the Realtor asked, glancing from one to the other.

"Definitely," Decker said, never losing eye contact with Morgan. He could fall and fall and fall forever into those eyes and never want to land. "But I think we already have a deal."

CHAPTER FIFTEEN

"I CAN'T BELIEVE I'm a ranch owner," Ben said, rocking up on his toes. The Realtor had gone, with promises to call as soon as the official paperwork was ready for signing. "My mom is going to be very proud."

"I'm sure your mom is always proud of you, Ben," Morgan said.

He nodded, the smile never leaving his face. "I'm a rancher," he said. "And I own my own horse."

"Congratulations, buddy," Decker said, shaking Ben's hand. "I couldn't pick a better partner if I had to."

"What about Morgan?" Ben asked.

Decker held his hand out for a shake. "Congratulations, partner."

"Thanks, partner," Morgan said, taking his hand and giving it a few good pumps.

"I'm going to go tell Scout the good news," Ben said. He hurried away, leaving Morgan and

Decker alone. Morgan concentrated on gathering her courage.

Everything had gone exactly as planned. But she wasn't done.

"There's more," she said, as Decker started toward the front desk. He turned. "Um…" She suddenly didn't know how to proceed. All of this planning, and she'd never planned exactly what she would say to him when she finally got the chance. She decided to go with the most straightforward approach she could muster. "I don't want to be your business partner."

He frowned. "But…you just said…this whole thing… I'm confused. I thought you did want to be my partner. We just shook on it."

"I don't want to *just* be your business partner," she clarified. "Decker, I'm in love with you. I thought I had let you go, but here I was, hopelessly in love with you all summer. When I got back to KC, I thought I would forget about you and move on with my life, but I couldn't stop thinking about you. I wanted to be back here, back with you. Working with you was so hard. Trying to act professional and pretend that there was nothing here. Trying to convince myself."

"It was hard for me, too."

She took a step toward him. "I know you have a history that makes it hard for you to trust, but I'm hoping that you will eventually come to trust me. At the dance, you asked me to let you love me. And I made a huge mistake running away from you that night. But I'm asking you now to let me love you. I'm not running away. I'm not going anywhere."

Morgan's heart was beating out of her chest. She feared that he might even be able to hear it all the way across the room. She'd laid it all out there, just like she'd promised herself she would do, but now that she had, she immediately worried that she'd made a mistake.

Decker stood stone-still, and she couldn't read the look on his face. She began to fear that she'd ruined everything. She felt a need to fill the silence, and, to her dismay, she started to back-pedal.

"Of course, if…if you want to keep it professional, I understand and I can do that. I still want to be your business partner, either way, and I swear I can keep it strictly business. It will be hard, but I can do it."

"No," he whispered, his voice a growl full of need. He took two swift steps toward her, whisking his hat off his head while he moved. He wrapped his free arm around her waist and pulled her in. "Maybe you can, but I can't."

He pulled her in closer, his mouth meeting hers, softly, slowly.

Everything—the ranch, the years, the hurt—

fell away as he kissed her. His hat dropped to the floor as he wrapped his other arm around her. And when they broke away, he touched his forehead to hers, his eyes closed, his hand stroking the back of her neck.

"I love you, Tweety," he whispered. "My family is finally here."

EPILOGUE

ARCHER WAS MISSING.

Again.

Annie burst into the office, her cheeks flushed, her breathing labored. The rest of the kids had all gone home, and Archer was supposed to help her get Ziggy untacked, but he hadn't shown up.

This was becoming a thing.

The ranch had made Archer bolder. They had been there for barely a year, and already he had so much more confidence. He was speaking short sentences, and they were understandable. He was bonding with more than just the hound dog. And…he was a runner.

Fortunately, he always seemed to "run" to the same place. He sure loved that tree house. Decker had spent a whole weekend gussying it up for him, replacing the rope ladder, painting the wood, sweeping out the inside, and even adding some small furniture.

Morgan couldn't really blame Archer for always wanting to be there. Sometimes, Ben and

Annie would join him, and Morgan would show up to find the three of them happily playing a board game or a card game or just indulging Archer's imagination.

"Where's Decker?" she asked, shutting off the computer and heading around the desk.

"I don't know," Annie said. "I think maybe fixing a fence or something?"

There was a broken fence? Morgan didn't know about it, if there was.

"And Ben?"

"Um. At his house," Annie said. "I think—I think he had something to do there."

"Okay, then. Is Tweety still saddled up?"

"Yes, ma'am. And I have Sugar."

When the deal had become final, Morgan's parents celebrated her homecoming by buying her a horse and Archer a pony. They'd gone to Decker for advice, and he'd found them a gorgeous, cream-colored perlino quarter horse. He'd wanted that color, he told her, because it was as close to yellow as he could find. He'd already named her Tweety.

Very funny. Aren't you just the comedian of the century, Morgan had said, but she loved everything about Tweety, who was patient and loving and intuited Morgan's lingering hesitation immediately. Tweety just seemed to know that

Morgan was moving on from something, and the horse was there for her, every step of the way.

Archer was still getting to know his pony. He still preferred June, and he liked to wander on foot. But getting him up on the pony was no longer a meltdown activity. Morgan was proud of him.

"Okay, well, let's go find him," she said, leaving her sandals behind the desk.

They jogged to the barn, where Tweety and Sugar were tied to a post. Annie immediately mounted Sugar. Morgan, still getting used to the whole process, grabbed the horn, put her left foot in the stirrup and kicked herself up onto her horse.

"First try!" she crowed, but Annie had already urged Sugar into gear and was taking off toward the woods. "Well, I'm proud of us, Tweets," Morgan said, leaning down to pat her horse's neck. "Let's go."

She and Decker had been working hard on getting her accustomed to a gallop, and now was her time to test what she'd learned. Tweety was a fast and eager horse, and in no time, Morgan found herself whisking along the path in the woods, trying to keep up with Annie.

Weird, she thought. *Annie seems to be making a beeline to the glade. She's like a woman on a mission. If she knows he's in the tree house, what's the hurry?*

The answer to that question dawned on Morgan as soon as they popped into the glade on the other side of the woods.

Their glade.

And then it all made sense.

Annie had been on a mission because this was all a ruse to get Morgan to the clearing.

Ben was there. Archer leaned out of the tree house window, waving at his mother. Cindy and Sareena were both there, as were most of the other teen helpers.

In the center of the clearing, standing next to a picnic blanket covered with a whole spread of food, was Decker.

Wearing a tuxedo jacket, jeans, white shirt and bow tie with his boots and hat. He held an oversize stuffed Tweety Bird at his chest.

Morgan let out a laugh, while her brain buzzed with questions. Was this what she thought it was?

"I've got her," Annie said, now off Sugar and reaching for Tweety's reins. Absently, Morgan handed them to her.

"Annie, I think you got me here under false pretenses. Did you know about this?"

Annie giggled but didn't respond.

Morgan nearly fell off her horse trying to get down, as her legs were weak and shaky, and she still wasn't used to the height of horses. And now she wished she'd left her sandals on, at the very least. She felt…underdressed. She was nervous and wasn't sure if she could make one foot go in front of the other to get to Decker.

But then her eyes met his. She saw his chest bounce in a laugh as he waited patiently for her. She was whisked back to that night, all those years ago, the tinkling carnival music behind them, the flashing carnival lights bathing his face. The way she felt pulled to him. Stopped without even thinking about it, drawn by the little curls at the base of his neck and the way his back rippled when he threw a baseball. She remembered demanding that he win her a stuffed Tweety Bird. And he did just that. Because he felt it, too, the pull between them.

If anyone had asked her back then what her vision was of the future, and if she really sat and thought about it, this would have been her answer. Twilight and fireflies and soft grass under her bare feet, and Decker's smile beckoning to her. Everything felt just right, like it had always been meant to be this way.

"I'm not gonna bite," he said, waving for her to come on.

She made her feet go forward. She felt numb and cold, despite the warm spring weather.

"You've got some explaining to do, Baseball," she teased. "A lot of people seem to be in on a secret that I'm not in on."

"Ah, it's not so secret," he said. "Is it?"

He held out the bird. Morgan took it, giggling like the teenager she was when they'd met. "Where did you get this?"

Hands on hips, he lowered his head and gave it a shake. "Don't ask."

"He got it at the Haw Springs Fall Carnival last year," Annie told her. "He's been hiding it at Ben's house."

"You won this at the carnival?" Morgan asked. "How? I was with you."

"Not when you were up on the square buying kettle corn."

Realization dawned on Morgan. "You had me stand in that enormously long line so you could buy a stuffed bird?"

"Nope." He scuffed a toe at the ground. "I had you stand in an enormously long line so I could *win* you a stuffed bird." He looked up at her and grinned. "Took a whole lot more baseballs than it did the first time. Guess I'm rusty."

Love washed over Morgan. She held up the Tweety and gave it a once-over. "You won me a Tweety," she said, feeling tears prickle at the backs of her eyes. Decker was sentimental. Just another tick in the Man of Her Dreams box. "Why?"

"Because I love you, goof." Decker touched the tip of her nose, a habit of his that she secretly adored. "And because…" He lowered himself to one knee on the picnic blanket.

Morgan would later muse over how hard it was for her brain to take in exactly what was happening. She knew, and she didn't know. Warmth bloomed in her chest as she lowered the bird to her side. Annie stepped forward and took it from her, and her fingers let loose without her even realizing it. Her gaze was glued to the handsome man kneeling before her, disbelieving that this was happening to her.

All those years of wondering why he'd broken up with her.

All those years of heartbreak.

She was sure that she'd lost him forever.

"Morgan." Decker had pulled out a black velvet box and opened it. A diamond glittered in the sun. "I never thought I would have a love like this. I was so terrified of it, I pushed it away. I pushed you away, and it was the biggest mistake of my life. I regretted it so much. But I'm tired of living with regret, and will never, ever push you away again. That's all in the past. I want a future with you now. You and Archer. A real future.

"Every time I think it can't get better between you and me, it does. You are the best thing that ever happened to me, and I never want to spend another minute of my life without you in it. I will promise you a lifetime of sunrises on that ridge over there, and footraces in the glade, and barn dances, and carnivals. I'll win you so many birds, you'll need to build a new wing on our house just for them. And we'll celebrate all of Archer's milestones together, and our grandchildren will ride horses from the moment they open their beautiful blue eyes. And we'll watch *Twister* every weekend for the rest of our lives, if that's what you want, even though *Goonies* is the superior movie. I'll give you everything, and when I've given you that, I'll find more to give. We make amazing business partners, Morgan. I think we'll be even better life partners. Marry me, Tweety. Spend the rest of your life with me."

Morgan wasn't sure if she should laugh or cry, so she was kind of doing both at the same time. She had no words; she simply nodded and held out one shaky hand for him to push the ring onto her finger. It was a perfect fit.

Decker stood, whipped his hat off his head and flung it to the sky, giving a loud *whoop*. Morgan was dimly aware of the cheering going on around them, but mostly she only had eyes for Decker. Her fiancé.

She wrapped her arms around his neck, and he grabbed her waist and gave her a good spin, whisking her bare feet right off the ground. She let out a delighted squeal as the sky spun above her.

Ben had come down from the tree house, bringing Archer with him. Decker set Morgan down and she crouched to hug her son while Decker shook Ben's hand.

"Congratulations, Decker," Ben said, then turned and tipped his hat to Morgan. "Future Mrs. Decker."

Morgan stood, laughing. "Can I hug you, Ben?"

He thought it over for a second and then nodded. "Okay."

Morgan wrapped him in a quick, but tight, hug. "Thank you."

Annie lumbered over like a freight train but stopped short of touching anyone. Instead, she gave an awkward wave, but she was all beaming smiles and fist bumps. "That was so romantic! Congratulations!"

"Thank you, Annie," Morgan said.

"I hope someone proposes to me just like this someday." She gave an irritated look at the sun. "Only maybe when it's not so hot outside. But also not nighttime because the woods are a little scary at night. Sugar doesn't like it. And there are mosquitoes."

Decker slapped Ben on the back. "Well, sounds like you just got instructions."

Ben blushed so hard he began to look sunburned. He settled his hat back on his head. "Annie and I will take Archer to the house and make him lunch," he said. "If that's okay with you, Miss Morgan."

"That would be wonderful," Morgan said.

"Have a nice picnic," Annie said, taking Archer's hand.

Morgan watched as Ben helped Archer mount his pony. Her son looked so comfortable and commanding on that pony. He'd made so many strides over the past year, it was almost hard to believe. He would start school in the fall, and for the first time ever, Morgan wasn't worried about how he would do. With all the people at McBride Pathways in his corner, he would do just fine.

Morgan watched until they were no longer visible in the woods and turned to Decker. He gazed at her hungrily.

Without a word, he grabbed her waist and pulled her to him.

"I love you so much it scares me sometimes."

"Don't be scared, Baseball. I'm right here."

He touched her hair, her cheek, her lips, then drew her in for a kiss that left her dizzy.

If this was what the rest of her life was going to be like, she could hardly wait for it to get started. He tried to pull away, but she twined her hands around the back of his neck, pushing her fingers through the curls that she loved so much, and pulled him in for another kiss.

They stood like that for the longest time, their foreheads and noses touching while they whispered dreams and promises of the future to each other between kisses.

And when the sun began to sink into the tree line, they finally lowered themselves to the picnic blanket and opened up the basket. They sat, knees touching, and watched the sun set while they nibbled fruit and cheese and crackers and chocolates. And when they were full, Decker pulled Morgan to him, and she leaned against his chest, wrapped in his arms, making wedding plans while evening rolled in.

I'll never miss another sunset. We will never miss one. Together.

When they finally decided that it was time to go, they gathered their things and headed for their horses.

"It got kind of dark on us," Decker said. "You okay to ride?"

"Please," Morgan said, hopping up onto Tweety like it was nothing. "I had the best teacher in the world. I'm not afraid of anything."

Decker lifted himself onto Tango's saddle, and, together, they rode through the woods toward the house.

Toward their future together, husband and wife.

* * * * *

Be sure to look for the next book in Jennifer Brown's Haw Springs series, available soon from Harlequin Heartwarming!